Novels by J.L. Weil

Saving Angel (Divisa #1)
Losing Emma (Divisa #.5)
Hunting Angel (Divisa #2)
Breaking Emma (Divisa #2.5)
Chasing Angel (Divisa #3)
Luminescence (Book 1)
Amethyst Tears (Book 2)
Starbound

Dedicated to those who believe in fate and love.

STARBOUND

J. L. Weil

ST. CHARLES PARISH LIBRARY
DESTREHAN, LA 70047
WITHDRAWN

Kindle Edition Copyright 2014

by J.L. Weil

http://jlweil.blogspot.com/

All rights reserved.

Second Edition April 2014

ISBN-13: 978-1497307995

Edited by Kelly Hashway

Cover design by J.L. Weil

Image Credits: Obsidian Dawn, Mirish, and I am Jenius

Kindle Edition, License Notes

This eBook is licensed for your personal enjoyment only. This eBook may not be re-sold or given away to other people. If you would like to share this book with another person, please purchase an additional copy for each person. If you're reading this book and did not purchase it, or it was not purchased for your use only, then return to Amazon.com and purchase your own copy. Thank you for respecting the hard work of this author.

This book is a work of fiction. Names, characters, places and incidents are a product of the writer's imagination or have been used fictitiously and are not to be construed as real. Any resemblances to persons, living or dead, actual events, locales or organizations is entirely coincidental.

All rights are reserved. No part of this may be used or reproduced in any manner whatsoever without written permission from the author.

Prologue

Katia

I had a hard time understanding why people didn't believe in magick. It was everywhere. Who could doubt it when the winds sung, the sky sparkled with stars, when rainbows appeared after a rainfall, and dewdrops glistened in the morning? Everyone in some way has been touched by magick. It was just simply a part of life.

Seth and I were living proof.

Chapter 1

Katia

I caught Seth Nightingale staring at me for like the umpteenth time, which wasn't that unusual really. We kind of had been playing this cat and mouse game since kindergarten. He would glare—I would grimace and glare back. And so the vicious cycle went.

What had me so worried was this undeniable pull I'd been feeling toward him lately. I thought I had gotten rid of my silly childhood crush years ago—apparently not.

Seth Nightingale?

I do not like Seth, I reminded myself—again—as if that was going to help curb this insatiable need to be near him. Ever since the start of our senior year, I noticed a shift inside me. It wasn't all centered around Seth, but he was the root of it. There were hundreds of boys to choose from, and I had dated my fair share of them, so why Seth? Why now?

What was it about this guy that made me want to throw all caution to the wind and leap into his arms, right in the middle of English nonetheless? There was something behind those smoldering green eyes that intrigued me. And no matter how many years had gone by, that intrigue only intensified.

Seth and I had a complex relationship, a love-hate relationship. We loved to hate each other, but it hadn't always been that way.

There had been a time when we had been friends—best friends.

Shocking, I know. I even had a hard time believing it.

Before all the eye glaring, name calling, and general loathing, we had been inseparable. Now, a span of the ocean stretched between us. Even our seating arrangements in class were affected—it was that bad. I sat in the first row; he sat in the last row. One year just for shits and giggles, I sat in the seat beside him. He had literally gotten up and told the teacher he couldn't be subjected to skank.

That burned my ass.

What he really meant was, he needed to be as far away from me as possible.

Asshole. And I didn't have a problem saying it to his face.

Daily. Or showing him just how deep my burning hatred was rooted. The one-finger salute became my signature greeting as we passed in the halls.

I had spent the remainder of my freshman year searing him with hateful scowls.

Yet, somehow we co-existed at Vermillion High without bringing it to the ground, but we'd come pretty close. If I didn't know better, I'd actually think he liked pissing me off.

Warped.

So I was back to my original predicament.

Why was Seth looking at me with a spark of interest instead of his usually irritation? Okay, I admit over the years I'd done my fair share of gawking. It was not like Seth was a hardship on the eyes. Just the opposite, he was sinful eye-candy. And the asshat knew it.

How could I find him both drool-worthy *and* stab-worthy? That was just wrong on so many levels. But for some unholy reason he both fascinated me and infuriated me. Embarrassingly, I knew way more about dark and dreamy than I would ever admit.

That was how screwed up I really was.

Seth was an amazing artist, always doodling in class, sketching instead of taking notes. He had these breath-stopping green eyes and black, messy hair that most guys couldn't achieve if they tried. It was adorable. But that was were adorable stopped on Seth. He oozed smexy and had that whole tall, dark, and dangerous persona going on. To say he made my mouth water was an understatement. But the real problem was...Seth was off limits. And we couldn't have been more of polar opposites if we tried.

As talented as Seth was at art, I was good at...being popular and pretty. If that wasn't cliché enough for you, I was also a cheerleader dating the basketball star. I made *myself* want to hurl. There was a time when I had been nothing but the girl in the shadows with Seth. It was amazing what one summer could do to a young girl's figure... and to her popularity.

My life sometimes felt meaningless, blah, except for one small detail.

There was goddess blood running through my veins that gave me power—I was a nixie. Descendent to Arachne—a greatly skilled warrior princess. Well, before a goddess turned her into a spider.

Pretty F'd up.

The cincher...Seth was a nixie, too.

It was what initially drew us together, the shared secret of magick. Actually our town was sort of a magickal haven for nixies. Vermillion had been were the birthright of nixies was forged. But most importantly, it wasn't that we currently ran with completely different crowds that kept Seth and me on opposite sides of the classroom. It was because he was a Nightingale, and in my family that was an enormous no-no.

STARBOUND

Our families despised each other. That was how it had been since the day I was born, going back more generations than I could count. A Montgomery and a Nightingale had always lived in Vermillion, South Dakota, and there had always been bad blood between our families. We had been forbidden from seeing each other, but that hadn't stopped either of us from being curious.

Rules were meant to be broken, and Seth loved to go against the rules.

At one time Seth and I had been best friends, in secret of course, just as our little sisters were to this day. There was just something appealing about going against your parents' direct orders. It was the whole Romeo and Juliet thing. All through elementary school we had found ways to meet in secrecy. It had been daring and fun.

Our parents never knew, and if they did, they never said anything. I was torn in half the day our friendship died. Young, stupid, and naive, I had thought that Seth felt something for me— a connection. I had made it bluntly clear how interested I was in him, not having a shy bone in my body. That lout rejected me our first year in junior high, and the sting of rejection had never left me. It was the start of our hate relationship, and I wasn't ready for a repeat performance of that kind of embarrassment any time soon.

My heart couldn't take it.

"Katia," Claudia, my best friend whispered in the desk next to me.

I tore my gaze from Seth and looked at her perfectly raised black brows and big blue eyes. "What?" I muttered.

The corners of her pink lips turned up. "You're drooling."

"I am not," I snapped, wiping the corner of my mouth with the back of my hand for good measure. After all, I had been doing some heavy eyeballing. What was wrong with me?

Biting the end of my pen, I snuck one last quick peek at Seth. He had stopped scribbling on his English textbook and was looking over at Claudia and me. By the dark expression on his face he looked irked, as if we were bothering him. Breaking his concentration or something, which was a total joke, since it was obvious he wasn't listening to Ms. Harper lecture about our next written essay.

"Are you and Matt going to the party Friday night?" Claudia asked as soon as Ms. Harper turned to the dry erase board.

I dug out my notebook, pretending to take notes. All concentration was shot for the day, thanks to Seth. "I don't know, probably." Out of the corner of my eyesight, I saw Seth's hands clench the sides of the desk. *What's got his boxers in a bunch?*

"You have to," Claudia whined. "Everyone is going to be there."

In her book, that meant anyone who was anyone was going to

be there. "I am sure Matt will want to go," I conceded.

"Good, we are going to get totally waxed—"

"Miss Jenssen, do you have something to share with the class?" Ms. Harper interrupted.

I slunk lower in my desk. Claudia, however, faced forward and smiled sweetly. "I was just telling Katia that we are going to get completely blitzed on Friday night."

I ducked my head, trying to cover my smirk. The entire class erupted in snickers, except of course for Seth, who looked ready to commit murder.

"I have a better idea. How about you spend Friday in detention?" Ms. Harper countered.

Claudia wasn't fazed. "Can't. I have plans."

"Miss Jenssen, you are trying my patience."

Luckily Claudia was saved by the bell as everyone shot up in his or her seat and started filing into the halls. She waved at an exasperated Ms. Harper on the way out the door. Claudia spent her life skirting the lines of trouble. She shot me a wink, and I shook my head as we parted ways. "See you at lunch, Katia," she called over her shoulder.

Seth

I watched her saucy little butt saunter out of the classroom and had to bite my lip. I still couldn't figure out why she hung out with Claudia and her other uppity friends. Kat wasn't a snob. At least not the Kat I had known.

Really, I shouldn't give two shits.

What Kat did—who she hung out with, who she kissed—was none of my business.

I scoffed at myself. That was all bullshit, because the truth was I cared.

I cared too damn much.

And that was *my* problem.

Sitting at my desk another moment, I thought legs like hers should have been outlawed from high school. She had long, sun-kissed legs that were toned in just the right places. All her cheerleading practice had paid off, but I was more of a butt kind of guy anyway, and I could tell you that Kat had a magnificent ass. She wasn't extraordinarily tall or short. Her hair was a long, angelic white with these soft waves that framed her heart-shaped face. And what a face, but it was her smile that made my heart seize. And the two dimples that appeared with it were the icing on the cake. Exotic was the first word that came to mind.

But where she was concerned, I had a hands-off policy.

That didn't stop me from being aware of her twenty-four seven, or appreciating what she offered. When Kat walked into a room, everything inside me became charged, electric. She had that kind of power over my treacherous body.

I hated the way she made me feel without even trying…and I loved it at the same time.

I was so screwed in the head.

It was unfair that the one person I wanted was the only person I could never have. Fate was a bitch.

The longest three months of my life felt like yesterday and had changed everything. It was the first time Kat and I had spent a summer apart. She had gone to her Grandma's beach house in Rhode Island, and I hadn't seen her at all. On our first day back at school, I had gotten a shock that rocked my system, especially for a pre-adolescent boy. Suddenly, I found myself attracted to her on a whole new level. My body had a mind of its own. When I saw her that dreaded Monday morning, all I could think was *Oh shit. That's Kat?*

She was the only girl to give me a boner in the school halls. Talk about awkward and uncomfortable. I had some pretty wild fantasies about her that year—fantasies were safe. Kat was drop dead hot.

My jaw had hit the ground.

Sweet Jesus. The beach had done her body good.

I'd been standing at the bottom steps of the school entrance as she passed me by. The scent of her shampoo teased the air around her, and she gave me a heart-stopping grin. I watched as she flipped her long curls, giggling with Claudia Adams and Harper

Thompson at her side—her two new besties.

Before she entered the double doors, she had glanced over her shoulder at me and ours eyes clashed. She flashed her dimples and her light iridescent blue eyes twinkled. Whether Kat had known it or not, that was the day our friendship had drastically changed.

Good God. I had been pretty sure Kat had just flirted with me. I had swallowed hard and slumped against the stair railings, feeling the ground slip out from under me.

It was no surprise that was the year Kat had shot up in her social status. She joined the cheerleading squad and was always surrounded by a flock of horny boys. What no one knew was I had spent that entire year fighting the urge to plant my fist in their faces. I'd wanted to scream at her groupies that she was mine. In my head, not one of those guys had the right to touch her, talk to her, or look at her like a piece of pecan pie.

Because Katia had been destined to be mine.

I'd wanted nothing more than to march up to them and slam their heads into the concrete block walls. And that was for just looking at her. Imagine how I'd felt when one of them touched her. I literally lost my shit the first time I saw her kiss another guy. Let's just say that the dent on the locker door was still there, and my poor knuckle had bled like a bitch.

It had done nothing to dull the ache in my chest.

Now, it was our senior year and nothing had really changed, except that I learned some self-control. I didn't want to smash Matt's face every time I passed him in the halls. I called that progress.

And I became an asshole. It was the only defense I had against her and the crazy-intense feelings she stirred inside me. It was far better for her to hate me than to have her love me. I didn't think I could have restrained myself if she loved me. Hell, even if she liked me a little, it would have been too hard.

Getting out of my seat, I trailed behind the group, catching one last glimpse of Kat before she disappeared into the crowd. The rest of the day was a breeze after that. Thankfully we only shared two classes this year, which in my book was two too many. First period and then English, I figured we should be able to survive our last year without killing each other—literally.

When the final bell of freedom rang, I sighed in sweet relief and trucked it home. I walked through the front door, and Dad took one look at me with sympathy filling his hazel eyes. "That bad, huh?" he asked, leaning on the fridge.

I sunk into the couch, mixed with rage, sadness, loneliness, and longing so profound it ate at my flesh like a zombie. "You have no idea."

He offered me a Coke. "It's for the best, Seth."

So I'd heard before. I was getting tired of hearing it, the same song and dance. Popping the top on the can, I took one long swig. My parents meant well and when you came from a family of magick, you learned to respect what knowledge they gave.

Dad sat down next to me and stretched his long legs under the coffee table. We had the same height and build, but I had gotten my coloring from my mom. There was not a touch of grey in his chocolate hair. "You know that this is the only way to keep her safe."

Yada. Yada. Yada. The warnings were etch-o-sketched into my brain, but that didn't mean it didn't suck serious monkey ass. "I know, Dad. You don't have to worry. Nothing will happen." But, for the first time, I didn't believe those words.

There had been something different in her silvery-blue eyes today. The usual scorn had been replaced with interest. I hadn't seen that glint of intrigue and possibility since sixth grade, right before I had smashed it to smithereens. Let's just say that back then, delicacy hadn't been one of my superpowers, and I might have been too harsh, but I hadn't known how to handle Kat. Or the feelings she enticed.

I wasn't sure I could handle them now.

"Harsh" really wasn't a strong enough word. I had broken her heart and stomped on it, crushing it with cruel words. I had been an insensitive jerk, though I think she'd had a few more colorful words for me that day. And who could have blamed her.

If she suddenly decided to flip the tables, how long would I really be able to stay away? How long would I be able to deny what my heart and soul demanded?

One year. One more year.

It wasn't just resisting Kat. It was giving up the girl who had been destined to be mine. Normally you don't mess with fate, being a nixie, you know better than to muddle with the greater powers, but she wasn't just fated as mine. She was my starbound. And that was harder to ignore for nixies than the next hit for a meth addict. It was impossible. Especially when finding your one true mate was so rare among us. The fact that I had known she was mine since birth was a freaking miracle.

But she was one miracle I could never have.

To make matters worse, her parents hadn't taken the same approach mine had when it came to the curse. For as long as I could remember, I had heard the warnings, was told to stay far away, but Kat's family kept her in the dark. She knew our families didn't get along, but she didn't know the truth.

Why we could never be together.

Chapter 2

Katia

It was my senior year.

Which meant late nights, more parties than I could stand, and in general, a whole lot of goofing off before having to make life decisions about my future.

Claudia and Harper excelled at all of the above. Claudia, our cheerleading squad captain, had skin that looked California tan all year, a Marilyn Monroe beauty mark, and ovaries the size of coconuts. She was not afraid to do or say whatever was on her mind, which quiet often was inappropriate and probably offensive to most.

I don't know why we were friends.

Harper was a blonde bombshell, smart and funny too. A triple threat, she had Hollywood written all over her. Harper wanted to see her name in lights, but that would never happen in small-town

Vermillion.

Neither of my closest friends were anything like me—a nixie—nor did they know what I was. I liked to think of myself as more of Glenda the good nixie versus the other alternative. There were definitely both sides of the coin—black magick and white magick. I had never met anyone who practiced the latter. Never wanted to either.

Magick always had a way of balancing the scales, and I didn't want to test those boundaries. And honestly, I wasn't all that great at being a nixie. I kind of sucked at it. Unreal, I know. As far as skills went, mine were virtually useless.

If any of my friends thought I was something other than normal, they never said. I think the people of our small town were used to the strange. Vermillion had always been home to nixiecraft, and there was plenty of goddess blood in our school, including the jerkwad Seth.

At one time we all used to hang out and do magick. The five of us had been a full circle, but that was eons ago. Now we avoided each other like the bubonic plague and had gone our separate ways, or maybe it was just me that had left. Not that I stalked him or anything, but I was pretty sure Seth and the others were still friends, including the hoodrat Elena. She always had her hands on him.

Not that I cared or kept tabs...

Who was I kidding?

For reasons unbeknownst to me, I did care, even when I tried to convince myself I didn't. Being at the top of the social chain, I heard the rumors about Seth and the others. They didn't exactly try to blend as I had, or hide that they were different. Of course, it didn't help that some of them dressed like they were part of a cult. The freak Elena's entire wardrobe was black, and she wore enough eyeliner to rival Kiss.

I had refined the art of blending. The most rebellious thing I'd ever done was add pink highlights to my hair. It hadn't lasted long, but that didn't mean I was a good girl. Far from it. Lately, my life was spiraling into nothing but trouble. Sure, I looked like the good girl next door who got away with murder, but looks were deceiving. There was a price for being popular.

And I was tired of keeping up the charade. I was tired of being something I wasn't. I was tired of denying who I was.

In a way, I envied Seth and the others.

They hadn't lost who they were. They had stayed true to their gifts. I was the one who was lost.

Not that Seth wasn't trouble with a capital T.

He definitely looked dangerous, like someone you didn't want to mess with unless you were looking for a good ass beating, but he also had this endearing protective streak. He had a way of making the people he cared about feel safe.

I used to be one of those people—part of his close circle.

Sighing, the last thing I wanted to dwell on was my past history with the dark and sexy Seth. It was Friday night. Tonight, I was going to have fun, let loose, and pretend all those doubts and uncertainties swimming inside me were gone. *I love when I lie to myself and mask my problems with booze.* My days of high school were numbered and college was looming in the distance.

New school.

New friends.

New set of problems.

I really didn't think that partying was going to make this empty feeling inside me disappear.

Slipping into the standby little black dress, I checked out my butt in the floor-length mirror, twisting from side to side. I pursed my glossy lips. It would do. I ran my fingers through my curls and tried to banish Seth's face from my head. Lately, he was consuming my thoughts—my dreams—my every waking moment.

I wondered if Seth would be at the party tonight. It was a stupid thought. I don't know why it had even crossed my mind. Parties were never Seth's scene. He'd rather munch on cockroaches than mingle with *my* crowd.

One last glimpse in the mirror to smooth a wrinkle from the dress and smack my glossy lips and I was ready to rock. I grabbed my wristlet off the dresser.

Downstairs, my little sister, Collins, was watching something on the Disney Channel. "Hey, Bug, whatcha watchin'?" I asked, leaning over the back of the couch.

Waves of cute curls cascaded over her shoulders as she lay belly down on the sofa, feet sticking up in the air. She popped a big, pink bubble before answering. "iCarly." She glanced over her shoulder at me. "Where do you think you are going looking like that? Dad is going to have a conniption if he sees you."

I rolled my eyes. "I'm going out with Matt. And *Dad* is not going to see me. I'm leaving before he gets home."

"Why don't you go out with Seth? He is so much cooler than Matt," she said, drawing out his name dramatically. I sometimes forgot that Collins and Seth's younger sister, Mya, were friends.

The doorbell rang. I straightened up and ruffled my curls. "You'll understand when you're older."

"When I'm older, I'm going to date Seth," she stated matter-of-factly.

I frowned, the doorbell momentarily forgotten. Why did it bother me that my little sister had a crush on Seth? "He is too old for you, silly."

She smiled. "He won't be in a few years."

The doorbell rang again. Ugh.

Collins's eyes were once again glued to the TV, her legs swinging happily in the air. "You better get that before *Matt* decides to ditch you."

"Aren't you a funny bug?"

She stuck her tongue out at me.

Little sisters were great.

I opened the door and there stood Matt Lang in all his athletic glory—sandy hair, perfect without a strand out of place. His jeans looked new along with the Rugby shirt. Sometimes I think he spent more time getting ready than I did. "Hiya, babe," he said in a lazy drawl, his hazel eyes twinkling. Someone was in a good mood.

He leaned in and gave me a peck on the lips. I smelled beer. Apparently someone had started the party early.

Collins made gagging noises in the background. "Get a room," she yelled, just before I stepped outside and shut the door.

I welcomed the cool autumn air as it washed over my cheeks. I knew later tonight I was going to regret wearing so little clothes, but for now, it felt good. We walked to Matt's BMW, and he immediately hopped into the driver's seat. No, *hey let me get the door for you, babe*. Chivalry was definitely dead in Matt, and I hated when he called me *babe*. It made my skin crawl.

In all honesty, I had no clue what I was doing with Matt. Just passing time, I guess. I wanted a boyfriend; what girl didn't? I just didn't want Matt, but no matter who I dated, none of them was right for me, and I had dated plenty. There was never that spark, that connection. Don't get me wrong, I wasn't looking to find the man of my dreams in high school, just someone interesting and fun to hang out with. Matt and I just didn't gel well together.

I think I was just about over us. Our relationship had dwindled. It was toast.

"No worries. I'll get the door," I muttered under my breath.

"What's that, babe?" Matt asked when I got in.

Grrr. If he called me *babe* one more time tonight, I might just make his tongue swell up like a sponge. I smiled through my teeth. "Nothing. I was just saying how much fun this party is going to be."

"I know, right? It is going to be a blast." He put the car in reverse, burning out right in my parents' driveway.

Ugh.

His idea and mine were so off left field. I imagined this party was going to be just like the last one. He was going to get plastered, and I was going to have to spend most of the night fending off his wandering, grabby hands. Then the next day, he would have no memory of the night. Fun.

My head fell back against the seat as we drove across town. Of course Matt drove too fast, but rules didn't apply when your dad was the sheriff. Staring out the window, a row of houses flew by, and I again couldn't help but wonder what I was still doing with Matt. It was evident I wasn't happy in this relationship. I heaved a long breath and cranked the radio. At least then I wouldn't have to think, or listen to Matt's buzzing nonsense.

As soon as we walked through the door of Brett Mancini's larger-than-life house, Matt was handed a beer. Shocker. There was a game of beer pong going on in the dining room. A DJ was spinning some beats, and Brett's parents were nowhere in sight. Like usual. They traveled extensively. Actually I didn't think I'd ever seen his parents.

"I'm going to get a drink," I hollered over the electric bass.

Matt was surrounded by a bunch of his teammates guzzling a bottle. I doubt he heard me or cared.

"Whatever," I mumbled and went searching for something more to my taste.

I found a bottle of white wine, the good kind, and things escalated from there. One drink turned into two and two into three. I was bored to tears. Claudia had ditched me to play tonsil hockey with some football jock, and Harper was doing the wild thang with some girl I didn't know on the dance floor. I angled my head from my seat on the couch. Wow. Those were some interesting dirty dancing moves, if you could call them that. How the heck did she get her leg like that?

This night couldn't have gotten any worse.

I was alone.

I couldn't stop picturing Seth's face.

And I needed to pee.

Apparently my bladder couldn't tolerate a few glasses of wine. Neither could my brain. The room swirled in dizzy hoops as I stood up. Immediately, I put a hand to the nearest wall in an attempt to steady myself and hugged it. Oh boy. I tried to scoot along the wall, using both hands with only mild success, meaning I stumbled more than once. And so the mindless search began.

Finding the bathroom in this joint was like winding through the hedge maze in Wonderland. Behind each door was a new surprise—and not necessarily a good one. I screwed up my face as I closed yet another door. Whatever had been going on behind door number three was going to scar me for life.

"Finally," I said out loud when the next door revealed the porcelain throne. My bladder was going to thank me.

Then, before I could close the door behind me, a pair of rough hands grabbed my waist and pushed me through the door. I let out a shriek as I was spun around and silenced by a pair of lips smashing mine. Putting both my hands on the culprit's chest, I shoved. "What the hell, Matt?" I should have guessed.

"What? This is what you wanted, isn't it?" he slurred. His mouth attacked again, clumsily slobbering on any part of me he could get his lips on. He smelled like a brewery, and my stomach turned.

Just like a guy. "No, Einstein. I need to pee. Now get out." I weaved and bobbed, trying to avoid his roaming lips. He didn't budge and neither did his hands, which were freely traveling on my backside. I let out an exasperated sigh. I was *so* not in the mood. "Matt, knock it off."

His hands moved from my butt to my bare legs then to my waist, and his lips were nibbling too hard on my neck. "Come on, babe. Live a little," he said between wet kisses.

"I'm trying, but I can't breathe with you smothering me."

"Don't be like that, babe." His hand slid awkwardly up the side of my ribcage, skimming my breast.

I was going to clock him in the nose. "Damn it, Matt! Stop!"

"We're just getting started," he murmured, sucking on my ear.

The hell we were. I was not about to have my first time in the bathroom at the house of some dude I barely knew, and most definitely not with a guy who didn't respect me.

I never should have come tonight.

This had to stop, and he really left me no other choice. I nudged my leg between his and he moaned. *Douche.* With as much finesse and strength as I could muster after a few too many glasses of wine, I brought my knee straight up into the center of his family jewels.

Suck on that, lover boy.

Matt instantly hissed in pain and clutched his junk. His sandy hair fell over his face as he groaned like he was dying. "Bitch. What was that for?" he spat between groans.

"That was for being an asstard." I snatched my wristlet from the counter.

His hazel eyes flashed. "Prude!"

"Go screw yourself, Matt! We're done!" I yelled and flipped him the bird. Then I promptly slammed the bathroom door, stumbling in my heels as I left the party.

"God, what an asshole." I couldn't believe that I had dated him for almost a year—365 days down the drain.

The brisk wind blew over my flushed cheeks as I ranted to the stars. My heels clicked on the road. I shivered. Without all my rage to overheat my system, I remembered that I was wearing next to nothing.

Why hadn't I brought a shawl?

What I wouldn't give to be able to snap my fingers and *poof,* one appeared. Unfortunately that was not in my power. Nixies all had different abilities, and summoning was not part of my repertoire. But if I recalled, it was something Seth could do. Where was he when I needed him now?

I giggled.

Damn wine. I had drunk a few glasses too many if I thought Seth would do something nice for me. I could blame that on Matt as well. If he hadn't been such a class act jerk tonight, I wouldn't have gotten so tipsy.

Actually now that I was thinking about Seth and his awesome

abilities, I also remembered how powerful he was and how captivating he looked wielding magick. He put my gift to shame. I was not even sure I would call what I could do a gift.

Now, while I was freezing, was not the time to start daydreaming about Seth. For God sake, I had just broken up with my boyfriend. Wrapping my arms around myself, goose bumps spread down my arms and legs. It was just the cold. A darkness had misted over the deserted road. Walking alone in the middle of the night no longer seemed like a smart idea.

My mind drifted to Seth, and I thought about the circle I was no longer a part of. An irrational sadness settled inside me, and a lump formed in the back of my throat. Everything had been less complicated before high school.

Oh God. I was a trainwreck.

My emotions were going haywire. One minute I was angry, then I was giggling like a crazy person, and now I was on the verge of tears.

Out of the blue, fat drops were spilling down my cheeks. They had nothing to do with Matt and everything to do with not wanting to be alone tonight walking the streets. I felt such a void. Sucking up a huge sniffle, I wiped the snot from my nose with the back of my hand. Then I smeared that on my black dress—attractive. What other choice did I have? I had gotten myself into this situation, and it was too much to hope someone was going to come and swoop me home.

A beam of headlights shone down the street behind me. My legs got tangled, and I cursed these heels to the hottest part of Hell. I contemplated sticking out my thumb, but I realized, even drunk, I wasn't that dumb—at least not tonight.

The car came to a stop. My heart quickened. *Dear Lord, please don't let them be kidnappers.* A car door opened, but I couldn't see past the blinding lights.

"Kats?"

I'd recognized that voice out of millions, and only one person ever called me by that name. This time my heart raced for entirely different reasons. It would have to be *him*.

Chapter 3

Seth

It might be Friday night, but I was at Eddie's Auto repair, my after school place of employment and the only mechanics shop in town. It was not glamorous, but it paid, and it beat smelling like a cheeseburger. I'd take smelling like a grease monkey any day of the week. On Friday's I stayed late, closing the shop.

It was after 11:00 pm by the time I'd finished counting the register, cleaning up oil spills, and locking up. I was in dire need of a hot shower. There was grease under my nails, car goop covering my shirt, and some unnamed substance splattered on my jeans. All in a day's work.

I liked working with my hands and loved cars, so it just made sense that I worked here. My auto teacher had put in a good word for me. I'd been employed by Eddie since junior year and couldn't complain. The work kept my mind off other things…

Digging my car keys from my pocket, I hit the unlock button to my GMC Sierra, and the beeping of the keyless entry echoed off the brick building. All I could think about as I started the truck was hitting the sack. Yep, it was Friday night, I was only seventeen, and I couldn't wait to get to bed.

Pathetic, I know, but I was beat. It had been a long day. Running a hand through my scraggly dark hair, I kept one on the wheel, cruising down the road. Driving was relaxing. It gave me a minute to myself, to clear my head without all the jumble.

On the downside, my mind wandered too often to the one person I tried so hard to forget, but when my body was bone tired, it was hard to keep her out of my thoughts. Girl's like Kat were unforgettable.

I was no more than a few blocks from my house when I saw a familiar figure walking down the road. If you could call what she was doing walking, it was more like stumbling. I blinked. And blinked again just to make sure my mind wasn't screwing with me. What were the chances that she would appear just as I thought her name?

Co-winkie-dink?

Probably not.

Pulling the truck to the curb, I put it in park and left it idling. I opened the door and called her name in disbelief. "Kats?"

She squinted in the dark at me, clearly blinded by my

headlights. "Seth?" White luminous curls framed her delicate face.

I walked in front of the truck so she could see me and got my first good look at her. She was a hot mess. "Are you drunk?" I asked, sounding icier than I intended. Being aloof to Kat had become such a habit it was hard to play nice.

"Nooo." She slurred the word, biting right back.

"Uh-huh. Get in." I slipped a hand under her elbow, ignoring the spark. I figured she needed some support before she toppled over. Wouldn't that have been a sight? The pretty and prissy Kat face planting the blacktop? "I'll take you home."

She shook off my hand and staggered. "I don't need your help."

"Oh yeah? You can barely walk." A beam of moonlight hit her face, and I frowned. "Have you been crying?"

"No," she insisted, swiping a hand on her glistening cheeks. "Why do you even care?" she asked surly. She stopped walking. Her face titled up, and she looked at me.

I could see the wet shimmer in her aquamarine eyes. It was all the answer I needed. My fists balled at my sides as I tried to ignore the pang in my chest. "Great. You're drunk and crying. And you're right. I don't care." Okay, so I was acting like a total dickhead, but it was my only defense against those sullen eyes. Then there was also the fact that I really, really wanted to hurt someone. At this point anyone would do, but I wanted whoever had made her cry to pay.

My eyes darkened, and she took a step back. "You're an asshole, Seth. Just like the rest of them. I don't know why I ever thought for a split-second you would be different."

I watched her swirl ungracefully on her heel and start walking down the road again. She tripped once, before plucking off her shoes and tossing them in someone's yard.

Classic.

On top of it, she was also going in the opposite direction of her house. I shook my head, wondering how the hell I got myself into these messes. Or rather, how Kat got into these messes. "You're going the wrong way!" I yelled.

She paused and just stood there in the middle of the empty road with her back to me. Letting out a huff, I trotted to catch up and turned her to face me. What I should have done was demand she give me her cell phone and called one of her sober friends to come get her. It would have been the wiser choice. Instead, I apologized. "Look, I'm sorry. It's been a real shitty night."

"You can say that again," she mumbled.

There was something in her eyes that hit me in the gut. Unhappiness. I wanted to immediately fix whatever was wrong, which was the first warning bell that I shouldn't get involved. "Let me take you home," I heard myself say. "I can't leave you out here alone. My dad would kick my ass." Not true. He would have probably given me the lecture of a lifetime about being alone with Katla Montgomery. And he would have demanded to know if I was trying to get us both killed.

No sir. I was trying to make sure she got home in one piece. Had you seen what she was wearing, you would have understood. That dress barely covered her fine ass, and I am not even going to mention how low the neckline was. I couldn't think about her bare shoulders and exposed neck. Not now.

"Fine," she finally gave in. "I'm too damn tired to walk anyway."

I figured adding that she was also barefoot wasn't a good idea. "Here." I offered her my hand. "Let me help you."

She walked right by me. "I've had all the help I can handle tonight."

I held up my hands. "Forget I offered." It was far better if we didn't touch. I followed closely behind her just to make sure she didn't trip and land on her face.

She planted her butt into the truck without much help from me, but I did have to refrain from laughing out loud a time or two. Kat made a cute drunk. After I made sure she wasn't going to fall out of the seat, I hightailed around the truck and hopped in before she changed her mind. Everything Kat did lately surprised me. She seemed lost.

And that was bad.

I could handle the spunky and sassy Kat all day long, but one glance at those gloomy eyes and I felt myself getting sucked in.

Before I did, or said something I couldn't erase, I put the truck in drive. She had her eyes closed with her head back against the seat. She shivered, and I leaned forward to crank on the heat.

She smiled, turning her head toward me. "Thanks. I can't believe how cold it is."

I caught a glimpse of her dimples and gripped the damn wheel tighter. This might just be the longest five-minute ride of my life. "Dressed like that I'm shocked you didn't freeze to death."

"There is nothing wrong with my dress," she snapped.

"That's a dress? I thought it was a shirt."

She gave me a dull look, eyes narrowing. "Seth…"

I glanced over at her, trying to ignore that my heart skipped a beat when she said my name. "Hmm?"

"Just take me home." She closed her eyes again and leaned back.

When she moved closer to me in the cab, I kept my eyes glued to the road. My truck had one of those bench seats, where nothing stood in the way of her and me. I thought about throwing up some kind of invisible barrier, me being a nixie and all, but I figured that might have been excessive.

The next thing I knew, she had her head resting on my shoulder and a hand on my thigh. *Oh holy God.*

I looked over at her. Gigantic mistake. The hem of her dress had hiked up while she had snuggled to my side of the truck. Her face was soft, and there was the lightest dusting of freckles on her nose. She smelled liked faerie roses and cherry blossoms, sweet and succulent.

By the time I tore my gaze from her legs I had passed her house and almost swerved off the road. "Damn it," I swore. Pulling the truck to the curb two houses past hers, I put the car in park.

Her eyes fluttered open, long lashes sweeping, and I found myself staring into eyes that looked like the center of a star. "Maybe you're not like all the rest, Seth," she mumbled, her hand still on my thigh. "Thanks for the ride." Then she shocked us both and brushed a feather light kiss across my lips.

Frozen, a second passed with us breathing each other's air. That tiny first taste of her lips was not enough. My eyes darkened, my body stiffened, and my gaze shifted to her soft lips. I was about to do something utterly stupid, yet it didn't change the fact that I wanted it.

Wanted her.

More than I wanted my next breath of air. I closed the distance between us. My whole wall of defense came crashing down the moment our mouths touched, and my world fell out of orbit. I had fantasized about kissing Kat practically every night. It came nowhere close to the real deal. She was…

Intoxicating.

Sensual.

Breathtaking.

Her fingers dug into my thigh as I wrapped my hand in her long curly hair, keeping her mouth sealed to mine. I couldn't let her go. Fireworks exploded behind my eyes as her taste invaded my mouth, our tongues dancing together. It was like the finest wine infused with sugary cherries.

My whole life I had waited for this…wondered, and now I would rather die than stop kissing her. Stop touching her.

Die… Die… Die…

That one simple word echoed somewhere in a small corner of my mind, snapping me out of it. I pulled back. Her lips were swollen and her eyes murky, but she wasn't easily derailed. I probably had the alcohol to thank for that. Her hand ran up my thigh, and my head dropped to the back of the seat as I prayed that I would have the strength to stop this before it went any farther.

God, she was lethal.

If the curse didn't kill us, then surely she would.

The moment my head hit the back of the seat, she moved, and her lips were on my neck, doing the most wicked things with her tongue. I moaned, twining my fingers in her hair again. Honestly, I didn't have the first clue how I had gone so long without kissing Kat.

"Seth," she whispered in my ear. "Kiss me again. Please."

Someone kill me now.

She trailed kisses down my jaw, stopping just above my mouth, our lips just a breath's length away. She looked into my half-closed eyes and took my lips into another shattering kiss that left me aching everywhere.

I don't know what happened next, one minute she was beside me, and the next she was in my lap—our kiss never breaking. We didn't need oxygen, not when we had each other. Her hands snuck under my shirt, making my stomach muscles jump.

I shifted and her back hit the steering wheel, giving me access to her body. I was dying to touch her. Leaning forward I—

Like a gunshot, the car horn blared through the night, long and loud, saving my sanity.

Appalled by my lack of self-control, I just stared at her. I could have gotten her killed tonight. Sure she might have had an awful night, drank a little too much, but what I had almost done was a thousand times worse.

This was the girl I loved, that I vowed to protect, and here I was doing exactly what I promised myself, my parents, and her parents I would never do.

I placed my hands on her waist and hoisted her to the other side of the car. "Stay there," I warned, my voice gravelly. I didn't want her to get any more ideas in her pretty head, because I couldn't take another round with Kat in the front seat of my truck.

Her hair was a wild disarray of curls. Her lips were red and swollen. And her eyes were still cloudy with passion.

"You should get inside," I advised in a voice of ice.

She tugged down her dress and reached for the door handle. "Whatever," she said.

Not that I cared. I would rather have her annoyed with me than dead. "You're welcome," I snapped as the door closed in my face. After I made sure she managed to get herself inside, I thumped my head on the steering wheel. "That was so stupid. What were you thinking?" I scolded myself and then slammed the truck into drive. It lurched forward at full speed, tires screeching and rubber burning.

Chapter 4

Katia

Oh. My. God. Please tell me last night had been a very vivid and bad dream. Please tell me that I hadn't thrown myself all over Seth Nightingale in the front seat of his pickup. That I hadn't begged for more.

I covered my face with my hands, rainbows dancing behind my eyes.

"Oh crap."

That was exactly what I had done.

And worse, I loved every second of it.

Wait, that was not right. I didn't like Seth. I hated Seth.

I didn't know if that made it worse or not. Matt and I had broken up and all I could think about was kissing Seth.

Lord have freaking mercy. Seth could kiss. He kissed like it was going to be his last. Never had I felt something like that before.

His lips were like an addiction. He had made me tingle from my head to my toes, and I was pretty sure the wine I'd had last night didn't even come close to making me feel that good.

I touched a finger to my lips, recalling how his had felt on mine.

Soft.

Demanding.

Possessive.

It felt like he had branded me with his kiss. Why had we never kissed before? I had known Seth my whole life. Sure, I'd thought about it. A lot. But it had never happened—until last night. And now, all I could think about was when I would get the chance to kiss him again.

Scientific reasons of course.

I needed to make sure what I thought I had felt was real. Not a one-time-alcohol-induced-mind-blowing kiss.

Somehow during junior high things changed. We drifted apart. I drifted. I left my circle of friends for a more popular group. Looking back, I felt ashamed of what I had done. It sickened me that I had turned my back on the circle.

Olivia.

Elena.

Zeke.

And of course Seth.

From the first day of kindergarten the five of us had become fast friends because we all shared one thing in common.

We all had magick.

Back then though, Elena hadn't been a bitch, and I hadn't been so shallow and self-absorbed. Things had been different. Simpler. Freer.

There was strength in numbers. A circle of five was the perfect balance to nature. Air. Water. Fire. Earth. Spirit. There were nixies that had affinities with the elements. Now if you had a complete circle of five with a nixie for each element it was divine—unimaginable power.

We weren't so sanctified.

Only one of us had an affinity with an element. Our circle had been formed more out of friendship and curiosity. We all had a love for magick, and our circle provided us with a platform to practice and experiment. What else did kids do?

Lying in bed, I stared at the ceiling, watching a prism of colors frolic from the sunlight and the crystal beads hanging in from my bedroom windows. Fragrant bottles of my favorite oils lined the old carved dresser in scents of lavender, rosemary, rose, and many more. If there was a part of the craft I hadn't let go, it was dabbling in oils and dried herbs. My room was infused with the essences of flowers that always smelled like high summer and cool misty mornings.

Candles with wax dripping down the sides hung in sconces above my bed, and I realized how much I missed them—the circle. How much I missed doing magick with them. I'd never felt less like a nixie than I did now.

I wanted to belong again. Have meaning to my life, because right now, I didn't feel like I was accomplishing anything. There was this huge chuck of my life that was lacking or missing. And I wanted to find a way to fill it. Something inside me told me that I needed to try to make amends with the circle.

And I could start by talking to Seth. Talking. Not sucking his face off.

But I might not resist if he tried to kiss me again…

First, I had to get the courage to face him in school on Monday. He didn't exactly make it easy. What was it about his loner the world-be-damned attitude that I liked? It probably helped that he looked the way he did, dark messy hair with eyes greener than emeralds. Seth was the guy at school every girl secretly wanted but would never admit to wanting.

Myself included.

I realized suddenly that Monday was too far way. I wanted to see him now. Throwing the covers off me, I shot out of bed, making a beeline to the bathroom. I shrieked like a banshee when I got a look at my reflection in the mirror. I looked like a member of an 80's punk rock band. My usual soft curls were spiking in every direction. My eye makeup was smeared around my eyes like a raccoon. And I imagined I smelled worse than I looked.

Christ. I hope I hadn't looked like this last night.

Downing two aspirins, I wasted not another second and hopped into the shower, scrubbing until my skin glowed. I dressed quickly and ran down the stairs two at a time. Just as I was about to walk out the door, Mom stopped me.

"And where do you think you are going?"

I took a step backward and spun around, facing her. Her blonde hair was pulled back with wisp of curls escaping the knot at her neck. She had a mixing bowl of cake batter in hands. The spoon was stirring by itself.

Everyone in my family had magick.

The TV was on in the other room with Collins monopolizing it as usual. "I'm meeting a friend," I answered.

"You got home late last night." There was undertone of disapproval in her voice.

"I know. I'm sorry. Matt and I had a fight, so I hooked a ride home." I really didn't want to rehash the details.

"Are you alright?" she asked, brushing a piece of hair behind my ear. Her soft eyes twinkled with concern.

"Yeah, I'm fine, but I am going to be late if I don't get going." Yes, I was fabricating, but I really wanted to get out of the house in this decade. "I'll see you later," I called, promptly slipping out the door.

The trip into town was a short one. Trees the color of mulberries lined the road, and the September sky was clear and blue. I pulled up to Eddy's Auto Repair with my nerves in my throat. Was it stalker-ish that I knew his work schedule?

Probably.

The door chimed as I walked through. Seth was leaning on the counter, his head buried in paperwork. There was a strong odor of grease and oil in the air. The shop was connected to the garage where loud clanging and the buzzing of drills sounded.

He glanced up at my approach, green eyes clashing with mine. "Kats," he said in surprise. Only Seth ever called me by that nickname.

My lips split into a silly grin, dimples and all, as I approached the counter. I loved seeing the way his eyes looked me over at first glance. It was like he was seeing me for the very first time. It gave me tingles.

"What are doing here?" he asked, surprised.

I'd never been in Eddy's before, for obvious reasons. "Looking for you," I replied.

"Well, you found me." He tapped a pen on a pad of paper.

I glimpsed down at the tablet under his hand. "You are still an amazing artist." I turned the slip of paper around so I could get a better view of the sketch. It was a landscape of a place I knew well.

"This is really good."

His brows slammed together. "Did you come here to discuss art?"

"No." I was confused by his sudden icy change in attitude. One minute he looked happy to see me, and the next he looked ready to boot my butt out of the shop. "I came to thank you for last night, but I think I've changed my mind."

He ran a hand through his dark, already messy hair. "Whatever. It was no big deal, and you could have done that on Monday. There was no need for a special trip."

His shirt was stained with what I thought was oil, and I didn't think he could be any sexier. Since when was I into blue collar? "I know." God, he was making me nervous. My stomach fluttered with butterflies. The last thing I wanted to admit was that I didn't want to wait to see him. I tucked my hair behind my ear.

Smooth, Katia. Way to sound like a dork. I was starting to think that kiss wasn't as earth-shattering as I'd imagined.

He shrugged like it wasn't a big deal. "Whatever, don't mention it. It's what any decent guy would do." Grabbing the piece of paper from my hand, he wadded it up and tossed it into the trash.

That was just it. I was pretty sure that Seth wasn't always a decent guy, but I knew in the depth of my heart, he would never really hurt me. Bruise my pride sure, but I got the feeling he would walk through fire before he let me get hurt.

"How about I repay you? I could buy you lunch…for the trouble and all." The words were tumbling out of my mouth before I even realized what I had said.

Had I really just asked him out?

"You don't have to do that," he replied, giving me an out.

My face fell. I hadn't expected him to say no. I guess I was used to guys jumping at the chance to go out with me, and I hadn't thought Seth would be any different.

God that sounded so superficial. When had I become such a snob?

Just then his boss Eddy walked into the shop from the garage. He had a streak of grease on his rough cheek, which was speckled with stubby hairs. "Did I just hear you refuse a pretty lady lunch? Seth, boy, what the hell is wrong with you?" Eddy's voice was gruff, just like the rest of him. I instantly liked him. It was nice to have an ally.

I grinned. "It's just lunch. I'm not asking you to marry me or anything."

Seth choked on air. "Fine," he agreed, not looking happy about it. "If it gets the two of you off my back, I'll go. But just lunch."

My smile widened. "Then we can talk about the number of babies we'll have." I was totally teasing, but Seth's face went pale.

Eddy laughed long and deep. "I like you, girl. It's about time someone cornered this one." He gave Seth a pat on the back.

Seth scowled.

We walked next door to a little burger joint, nothing fancy. Being so close to him, I couldn't stop thinking about the kiss. I wanted to apologize for my forward behavior, yet at the same time I wanted to tell him that I hadn't regretted what happened.

I didn't have the first clue where to start.

My arm brushed his as he held the door open, something Matt never would have done. A spark shot over my skin. I met his eyes, curious to see if he had felt anything. His green eyes darkened. I gulped. Everything about Seth was so…intense.

I pushed aside my hair and walked through the door. As we waited in line for our food, I could feel the heat from his body. It was exciting and comforting at the same time, and I might have stood a little closer than necessary.

I struggled for something to say to break this awkward silence that had settled between us. "You probably eat here all the time."

That sounded so lame. Just attach a giant L to my forehead please.

He glanced down at me from the oversized menu plastered on the wall behind the registers. "It's convenient."

I could feel the scrutiny from his mossy eyes, trying to figure me out. *Good luck*, I thought. I couldn't even understand who I was anymore. But I wanted to change that. I no longer wanted to be that stuck-up, popular girl who thought her shit didn't stink.

After we got our food, we took a seat in one of the red leather booths. I didn't know what to say, so I munched on a fry while I studied Seth. He was so darn good looking. Why had we lost touch again? Right now staring at him, I couldn't think of one valid reason. He was ten times the guy any other boy at school was.

And I didn't just mean his insane looks. He also had manners under his bad boy exterior. "I'm glad you still draw," I said, picking up another fry.

He shrugged. "It passes the time."

"You're really good. Are you thinking about going to an art school next year?" I thought it might be totally creepy if I mentioned I still had a few of his drawings he had given me in fifth grade. I couldn't seem to stop staring at his face, like I was trying to memorize every detail.

"Look, Kats," he said, pulling me out of my drool-fest. "I don't know what you are trying to pull here, but I don't have time for games."

My back stiffened, and I dropped the fry that had been in my hand, taken aback. *Jerk.* "I'm not playing any games. Forgive me for trying to be nice and thank you."

"Since when is Katia Montgomery nice."

Ouch. That stung. I take back any thoughts of Seth being a decent guy. He was an asshole. But in reality what he said wasn't any less true, at least for the old Katia. I didn't want to be that girl anymore, especially with Seth. I looked down at my plate. "Maybe I'm turning over a new leaf."

"Yeah right, and the grass is pink," he said gruffly.

My head snapped up.

"You haven't spoken more than two words to me at a time since sixth grade and you suddenly want to be my best friend. Let's be real here. You and I don't run in the same circle. Not anymore." There was anger in his voice.

I slumped in the booth like he had slapped me. "Rot in hell, Seth. I can't believe we were ever friends." I did the most mature thing I could think of. Actually at this point, I wasn't thinking at all. I just grabbed the first thing in front of me and dumped the contents all over Seth's lap. It just so happened to be my chocolate mint milkshake. Then I marched my pissed-off butt right out of the restaurant, leaving him alone at the table to finish his cheeseburger, soaking wet.

Chapter 5

Seth

I sat at the table covered in minty glop and watched her storm out of the restaurant. Chunks of chocolate were on my shirt. Sitting plastered in goo, I ignored all the curious glances and snickers from the other patrons. They could all screw themselves.

Damn.

That hadn't gone according to plan. The only thing that had come out of it was maybe it would keep her away, which had been why I acted so harshly. It was for Kat's own good. I hated the look that had sprung into her eyes. Hurt. Pain. The fact that I had caused it sliced at my heart.

Damn it.

Why had she come into the shop today?

Why now?

We had successfully avoided each all through high school,

now in our last year before we went our separate ways, she wanted to be my friend? One year. That was all that was left before I put continents between us.

She had been right about one thing. Art school. I had applied at a foreign art academy in Europe. It was both pleasant and alarming that Kat knew me. Really knew me, even after all these years. She had known how drawing was my escape, just like I knew that the real Kat wasn't shallow and heartless. She never could be.

But that was not what I had implied. What I said hadn't been entirely true. There was still very much the old Kat in there. She had proven it. I wanted to kick my own ass. There was this overwhelming urge to run after her and beg her to forgive me. I clutched the edges of the table, wrestling with the need. Kat needed to keep her distance from me. *I* needed her to keep her distance. It was the only way.

I could still see the flames spitting from her eyes. Kat was a hellfire when she got mad. There was a fire crackling behind those incandescent eyes that had always been there. It was part of why I loved her.

I grabbed my heart and gritted my teeth.

Blast it.

Pangs shot in my chest. Admitting how I felt hurt like a mother trucker, knowing that I could never have her.

Fate was the biggest bitch.

I pushed my food aside, no longer having an appetite. I kept telling myself this was for the best. I repeated the phrase the whole way back to the garage in tempo with my feet crunching on gravel. *For. The. Best. For. The. Best.* It had no bearing on my mood. I was just as temperamental.

When I sauntered back into the shop, Eddy took one look at me and laughed his ass off. "What the hell happened to you? Wait. Don't tell me. Let me guess. She was about five-five with angel curls and killer dimples." In his own way, my boss cared about me. He had no kids of his own and took it upon himself to harass me at every opportunity.

I stabbed him with a dry look, and then headed in the back for a clean shirt. Maybe if I wasn't a covered in ice cream I might have found humor in the situation. Tossing the milkshake-covered shirt into my bag, my lips twitched. I would never be able to look at that shirt again without thinking of Kat.

She was something else.

Katia

Seth was such a jerk. Jerk didn't even cut it. He was the scum on the bottom of my heels. It was such a pity, because he was an amazing kisser. And he made me feel more alive than I'd felt in a very long time. He ignited something inside me. If he didn't open his mouth, he'd be damn near perfect.

I drove home in a blind rage and even had to circle the block a few times before I let off enough steam. When I pulled into my driveway, I sunk into the seat and hit the steering wheel with my hands. "How could I be so dumb?" I seethed, and then I swore.

The last thing I wanted was to face my family. My emotions were written all over my face, and the downside of having a mom with goddess blood was that she could detect every emotion. Mom had a knack for knowing when something was wrong. Mother intuition. Magick. Clairvoyance. Whatever you wanted to call it, she had it, which could be annoying or consoling, depending on your mood.

Today, I did not want my feelings picked apart. I just wanted to escape to my room and wallow in my own self-pity. I didn't want to see another human all day. Not until I finished licking this wound Seth left on my heart. Or maybe it was Matt.

I was an emotional wreck. It was possible I was projecting my breakup baggage on Seth, looking to grasp onto something that had never been there. Or maybe Seth just wasn't into me and he really did loathe me.

The thought made my stomach drop.

Creeping from my car to the house, I made it up into my bedroom undetected. Someone upstairs must love me. Once I clicked the little lock in place, I let out a long swoosh of air and collapsed on my violet bed. I stared at the white butterflies on my wall, contemplating my life.

School had barely begun and already I was dreading the rest of the year. I didn't want my senior year to be a repeat of the last three: homework, cheer practice, basketball games, and endless parties.

I wanted my last year to be memorable, exciting. I enjoyed hanging out with my friends, but I felt like all we did was talk about the same trivial things over and over. They didn't really know *me*. How could they when I was keeping such a huge secret? Being a nixie had suddenly become a small piece of me. It had taken a back burner. I hardly ever practiced anymore in my attempt to be *normal*. I was just now realizing how special it was to have magick and how much I missed the exhilarated rush flowing through my veins.

Part of the reason I stopped practicing was because I thought my magick was insignificant. It felt so lame compared to what the others in my circle could do.

Olivia, the free-spirited soul, was the only one of the group with an affinity. Hers was with fire, and she had the flaming red hair to match.

Elena, though she was moody and hard to get along with, could bring anything she touched to life and had the power to heal.

Zeke, sweet Zeke. With his fair colored hair and blue eyes, he had been the prankster of the group and Seth's best friend. Zeke played with people's heads. He could make you think things, erase memories, and much more.

Then there was Seth. What couldn't Seth do was a better question. Besides having a talent for drawing, he was also a gifted nixie. I'd seen him turn water into fire, rocks into crystals, and pluck a star from the sky.

No joke.

Seth was mesmerizing.

And then there was me. What were my magickal abilities? Puzzles. I could solve puzzles, mazes, anything problematic in seconds.

Ugh, why couldn't I have gotten something kickass like invisibility or teleportation?

As you got older, you honed your ability, strengthened the gift you were blessed with. Just like anything in life, practice makes perfect. I really hadn't seen the point. I wasn't going to be able to use my gift to save lives, so I just stopped altogether—cold turkey. Why? I hadn't felt blessed. I felt like the goddess blood in my veins had been wasted on me.

Thinking about the circle brought back memories I had buried. The five of us had gotten into trouble, but it had been fun. Not at all like my current friends' idea of *fun*. It made my heart heavy and achy remembering.

If I tried to befriend them now, would they even accept my

place in the circle again? Without me, the circle had lost its balance. They could still practice as a group, but their combined powers would have weakened immensely without the fifth. If with my measly powers, I would have amped up magickal juice.

There was a huge part of me that was scared to be rejected, although I had rejected them years ago. It would serve me right if they shunned me.

I was past the point of caring what everyone thought of me. Being popular was not all what it was hyped to be, and ironically I was more alone than ever. I stared at the white butterflies on my walls until the sun went down.

***

"What happened to you Friday night?" Claudia asked Monday morning.

I leaned against my locker, the cool metal at my back. "Don't even ask. It was a disaster."

She folded her arms, her black ponytail swinging with the movement, and waited for me to elaborate. I huffed. She was bound to find out sooner or later. "Matt and I broke up," I said, the back of my head hitting the locker.

"Totally saw that coming," Claudia replied in her know-it-all tone.

She was getting on my nerves. "What's that supposed to mean?"

"Just that you haven't been happy in months, Katia." I was surprised at how intuitive she'd been to figure that out. So not normally Claudia. "It was guaranteed to happen. That, and there have been rumors that Matt's been sleeping with Jessica."

My head snapped up. "What! And you are just now telling me this?" Some best friend.

She shrugged, biting her lip. "I figured maybe you didn't care. You've been distracted by a certain someone else lately."

I gave her a weird look. "What is that supposed to mean? If you've got something to say, just spit it out for Pete's sake." I wasn't in the mindset for games.

She gave me a half smile. "What's the deal with you and Seth Nightingale?" she asked.

Gulp. Had someone seen us kiss? Had he told the whole school that we swapped spit? I didn't peg Seth as the kiss-and-tell type of guy. But God knows I didn't have the best judgment when it came to boys. That was for sure. "I don't know what you mean," I said, playing dumb. I hiked up the bag that was beginning to slip off my shoulder.

Claudia snickered. "The heck you don't. You can't fool me, Katia. The two of you have been having some kind of twisted eye-banging thing for the last two years."

"We have not," I denied and took a deep breath. "There is nothing going on with me and Seth."

"Uh-huh. So you are telling me that you don't undress him with your eyes every day in Ms. Harper's class?"

"I do not," I insisted more forcefully. A few heads turned our way as the halls started to fill with students shuffling to get to class.

She rolled her dark blue eyes. "Why don't you just do him and get it over with? Then you'll satisfy that curious mind of yours and you can concentrate on something other than Seth's glorious body."

My mouth fell open.

"See you at practice," Claudia called over her shoulder, grinning like a shithead.

Claudia had lost her freaking mind.

I did not ogle Seth every day like he was a piece of cherry pie. Man, I love cherry pie. Add vanilla ice cream on top and I'd be putty in his hands. Okay. Fine. I'd been caught gawking at him a few too many times, but that was only because he was gawking at me.

Not that it really mattered how I looked at Seth. I had apparently totally misread the signs. He made it clear that he wasn't interested in me like that—twice. Still didn't change the fact that he made my heart jump out of my chest.

His name alone made my belly dance with butterflies.

Being a teenager sucked.

Chapter 6

Katia

If I thought my day started off rocky, it only got worse. Matt Lang was the biggest dickhead this side of the Mississippi, or maybe in the whole goddamn universe. I should have known Matt would make a scene at school. He lived for drama.

Just to sweeten the pot, when I was on my way to English—the class I had with Seth—I bumped into my ex.

"Well, if it isn't Katia, the school slut," Matt sneered, and his basketball buddies snickered. He turned to his circle of d-bag friends. "Which one of you guys wants her next? I've grown bored, and she isn't that good anyway."

Assholes.

I was two-seconds away from punt-kicking him in the junk. Again. It was effective enough the first time. Why not go for round two? My cheeks blazed with anger. Was it just too damn much to ask that Matt actually talk to me in private? Oh no. The whole school had to be involved. Mature. What I was twitching to do was turn him into a fly and smash his five-eyed butt.

"Matt, let me break it down into small terms for you. I. Broke. Up. With. You. Do you understand?" I asked condescendingly.

He took a step closer to me, evading my personal bubble. Matt loved intimidation, but this was one girl who didn't back down. That little trait was definitely going to get me in trouble one day. Just hopefully not today. I contemplated hocking a loogie in his face. "Katia, you're a slut. Everyone knows it, so cut the little virginal act. You aren't fooling anyone."

My blood boiled, and I felt the first tingles of magick spread to my fingertips. Maybe everyone did think that I had a loose reputation, but it couldn't have been further from the truth, and that was what really bruised Matt's inflated ego. He was pissed I hadn't slept with him. I wanted to cause him bodily harm. I wanted to deck him square in the face. "Listen, douchebag, I don't care—"

I never got to finish my verbal thrashing. Seth had materialized out of nowhere and quicker than I could blink, he had Matt pinned against the lockers. Metal screeched under the weight of Matt's body. Suddenly, there was a crowd surrounding us, growing like wildfire.

Oh shit.

"Watch what you say about her," Seth growled, eyes flashing with barely contained rage.

My heart leaped into my throat. Confusion couldn't begin to describe how I was feeling. Why was he jumping to my defense?

Every muscle in Seth's body was taut, poised to crush Matt. The vein in his neck pulsed, and whether Matt knew it or not, Seth was a much bigger threat. He had more than just his fists to pummel Matt with. I held my breath as I waited to see what Seth would do, what he might say next. Then he shoved Matt into the locker, smacking his head against the steel, and released him. Matt stumbled. His basketball buddies hadn't been very quick on the draw, and they hardly had time to realize what had happened. Seth didn't wait around, he pushed his way through the cluster of kids, and as he passed by me, his fingers clasped mine.

Half dragging me, half guiding me, he led the rest of the way to class. I stole a quick glance over my shoulder and smiled to myself. Seeing Seth jump to my defense was almost as satisfying as ninja kicking Matt's balls.

"You sure know how to pick them, don't you, Kats?" he grumbled, his voice still vibrating with anger.

Tongue-tied, I watched Seth stalk to his seat, leaving me more muddled than ever. My mind felt like a cherry slushie. I wanted to ask him a gazillion questions, but not in a room with an audience. So for the next forty-five minutes of Ms. Harper's class I peeked at

Seth from under my long lashes, studying this complex guy—the vein at his neck still ticking and his body lined with tension.

What gives?

Why would he care about the nasty lies Matt spread about me?

What was he so pissed about?

Even after class had ended, Seth still looked ready to commit murder. On my behalf? Or maybe he was annoyed that he had to rescue me—again. Either way I didn't get it. One minute he insulted me, and the next he was defending my honor. Talk about making a girl's head spin.

He shot out of the room before his name even left my lips. I slumped in my seat, running a frazzled hand through my curls.

Damn it.

Obliviously he was back to pretending I didn't exist.

Whatever.

Two could play that game.

When the final bell rang, announcing the end of yet another day, I immediately changed into my cheerleading clothes. The black and red short shirt swished against my bare legs as I walked to the gym. Vermillion high was home to the Tanagers—a little bird, not precisely fierce.

Slugging my athletic bag over my shoulder, I walked into the gym and the lively buzzing of the gossip bees went dead. My newly single status and the commotion I had caused in the hallway must have trickled down the grapevine. I dropped my bag in the corner with a loud thump that echoed through the gymnasium.

This ought to be interesting.

You could have dropped a pin in the room. "I am not going to have a breakdown," I said to the group, pretending to be stretching my limbs. "Let's just practice."

After that, energetic chatter once again jam-packed the gym. They really weren't overly concerned about my feelings, just waiting to see if I would give them something new to start spreading over the gossip mills.

I sighed and sat on the mats to finished my stretch routine.

Seth

I should have done a lot more than body slam Matt Lang. He deserved so much more for his treatment of Kat. And I didn't just mean for today. Matt was a prick. What she ever saw in the jerky-jock escaped me. But God did it feel good to lay my hands on him. I had been itching to pulverize that pretty boy face of his for a year.

It had taken all my strength to not lay into him. I hadn't realized the amount of pent-up anger I had at him, at the shitty deck I'd been dealt. He was just the lucky sap I'd projected it on. Even now, hours later, I was still fuming and was looking for something to hit.

Shoving my books into my locker, I paused, feeling the familiar tingle. Kat was near. Shoving the metal door closed, I leaned against it and waited. A moment later she came into my eyesight from the girl's locker room, walking toward the gym. My head hit the locker as my heart back flipped.

Kat in her cheerleader skirt was like every teenage boy's wet dream.

Well, at least mine. My eyes followed her through the hall just to make sure Matt the punk left her alone…so I told myself. It had nothing to do with the fact that I found her utterly spellbinding.

"Are you ever going to hit that?" Zeke asked, sneaking up behind me.

I still hadn't taken my eyes off her. "Sheila Michaels?" I said, playing dumb. "Hell no. I wouldn't touch her if my life depended on it."

Zeke snorted. "You know that is not who I am talking about. And, dude, if you touched Sheila, I would disown you as my best friend."

I wanted to pretend ignorance, but there was really no point. I'd been caught red-handed ogling. Sheila and Kat disappeared behind the gym doors, and I finally looked at Zeke. "Nope. I don't plan on going anywhere near Katia Montgomery." I pushed off the lockers and started to strut toward the exit. Zeke was quick on my heels.

"Why the hell not? That girl is bangin', popular, one of us, and clearly into you. She is a cheerleader for frick's sake. Enough said."

My brows buried together. "I just can't. So drop it." There was a warning in my tone not to push the subject. Zeke pretty much never listened to warnings.

The sun hit us overheard. "You literally bare teeth and growl if anyone mentions her name."

I blinked, adjusting to the sunlight. "I do not," I argued.

Zeke shook his blond head. "I don't understand. We used to all be friends."

The parking lot was packed with cars zipping to get off school grounds. "Keyword in that sentence, *used* to be friends. As in not anymore." We weaved through the parking lot, barely escaping being run over by some overzealous sophomore who probably just got their license.

"If you tell me that you aren't interested, I'll call you a liar."

Man. He just wasn't going to drop this topic. "Trust me, Zeke, when I say that it will never happen."

He leaned against my truck, preventing me from opening the door. "I'm not an idiot, Seth, but *you are* if you don't take a chance with Katia. She is one in a million, and she is *so* into you. I can feel the sexual tension between the two of you. It's thick enough to cut with a samurai sword."

I didn't need a reminder. I already knew how special she was, but that changed nothing. I never told anyone about the curse, not even my best friend. The only people who knew about the dark cloud that hung over my head were my parents and Kat's. Maybe the only way Zeke would shut up about her was if I told him. I was getting sick and tired of always shouldering this fucking curse alone.

"Look, man," Zeke said when I remained silent, stewing in my indecision. "If you aren't going to take a shot, then I will—"

He barely finished the sentence and I was in his face, my vibrant eyes narrowing. "I will break you in half if you touch her."

Zeke grinned. "So you *do* care…"

I sighed heavily, taking a step back. "It doesn't matter, Zeke." My gaze wandered off over his shoulder, looking at the white peaked mountains in the distance. "Kat and I can never be anything."

His blue eyes shot me a puzzling look.

"We're cursed." There, I'd said it. Surprisingly, my chest felt lighter. I wasn't sure how I expected to feel, letting go of a secret I'd kept my whole life.

I'll hand it to Zeke; he took it in stride. "You're freaking shitting me."

Or not.

I met his astonished gaze. "No. I wish I was though," I admitted, my voice thick with unmistakable regret

He ran a hand through his short hair. "What kind of curse? Why have you never told me?" There might have been a little bit of hurt behind his words.

I slouched, my whole body supported by the truck. "The kind that will get Kat killed."

He squinted his eyes. "And you're sure about this?"

I understood his doubt, but bad things happened if Kat and I got too close. That was all the proof I had needed to keep my distance. The sinking sensation in my gut got worse. "Yep. Positive. We're starbound."

I heard him suck in a sharp breath. My thought exactly. The idea of not being with Kat stole my breath. It made my chest ache. It splinted my heart into a thousand pieces.

Being starbound meant there was one person chosen to be yours by the stars—like a soul mate juiced up on steroids. It infused magick, heart, soul, flesh, and spirit, binding two nixies for all eternity—the five points of a star. Starbound was rare, and if you found yours, you never let go.

After a moment of deadpan, I told Zeke the tale, one I knew by memory and could recite in my sleep. "This curse has been plaguing our families for centuries. It was cast by Arachne, Kat's ancestor."

"The one who was turned into a spider?" Zeke asked, interrupting.

"The one and the same, except this happened before she offended Athena. Archne had been starbound to my bloodline. She was hopelessly in love, but their love came at a price—a fatal price. Before they took the starsoul pledge, Avery, my ancestor, was with another goddess. He betrayed her with Arachne, and the scorned goddess lost her shit. The warrior princess, in her grief at catching him in the arms of Arachne, was blinded by her broken heart. She cast a spell. It didn't matter that Arachne and Avery were starsouls. And so the curse was born—my bloodline could never love a Montgomery without them killing each other. But in a cruel twist of fate, the curse also binds our bloodlines as starsouls, so that our destiny is always the same. If Kat and I accept our fate and utter the sacred words, the curse will be activated and it would kill her. And eventually kill me."

A starsoul could never live without his or her love. Their hearts—their lives were woven together. If one stopped beating so would the other, and their souls would follow one another into the afterlife, where they could be together forever. Every nixie knew about starbinding and how exceptional it was.

Zeke's expression turned thoughtful as he digested the heavy information. "Does Katia know?" he asked after a moment.

I shook my head. "She doesn't have a clue."

"That's just wrong. Don't you think you owe it to her to tell her?"

"Honestly, I don't know anymore, Zeke. I've spent so much time pushing her away, making her despise me…"

He could hear it in my voice, how much it tore me up inside. "Oh, man. That is one seriously messed up curse. And you are sure there is no way to break it?"

I shook my head.

"Have you ever tried?" he asked. Zeke was the kind of guy that wanted to help. If you had a problem, he would be the first in line to offer his services.

My eyes sobered. "And risk her dying. I can't. I won't."

Silence stretched out between us in the nearly empty parking lot. The sun was slowly beginning to fall, just reaching the tips of the trees. It blasted rays of orange, red, and purple across the horizon.

There was nothing else left to say.

Chapter 7

Katia

"Not before you have breakfast," Mom urged, as I was getting ready to walk out the door.

Today was the first home game of the season. Sometimes Saturday games just plain sucked, especially when I had to get up almost as early as a school day. "I don't have time, Mom. I have a game." And I was dragging ass.

She had her no-nonsense face on. "Katia, at least eat something, or you'll collapse on the court." She set a box of cereal at the table and kissed my head.

Dad winked at me from over the paper, taking a sip of his black coffee. There were sprinkles of grey at his temples in his otherwise sandy hair. The sun streaming from the bay window picked up hints of red, and a five o'clock shadow covered his chin. I took a seat next to him at the table and slammed down a bowl of

Lucky Charms just to appease Mom. Dad chuckled occasionally at the comic section like a knucklehead.

I rolled my eyes.

Dad didn't have a serious bone in his body. "So you have your first game, Sprite?" he asked, setting aside the paper.

When I was born, Mom told him that I looked like a tiny faerie sprite with my downy white hair. The nickname stuck. "Yep," I replied, swirling my marshmallows in the bowl with my spoon.

He took a sip of his coffee. "I don't hear the usual enthusiasm. Where's all the rah-rah-rah?"

I sighed. "I think I am done with cheerleading," I admitted, something I'd never thought I would say.

His brow arched. "Really? Wow, that is a surprise. I thought you loved it."

"I do, or at least I used to. I don't know anymore." I heaped a spoon full of marshmallows into my mouth. Does anyone actually eat the cereal part?

Mom joined us with her own steaming mug of caffeine in her hands, warm blue eyes smiling at me. "I think you are starting to feel the pressure of being an adult. This is your last year in high school, and there are so many big decisions for you to make. It's okay to be confused about what you want, Katia."

She made it sound so easy, but it really wasn't—at least not for me. "Maybe," I conceded. "I've been thinking about Olivia, Zeke, and Elena a lot lately, and how we used to be friends." I left out Seth. That would have been a big blunder.

There was a brief hesitation before she said, "I think that is a great idea."

Under normal circumstances Mom would have jumped all over the idea of me hanging with other peers who had magick. I didn't understand her hesitation. Wasn't she always telling me that I needed to use my gift more? "I better go before Claudia chews me out," I said, gathering my bowl and bringing it to the sink.

As I got up from the table, I couldn't help noticing the look that passed between them. Something was up that they didn't want me to know, or didn't want me to worry about. It wasn't the first time I had gotten that inkling.

As if I needed something else to add to my plate.

The October air was getting chilly, and my spanks just weren't going to cut it for the short trip to school. A shiver ran through me before I even reached my car, and I turned right around and headed back inside. Taking the stairs two at a time, I ran up to my bedroom to grab a hoodie. I didn't feel like looking fashionable and freezing to death. I'd learned that lesson the other night and was in no hurry for a repeat.

But there wasn't time to dwell. If I didn't blow at least one stop sign on the way to school, I was going to be late. I had my hand on the front doorknob when I heard whispering coming from the kitchen. Collins was still fast asleep, and I knew I shouldn't eavesdrop on my parents, but…

Creeping around the corner, I suddenly wished I had supersonic hearing. Their voices were low and somber. A ribbon of unease wound itself inside my belly. Maybe I would hear something I didn't want to know. Maybe they were getting a divorce, or maybe my grandma was terminally ill. None of these irrational conclusions were making my unease less.

Pressing my ear to the wall, I listened to see if I could pick up pieces of the conversation. "We have to tell her," Dad said, and I assumed *her* was me.

"I know. We will soon," Mom's hush voice agreed.

"Before it's too late," Dad warned worriedly.

"I'll talk to him." Mom didn't sound exactly thrilled to do so.

Who the hell is him?

God, I hated cryptic snooping. It was the pits.

I snuck out of the house feeling more confused and tangled. What was I supposed to make of that? I glanced at the clock on the dash and swore, slamming my foot on the gas. I was so going to be late for the first game, and Claudia was going to serve me my ass. Friend or not, when it came to cheering, Claudia was a hardass.

Squealing the tires on my Jetta, I pulled into the parking space cockeyed at Vermillion High. Whipping off the seatbelt, I bolted for the double doors that led to the gym.

"Where the hell have you been?" Claudia pounced as soon as she saw me.

Breathless from the run, I winced. "Sorry, Claudia. Crisis at home."

Her olive-complexion looked amazing in red. Even when she was scowling, as she did now, she still looked good. "Don't let it happen again, Katia. There is no special treatment just because you are my best friend."

It was best to agree with her. I didn't feel like arguing. "Got it."

I took my place with the other girls gathered by the left side of the bleachers. The rows of benches were already filled with parents, classmates, and the rival team's cheering section. Open season always brought a crowd.

The whistle blew, the ball was tossed in the air, and the squeaking of snickers filled the court. Our basketball team was state champion material. I watched as Matt setup a shot and the ball sailed through the air, swishing into the net. The other girls around me jumped up, screaming and cheering for their team. I just glared, unable to muster any enthusiasm for my ex.

Claudia gave me the death stare, and I threw her a fake grin. I was so going to get an earful after the game.

Harper poked me in the side with her arm. "What's going on with you? Claudia looks ready to summon an evil spell on you."

I coughed. I knew it was an offhanded comment, but it hit a little close to home, being a nixie and all. Cursing someone was a real possibility whether you meant anything by it or not. We don't take that lightly. "Nothing. Just shit at home, and I'm totally PMSing." That usually stopped people from asking prying questions.

Harper tossed her blonde hair into a ponytail. "Great. Two raging bitches. This ought to be a fun game."

For some stupid reason, I scanned the stands for Seth, which was a pointless endeavor. He never came to school games, and I knew that he worked at the garage on Saturdays, but it still didn't stop me from looking, on the off chance that he was here.

Illogical disappointment sprang inside my belly.

I was mad at him—really mad. Why should I care that he didn't come to a stupid basketball game? Hell, *I* didn't even want to be here. Hadn't I just a week ago cursed Seth to seven different kinds of hell? And now I wanted to see him every chance I got?

God, what was wrong with me?

Just then the buzzer went off, announcing the end of the first quarter. Matt strutted off the court, dripping in sweat like a pig. I paid him no attention, still lost in my own argument over my mixed feelings for Seth. But when a hand slapped my butt, I was jarred back from what was starting to be a spicy memory of Seth's lips.

Spinning around, I was ready to condemn the asshole who put his hands on me. "What the he—" I yelped, coming face-to-face with Matt, the two-face scumbucket. I gritted my teeth. "Keep your hands off me."

"Whatever you say, toots." He gave me a smug grin and went to the sidelines with his teammates all snickering.

Toots? I wanted trip him and watch him kiss the court, but as I took a step forward, Claudia placed a hand on my shoulder.

"Not now. We have a routine to perform," she all but scolded.

How could I concentrate now?

Reluctantly I put my need for revenge aside and mechanically got into formation. Later, Matt Lang was going to feel my wrath. I'd had enough of his shit, and his lies, for a lifetime.

The music started, and I tried to shut down my brain and focus on my dancing. I failed. Seeing Matt brought memories of the night I kissed Seth. Funny how I felt nothing but hatred for Matt, yet Seth…well, he made me feel feverish, annoyed, and achy. Talk about messed up.

I craved Seth's presence, and I couldn't ever remember my palms going damp because of a guy, if ever. Seth intrigued me, and there was no denying the air sizzled between us. Whether we were locking lips or spitting fire, there was heat.

In my distractedness, I missed a step, followed by another one. My rhythm was thrown off, and I scrambled to get back in time with the others.

"What is your deal?" Claudia hissed between her teeth next to me and still managed to keep a smile on her face for the crowd. It was sort of impressive.

"Nothing," I mumbled, recovering the steps.

I had a feeling this was going to be a very long year. It was only nearing the end of October and already I was losing my footing.

Chapter 8

Katia

All Hallows' Eve.

It used to my favorite holiday as kid. Still was. The circle would meet in our secret place, and we would celebrate in our own way.

It was magickal. The whole night was filled with candlelight, laughter, an eerie ambience, and the security of each other. There was the scent of spices, crushed flowers, and damp earth. The secrecy of our group, and what we could do, added to the thrill of the night and the possibility of exposure.

It was so much fun.

We were able to let go, cast spells, giggle, play games, and in general cause mayhem. I lost count of the number of pranks we pulled on All Hallows' Eve. Zeke was in seventh heaven. I missed his infectious smile.

Out of everyone, I expected Zeke and Olivia to be the least judgmental. It was going to be Seth and Elena that got their backs up if I showed tonight. That was if they still met at the clearing in the woods, not far from the cemetery. It was a spot that radiated with natural spirits and energy. The perfect place to cast spells. It added potency to them, strengthening our magick.

All day I struggled with the decision.

Do I or don't I try to make amends?

Do I or don't go to the clearing?

Do I or don't I leave myself open to getting hurt?

Nothing had changed over the last week with Seth. He still wasn't talking to me. He still avoided eye contact. And he went out of his way to put as much distance between us as possible. It was almost as if he was afraid to be close to me. Except, I couldn't help but feel like things were different. Something had changed between us, whether Seth liked it or not. I could sense it shimmering in the air. There was this twinkling ribbon of some unknown force pulling me to him. I didn't know how else to explain it.

So what exactly made me think that tonight of all nights was a good time to try to reconnect broken bridges was a mystery. I not only felt a pull toward Seth, but there was also this overwhelming need, beckoning me to seek out the companions of the circle. I didn't know why, but I felt like something big was going to happen tonight. Though, there were many other All Hallows' Eves I'd felt the same.

As night approached, I finally made up my mind. I wanted to spend this sacred holiday with friends who understood what it meant to have power. The circle had once been a second family to me. This was as good as any time to see if the circle would let me back in—maybe at least for the night.

I took a seat in front of my vanity, digging out makeup I had reserved for just this night. While the other girls in my circle went for the darker approach, I had always gone in the opposite direction. We would tease each other mercifully, but it had all been in fun and games then.

Lining my eyes with a white glittery shadow, I took time with the application, and when I finished, my face sparkled with a celestial glow. Tossing on a white cardigan, I grabbed my keys from my nightstand and took a deep breath.

Here went nothing.

"Mom!" I called as I skipped down the stairs. "I'm going out."

"Okay, Katia. No need to yell." She was at the bottom of the stairs passing out a giant bowl of Halloween candy—the good stuff. It was kind of a family joke that Mom dressed up as a ghastly witch every year. The best part was it looked amazingly real. A few twists of her nose and she suddenly had long grey hair, warts, and the sickest green skin I'd ever seen on a human. And Mom could cackle with the best of them.

When Collins and I were little, Mom used to chase us around the house. We loved every second of it.

I snuck a piece of chocolate from the bowl and got my hand smacked. "Don't get into any trouble," she said and then gave me an eerie laugh.

I grinned, unwrapping the candy as I strolled out the front door, leaving Mom to the little goblins and princesses. My Jetta purred to life as I backed down the driveway, careful of the little kiddos. The streets were lined with parents, some in costume, some not. Mine had always been the ones decked out in full gear. There were wagons piled with toddlers in them, candy wrappers tossed in the grass, and the spooky sounds of chains rattling, ghostly moans, and chainsaws.

Parking my car at the edge of the road, I took a breath. This was it. There was still time to change my mind and possibly save myself the humiliation of being rejected. It would be pretty sad being told off by a band of misfits.

I had come this far, no point in turning back now. I wasn't a coward. Every bone in my body told me that this was the only way I was going to fill that void inside me, the one I had been searching blindly the last few years to satisfy—unsuccessfully I might add.

After adding a quick coat of lip gloss, I got out of the car and began to trudge up the hill that led to the woods. I could walk this hike blindfolded. It was second nature to me. Being back here was like a blast to the past. With each step I took, my heart accelerated, whether it was because I would soon see Seth or because of the circle, I could not say. Regardless, my palms had started to sweat, and a streak of nerves shot through me.

God. This was probably such a horrendous idea. I was just full of them lately.

Finally, I peeked behind a bush, staring into a small circular glade. As I pushed aside the colored tree branches of autumn and stepped into the clearing, I saw a sight that never failed to steal my breath. It was just as mesmerizing as the first time I'd seen it. White pillar candles were lit around a circle of stones, which I knew had been lit by Olivia. She could make anything go up in flames, including her hair in the fourth grade. If I concentrated I could still smell her charred hair. It was nasty, but tonight the air was infused with lavender, rosemary, and other herbs. Sweet, like homecoming.

The moon's glow bathed over my skin as I gathered the last of my courage and stepped farther into the clearing, leaves crunching underfoot. There were voices coming from just outside the circle, and I could make out four shadows from the moonlight. I gulped.

They were all here. And I made five.

At the sound of my footsteps, heads whipped in my direction.

A branch snapped as I stopped, afraid to go any farther. There was a moment of dead silence. Not even the woods around us spoke, and I waited, teetering on their decision. I should have known the quick-tongued Elena would be the first to speak. She had something to say about everything.

"What is *she* doing here?" Elena spat. Her short and sassy midnight hair was streaked with bright purple strands. In all black, with bold red lips and pale skin, she looked like a vampire.

I hadn't expected a warm welcome, but I also hadn't expected such contempt. It was on the tip of my tongue to tell her to kiss my ass and storm back the way I had come.

Elena and I didn't have a stellar past. I think out of everyone in the circle, my departure hit her the hardest. While the others might have understood my need to try and be normal, Elena never would.

She took magic very serious. My rejection of my gift was in her eyes worse than kicking a puppy. She never could comprehend that I might see my powers as more of a hindrance.

I also believe a part of her had been jealous of my relationship with Seth. Even at a young age, we had this unspoken bond. I think Elena had been bitter that Seth and my connection went deeper than just the circle.

We never really talked about it. It was just there, a spark between us, but now, I wondered if it was something more...

Maybe if I hadn't run off, Seth and I would be different, maybe I would be happy.

Luckily Olivia saved Elena from my backlash. Typical.

"Elena!" Olivia hissed. The soft glow of candlelight bounced off her glossy dark red hair. Out of all of us, Olivia looked the most like a fae. She had the dainty features of a pixie faerie with a cute button nose, a petite frame, and the brightest violet eyes.

I stood still, nibbling on my lip, seeing what they would say or do next. I hadn't ruled out my "aborting mission" option just yet.

Zeke was the first to move. He gave me a devilish grin and then embraced me in a bear hug, lifting me off my feet. "Christ, Katia. It's been a long time." His voice had a sparkle of mischief in it and genuine glee.

I wrapped my arms around his neck, squeezing my eyes shut, and held on. "I'm glad someone is happy to see me," I murmured. A feeling of relief spiraled through me. I wasn't being burned at the stake…yet.

"Always, Katia." He set me on my feet, and I couldn't stop smiling. His summer-blue eyes were full of humor. "You're one of us." Zeke was always so easygoing, easy to forgive.

Olivia took his place the second he released me. "We missed you," she said, her quiet voice filled with emotion.

"Me too," I replied, my eyes misting with hers.

She wiped her eyes with the back of her sleeve, smiling. And just like that I felt something click inside me. This was what I had been looking for. The same thing I had run from in my youth was the one thing I needed. Being with others who embraced our gifts made more sense than anything else right now in my life.

"I can't believe you are guys are just welcoming her with open arms. Um, hello. She left the circle. Why does she just get to stroll back because she is bored?" Elena's expression was darkened with outraged and eyeliner. She stepped forward from the shadows.

I took a deep breath. I'd known that not everyone would be openhearted.

"Cut it out, Elena," Zeke replied, slicing Elena with a look of warning.

Elena stabbed me with hateful daggers. "She is the biggest joke."

I bit my lip and returned her glare with one of my own. I could only take so much.

This time is was Seth who spoke. He had been absolutely quiet since I had stepped through the clearing, but that didn't mean I hadn't felt his eyes one me. "Knock it off, Elena. Kats has every right to be here—as much as we do."

She glanced at Seth who had stepped beside her. "You guys sicken me. I can't believe you."

"Give it up, Elena. We don't want to spend the whole night listening to another one of your bitchy rants," Zeke cut in before

Elena could continue in a full-blown tantrum. She was prone to them when she didn't get her way. Some things never changed.

I met Seth's eyes and the world stood still. I hadn't known what to expect or how I would feel when I saw him again. We hadn't exactly been on the greatest of terms the last week, so I figured it was going to be awkward to the tenth power.

I was right.

"Hey," I said, unable to think of anything intelligent or sarcastically witty.

"Hey," he replied. The sound of his voice squeezed my heart.

Why does *he* have to be the guy that made me feel lightheaded? Why did it have to be Seth who made my breath catch? Why was it when I looked at him, the rest of the universe disappeared?

Even when I probably should have been miffed and irritated with him, I couldn't be. There was something about Seth that made me want to ignore his less than stellar qualities. Like that he could be a little rough around the edges. He might have a quick temper, a protective streak a mile long, and he could be an insensitive jerk, but under all those jagged edges, there was a guy with a huge heart. And even with his flaws laid out on the table, I knew that I didn't just want to be friends with Seth.

Shit. I was in so much trouble. My heart was in so much trouble.

I couldn't figure out why it took me so long to realize that what I wanted was him. I wanted Seth.

With our gazes still locked and my heart pounding in my ears, I found myself lost inside eyes like the rolling plains of Ireland. It felt like he could see inside my soul. As if he knew what I had just come to understand. His eyes warmed the same time my body flushed.

"I can't believe we are all here again," Olivia squealed excitedly, snapping me back from la-la land. "I am so glad you came." She grabbed my hand in hers and pulled me to the circle.

Elena stuck her finger in her mouth, making gagging noises. Everyone ignored her.

We all sat around the circle, candles lighting our faces. Seth and Elena sat on the opposite end, obviously to put as much space as necessary between them and me. I tried not to show the irritation I felt. There was this absurd voice inside me that wanted to stomp across the circle and claim my stake on him. I didn't want another girl near him.

What the flip is wrong with me?

Instead I folded my hands in my lap and clenched my jaw.

Elena sat practically on top of Seth, and she was constantly finding ways to touch him. I ground my teeth and seethed. It was pitiful how evident she made her desire for Seth. I couldn't decide if she was turning up the flirting because of me or if she was just that much of a skank. I had an inkling she was just a skank. But if she put her hand on him one more time…

My eyes narrowed as her black painted nails rested on his shoulder.

I wanted to puke. I wanted to gouge her eyes out.

Glancing at his face, he didn't seem to care what Elena was doing or saying. He was far too busy staring at me. A shudder ran through me. I couldn't look away if I tried.

"Seth!" Elena shouted, and we both dropped our gazes as if we'd been caught stealing from the cookie jar.

He wrestled a hand through his dark hair, and Elena pressed her leg against his. I tried not to let my irritation show. If I ever needed a poker face, it was now.

"So what should we do?" Olivia asked the group after we all were seated.

"I think we should do something special—you know, now that Katia is back," Zeke replied, smiling beside me. I grinned back.

"I got it." Olivia all but jumped up. "This is our last All Hallows' Eve before we go off to college. Let's do a starsoul spell. I've always wondered if my true love is out there." She got all dewy-eyed, fluttering her long lashes.

Seth's eyes slammed into mine. "No," he quickly shut her down.

"I think it is a great idea," Elena purred, completely

disregarding him. Her leg was basically in Seth's lap now, and she gave him a pointed look. If she kept looking at him like that, I was going to blind her.

"Come on, guys," Olivia encouraged. "It will be a fun. Haven't you ever been curious if you've met your soul mate?"

Maybe it was more a girl thing, kind of like planning your wedding, something little girls dreamed of. I wasn't sure guys were wired the same way.

"Olivia, you know that spell is inaccurate. It only works if you have had some form of contact with the person," Seth argued, clearly against the idea.

She shrugged, not deterred. "I know, but it's worth a shot. And so what if it doesn't work? No harm done. We will be left to still wonder if they are out there."

"Hell, why not?" Zeke replied. "What else do we have to do tonight?" He gave me a sideways half-smile.

"I can think of plenty," Seth grumbled.

Zeke eyed Seth across the circle. "What's the big deal, Seth? Afraid of what you'll see?" he asked, arching a brow at his best friend. There was a glint of challenge in his eyes.

Something was definitely going on between those two. I glanced between them, wondering what was going through their heads.

Seth folded his arms. "Whatever. Fine. If this is what you guys want…" He stretched out his long legs, appearing blasé, but the tightening of his jaw said otherwise.

"Well, I vote yes just because Seth doesn't want to do it." I gave him a glaring-smirk.

Zeke chuckled beside me.

"I'd be careful what you ask for," Seth warned, his eyes sharpening.

My mouth thinned. "What is that supposed to mean?"

He shook his head. "Nothing. Let's just get this over with."

If I wasn't mistaken, Seth was uneasy. There was something he was hiding, and this spell was making him edgy. Maybe he already knew who his starsoul was. The thought made my gut twist. It was bad enough that he had Elena stuck to him.

Biting my tongue, I decided to suck up my irritation and try to have fun for Olivia's sake. Maybe it hadn't been a great idea to force my way back into the circle. Being this close to Seth was driving me bonkers.

I ripped my gaze from his. If it took all the strength I had inside me, I was going to avoid being caught by those startling green eyes. Instead, I concentrated on centering my energy and feeling the burn of power trickle in my veins.

There was magick in this place. I could feel it seeping from the ground, swirling in the air, and vibrating from the tree roots. As the five of us joined hands, sparks ignited on contact. It was a thrill feeling our magick flow from one another. Together we had more power and control. Together we were united.

Olivia had the most knowledge, so it was no surprise she cast the spell. Her voice was musical, steady, and true. "If there be a perfect match, this spell under moonlight will surely catch the one who is meant to be and shall be revealed to me. I cast this spell from a part of me, one of five, free will of who I see."

A gentle breeze picked up my hair and tingles ran down my spine. I watched in awe as a fire of blue flames erupted at the center of the circle. The flickering flares were cool to the skin, emitting magick, not heat. Inside my blood was singing in rejoice. It had been so long since I'd given in to the magick. It engulfed me with love and trust.

I missed this.

"I'll go first," Olivia offered. The material of her long, black dress draped on the ground. She plucked a strand of her hair and dropped into the center of the dancing blue flames.

Zeke snickered beside me. "I pity the poor sap that gets saddled to Olivia."

Olivia tapered her eyes. "Just wait, Zeke. I'll be laughing when some girl knocks you on your ass."

We all waited for something to materialize out of the unearthly flames. A shimmer. A face. When seconds turned to minutes and nothing happened, I felt cheated. It was a reminder that having goddess blood didn't mean you always got what you wanted at the snap of your fingers.

"You go next," Olivia prompted, looking at me. There was a tint of disappointment in her crystal-violet eyes.

My heart went out to her. She, out of all of us, had probably wanted to know the most. Maybe this spell wouldn't work on any of us, and it would be just a big waste of magick. I took a deep breath. Did I really want to know who I was destined to spend all eternity with?

"You don't have to do this, Kats," Seth said, staring intently at me over the blue fire. His voice was hard and icy.

It instantly put my back up. God, I hoped my starsoul was drop-me-dead-gorgeous, just so I could rub it in Seth's face—hell, Elena's too. I plucked a piece of hair, eyes defiant, and dangled it over the glowing flicker. Then I looked at Seth and Elena on the other side of the circle and let the single piece of hair slip from my fingers.

Shifting my gaze to the blue light swirling within the circle, my heart was in my throat. I didn't know why I was so nervous, but my palms were damp. Was I really about to see the guy of my dreams?

At first I thought that the spell was going to be another dud. The azure flames held steady, frolicking in time with my pounding heart. And then it happened, a twirling motion in the fire that slowly began to emit a colored smoke. My eyes clashed with Seth's over the ethereal light, and I lifted my chin. Nervous or not, I wasn't about to show it, yet he looked just as anxious. Or maybe I was mistaken and it was just because Elena was whispering something in his ear. I probably had it wrong. Why would Seth care whose face would be revealed?

Slowly the sapphire mist began to curl and take form. I sat at the edge of my seat with clasped hands. The face reflecting from the smoke was… *No! No! No! It wasn't possible.*

My breathing became labored. I thought I was going to pass out.

Seth's?

What the hell?

I froze.

No one said anything. No one moved.

It was Elena who broke the thick silence. "Fuck me."

I couldn't have said it better.

Olivia gasped beside me.

I could feel my whole body shaking, but was it from anger, fear, or shock? "Real funny, guys," I said cynically. This couldn't be real, right? There was no way that *Seth* was my starsoul. I stood up. "If you didn't want me here, you could have just said so. There was no reason to be assholes about it." I had never been so embarrassed.

"Katia, this isn't a joke," Zeke added stonily. "I swear on the full moon it's true. But he should have told you in a less tacky form. I'm sorry. I wasn't thinking you would get hurt."

Looking over my shoulder at Zeke, my emotions were tripping over one another. How could this be real? How did Zeke know? Had they all known, and I was the only idiot here? "Seth told you?" I accused, addressing everyone.

Zeke nodded. "The others didn't know," he said, heavy with regret.

Maybe somewhere in all the craziness running through my head, I knew that Seth had always been more than just a guy. I shot to my feet, glaring at him, and he was quick to follow. "Y-you knew? You knew that we were starbound?" I could barely get the words past the lump in my throat.

His jaw ticked. "Yes."

I felt the air leave my lungs. "For how long?"

Frown lines creased the corner of his lips. "Practically my whole life."

I was speechless. *His whole life?* "I—I don't understand. Why didn't you ever tell me?"

I couldn't believe we were having this discussion in front of the whole circle. They all pretended to be interested in something else. I was still having trouble believing it. Seth Nightingale's heart was twined with mine. Seth. How had *I* not known? I mean this was my soul mate, and he had been here, in front of me the whole time. A range of emotions tumbled inside me. Disbelief. Rage. Longing. Excitement. Hope.

Hardness settled over his dark eyes. "Because I don't want this. I don't want you," he said, his voice strained and harsh.

I felt like I had just been sucker punched. I gasped. "You don't want me." My mind was reeling, and then I was seeing red. I wanted to hurt him. "Well, the other night you sure as hell wanted me," I spat.

Beside him, Elena's painted red lips sneered. I had to get out of there. Pain lanced through my chest, and I turned away before Seth could see the effect his words had on me, before he could tell me again that he didn't want me.

I ran.

Chapter 9

Katia

"Kats!"

"Katia!"

I heard both Seth and Zeke yell my name, but I kept on going without looking back. Just as I reached the edge of the woods, uncontained tears streamed down my cheeks. I ran without any destination, just away from him—away from the circle. My vision was cloudy, my makeup was smearing, and my body felt heavy and sore, but none of it mattered.

My heart was...

Breaking.

Confused.

In pieces.

And I never felt so humiliated and exposed in my life. He didn't want me? Fine. I never planned to talk to Seth Nightingale again. He could roast in Hell for all I cared. Even as I thought the words, I sniffled back another round of tears.

None of it made sense. How could he be my starsoul if he felt nothing but hatred for me? That was not how starbound worked. The spell had to be wrong. Seth had to be wrong. We weren't destined. Our love wasn't written in the stars.

Occupied with the events of the night, I somehow ended up in the old cemetery, on All Hallows' Eve nonetheless. That was a bad omen all around. Just as my legs were burning in protest and I was about to stop, I felt the ground slip out under my feet. Suddenly I was staring at the twilight sky, when moments ago all I could see were blurry headstones and graves. My belly dropped at the rush of falling, and I had no time to catch myself.

Arms flailing, I fell backward. There was a loud thump followed by a searing burn on the back of my head. Blinding pain speared behind my eyes, and I thought maybe I had screamed Seth's name. Or maybe that had been inside my head, because then the lights went out.

And there was nothing.

Seth

"That was low," Zeke said frowning, and I couldn't have agreed more. It was by far the lowest thing I had ever done. "I am actually ashamed that we are friends. I never thought that would happen."

My belly sunk, and remorse unfurled, growing like a wild weed. Everything Zeke said was true. He couldn't possibly make me feel any worse than I already felt. By hurting Kat, it was like stabbing myself in the heart again and again. Her pain was my pain.

And right now I was drowning in it.

I wanted to karate chop something.

Zeke continued, making me feel like shit, but I knew it was deserved. "It was wrong and you know it. She deserves the truth. The *whole* truth."

He had thought that if he forced my hand, I would tell her about the curse, but I couldn't. I had made a promise.

"How could you, Seth?" Olivia asked, tears swimming in those violet eyes, and I was hit with a fresh wave of pain. Olivia was like a sister to me. She wore her heart on her sleeve. If others hurt, Olivia felt their pain. Plus, she could incinerate me with a twitch of her pinky finger.

I had done some pretty shitty things before, but this took the cake. The look in Kat's eyes would haunt me for the rest of my life, I was sure. My hand reached out, steadying myself on the trunk of a tree while I tried to catch my breath. I couldn't breathe. It felt like the air had been sucked from my lungs.

Digging my fingers into the tree bark, I fought with the

crushing urge to chase after her—to beg her to understand. What I had done had been for her wellbeing. Deep down I wanted to believe that she knew that—knew me.

But even as I tried to convince myself, I knew that Kat didn't really understand the sacrifices I was making for her. How could she? In an attempt to protect her, no one had bothered to explain, but were we really protecting her? Because if the amount of pain that I had seen in her eyes was any indicator, then I was doing a bang up job of destroying her.

Elena slinked up next to me. I wasn't in the mood. "Go away, Elena," I growled.

Her head titled up, and she had this secret smirk on her lips. "And leave you to suffocate in guilt? Nah. I don't think so."

My eyes flashed in anger. "I don't want to be coddled. Not by you."

"Oh, don't I know it. Only Katia could cure what ails you, lover boy, but you sent her away." She trailed a black nail up my T-shirt. Elena loved to stir trouble. "Now why would you do that?"

"It is none of your business," I said with clenched teeth, feeling my anger rising.

She wasn't discouraged. If anything, I had piqued her interest. "Hmm. It makes me curious."

My fists balled at my side. If she were a guy… "Well, you can shove your curiosity up your—"

"Guys," Olivia interrupted. "This isn't helping."

"You're right," I agreed. "We need to find Kat."

Elena pouted, her hand flattening on my chest. "Do you ever stop thinking about her? It's exhausting, and we are supposed to be having fun."

I frowned. "Knock it off." I batted her hand away, and she scowled.

"Something isn't right," Olivia said, hugging her arms around herself while her eyes clouded in worry.

Elena sauntered into the middle. She enjoyed being the center of attention. "You guys are pathetic. She probably went home with her tail between her legs."

I'd had enough, plus Olivia was right. Trouble brewed in the whistling winds.

Straightening my shoulders, I shoved my hands into my pockets. "We should break off in groups, cover more ground. Olivia's right. We need to find her."

No one argued, for once. Elena and I went off in the direction Kat had run, while Olivia and Zeke headed back toward the road. Hopefully, this way, we could eliminate where she wasn't. I tried her cell phone with no luck as we split off, but then again, I really hadn't expected her to take my call.

We approached Hilltop Cemetery, a place I'd rather avoid tonight of all nights. The high moon cast shadows over the chipped headstones that my imagination went wild with. An owl hooted from the woods surrounding the old cemetery.

"Tell me she isn't this stupid," Elena grumbled in discomfort behind me.

She wasn't the only one who felt apprehension. "Come on," I replied, cautiously treading around graves, careful not to disturb the dead.

We weaved between the rows of graves, both aware that we weren't really ever alone in a cemetery. Not with all the spirits running amuck. Something was definitely wrong, I could feel it with every fiber of my being—Kat was in trouble.

Just as I was about to suggest we move on, something caught my eye—a glisten of white. Before I looked any further, I knew it was Kat. Snowflake curls spilled in a ring on the cold ground. Seeing her motionless, stark fear encompassed me. "Kats," I called in desperate hope. She didn't move, and I reached her in two long strides.

Her face was so pale, and her body lay awkwardly in the grass. Sticky blood oozed from the side of her head, staining her hair and seeping into her cardigan in stomach-turning red. "Kats." She was unresponsive. "Kats, open your eyes," I demanded.

I sunk to my knees next to her, unable to believe what I was seeing. Less than an hour ago she had been full of life, smiling with the circle. Now she looked on the verge of death, and there was too much blood.

A shadow fell over me, Elena. "Heal her," I demanded as she stood over us. Kat's blood covered my hands as I laid her head in my lap. Her breathing was shallow, and I was scared out of my mind.

"No," Elena replied without hesitation. I had to wonder if she even had a heart.

"Elena, please," I pleaded. Never before had I asked her for anything, let alone begged her. It killed me that she was the only one among us with the power to heal. "Please. She's lost so much blood."

"Why should I?" She sounded self-righteous.

All I could think was fate couldn't be so cruel as to take Kat from me before she really knew how I felt about her. She couldn't leave me after I had just thrown what we had in her face—rejected her. It was so absurd, I almost laughed out loud. To lose Kat not from the curse but from something as tragic as this was too bitter to accept. I refused to let her go.

"Elena, come on. Don't be a bitch. She used to be our friend," I said, desperate and not thinking.

I looked back down at Kat's colorless face and asked, "What do you want?" I knew how Elena operated. She wouldn't never do anything for free or out of the kindness of her black heart. One thing I did know—I wasn't going to like where this was going, but what choice did I have? Kat's heart was wavering. "Just name your price. I'll do anything." My voice had gone cold as steel.

"You," she simply stated.

I stiffened. I really shouldn't have been surprised. Glancing up at Elena, I met her with frigid eyes. "You want *me?*"

"Yep. You got it. That's my offer." She crossed her arms. "Going once…"

Looking down at Kat fading in my arms, I knew there was no other choice. I didn't have time. "Fine. Just do it."

Elena smirked and kneeled down on the other side of Kat. "It would be my pleasure."

I squeezed my eyes. It felt like I had just made a deal with the devil. What was done was done. The important thing was that Kat got better—that she lived. And maybe when I had time to digest what I had done, I would think it was better this way. I couldn't have Kat regardless, so maybe if she saw me with someone else, she would move on.

Without me.

Elena's hands hovered over the seeping wound on Kat's head, heat radiating off her touch. I brushed the hair from Kat's forehead, needing to touch her. It might be the very last time that I had the chance. Elena's cat-eyes closed as she concentrated, muttering words under her breath, and the air fizzled.

Only a few minutes had passed and already the opened flesh

wound had closed. There was still dried blood caked on her forehead, but no new blood flowed.

Elena opened her eyes. They were bright and a little tired. Her shoulders dropped, and her body relaxed. "She will have the mother of all headaches when she wakes, but there will be no scarring. She'll live to annoy me another day."

"Thank you," I whispered, gathering Kat's lifeless body in my arms. I stood up, overwhelmed with the desire to get the heck out of the el-creep-o cemetery.

"Where do think you are going?" Elena asked, her yellow eyes glowering.

"I'm taking her home. I'll be all yours tomorrow." I cringed even as I said the words.

God. What a catastrophe.

Me and Elena? I was going to puke.

"Call Zeke," I added bitterly over my shoulder and took off to where I was pretty sure I'd parked my truck. I didn't care that I was leaving Elena fuming and alone.

Kat fit extraordinarily in my arms. Her head was nestled in my neck, and her soft, even breaths teased my skin. Now that I knew she was going to be okay, I was assaulted with a wave of relief. Without her, I would have eventually faded and withered away. Kat was my life, she gave me life. We might not have spoken the scared vows, but that didn't mean she wasn't already a part of me.

With or without magick she was already mine.

I slid into the seat of my truck with Kat still in my arms. Laying her down as carefully as possible, I brushed the hair from her heart-shaped face. I couldn't stop myself. Not after what I had just gone through.

I kissed her still lips. "I'm sorry," I whispered. Then I picked up my phone and punched in Zeke's number. He answered on the first ring. "I found her, but Zeke…I need you."

"Elena told me. We're on our way," he advised without question.

I could always count on Zeke.

He and Olivia arrived at my truck in mere minutes. Kat was still unconscious, which was probably better, because she would most certainly not go along with what I was about to ask Zeke to do.

"Are you sure you want me to do this?" Zeke asked.

I nodded. "It is the only way."

"I don't understand, Seth. Why do we have to erase her memory? I like having her back," Olivia complained, nibbling on her bottom lip.

"I don't have time to go into the details." My words were rushed. "I'll let Zeke take care of that, but Olivia, she will still remember coming to the clearing tonight, she just won't remember who she saw in the smoke, or how she hit her head."

"This is such a bad idea. I can feel it my gut," Olivia grumbled.

"It's the only way. I swear."

Olivia relented, but the doubt never left her silky violet eyes.

Zeke placed a hand on either side of Kat's head. "Here goes nothing," he mumbled, and then he cast a spell to make her forget most of the night. At least right up to before she learned that we were starbound.

It was done.

And I felt sick about.

Katia

I opened my eyes with what sounded like sirens blaring through my head and grimaced. My head felt like it was going to explode. I touched a tentative hand to my tender and sore forehead. Moaning, I stumbled into a pair of green eyes watching me with concern.

"Seth," I said, my voice scratchy.

"Hey there." His voice washed over me, soothingly.

"What happened?" I twisted my head to the side. Pain blasted, and I regretted the movement.

"You took a nasty hit on the head. That rock did a number on you." Seth's fingers were in my hair.

It was then I realized that I was lying in his lap. I felt my cheeks turn five shades of pink. Several long moments passed before I tried to sit up, and when I did the world spiraled on its axis.

Oh crap. I closed my eyes against the whirling colors.

"Hey, take it slow." He guided my head to his shoulder, and I leaned my full weight into him, grateful for the support. "You're probably still a little fuzzy. That was a wicked gash you took to the head."

"Oh." Why couldn't I remember that? Probably because being so close to Seth, I couldn't remember my name, let alone details. His body was firm, warm, and enticing, even with a splitting migraine.

Of course, I wasn't supposed to notice those kinds of things. *I. Don't. Like. Seth.* Now if only someone reminded my heart, so it would stop jackhammering against my chest.

"Here, let me help you inside." He kept his voice low and quiet, like he knew my head was in agonizing pain.

I gripped his shirt, as the car felt like it was flying. "No." My voice was hoarse, and I dropped my head back against the seat.

He arched a brow.

"C-could we just stay here for a little bit? Just until the car stops spinning?"

The corner of his mouth lifted as he tucked a strand of loose hair behind my ear, his hand lingering. "Whatever you want."

Oookay.

Either someone had taken some happy pills, or I had hit my head a lot harder and was hallucinating. He was being far too nice and accommodating, which made me very suspicious. It didn't help that his touch was fire-bolt electric. "What happened? The last thing I remember is being in the circle."

"You slipped and hit your head on a boulder." A flash of pain shot through his eyes. "It wasn't pretty. I'd rather not relive that moment."

I cracked a small smile and winced. Even that hurt like something fierce. "Oh God. Don't make me smile."

A lopsided smirk started to form on his lips.

"I'm serious. It's painful," I said not all that convincingly.

"I'll do my best, but I make no promises." Amusement betrayed his words.

"You're such a jerk-face. I'm remembering that I hate you." I took a glance at myself in the rearview mirror and hissed. There was dried blood plastered on my forehead and in my hair. I looked atrocious. Tentatively, I pushed back my hair, assessing the damage. "Elena?"

He nodded. "Yeah."

"And she healed me willingly?" It was hard to believe. If there was one thing I remembered about Elena, she never did anything without getting something in return.

His eyes flared. "I didn't give her a choice."

Whoa. There always was a shadow of darkness lurking in Seth, but getting a glimpse up close was intense. If pushed, he could be ruthless. "I should thank her," I replied, looking down at my hands. It was the polite thing to do, but it didn't mean I had to like it. Actually I was surprised that she had even wasted her magick on me.

"Later. Right now you need to get to bed and lie down. A couple of aspirins wouldn't hurt either, might take off the edge. I'll call you tomorrow and see how you are feeling."

God. That sounded like bliss. "Thanks, Seth. You seem to always be there when I need you, even if you're an ass most of the time."

His eyes lost their luster. "Don't mention it."

As I got out of his truck for the second time in the last month, I glanced behind me for one last look at his face. I couldn't explain it, but sitting in the cab of his truck, I'd never felt so close to anyone in the galaxy—human or alien—if you believed in that kind of thing. But I couldn't say the same thing for Seth. He wore a dark frown as I waved from the porch.

Was I destined to always want what I couldn't have?

Chapter 10

Katia

A bath was just what I needed. My body was chilled to the bone, I felt grubby, and my muscles ached along with my head. Taking Seth's advice, I popped two little white pills before filling the tub with steaming bubbles that frothed to the top of the tub. I added a subtle hint of rose-infused oil I'd made myself. It would do wonders for the pain and make my skin smell like a bouquet.

Sinking into the foam, I sighed and closed my eyes. My mind wandered, thinking about Seth and the circle, how nice it had been to use magick again. But that was where I hit a wall. My memories went no further. Every time I tried to think past the casting of the spell, I got nothing but blackness. It was frustrating.

Finally exhaustion won, and I crawled from the tub straight into bed. I fell asleep almost instantly, with the soft rainbow of colors dancing behind my eyes from the moonlight hitting the prism of crystals.

I spent the next day gnawing away at this blank spot in my head. It was like a pesky mosquito buzzing around my head on a humid summer day. Nothing I did brought back the memories I'd lost on All Hallows' Eve, yet I couldn't shake this feeling that something big had happened. And I was determined to remember.

Staring at my reflection in the mirror, I lifted the hair off my head, inspecting where the wound should have been. The skin was smooth and flawless, no lingering evidence that I was a klutz. The funny part was I could almost convenience myself it hadn't happened. After all, I had no memory of it. My mind was as swirly as the blue smoke from last night, before it all went black.

When I got to school, I couldn't concentrate to save my life. The morning was brutal and long. By lunch, I'd had enough and was ready to call it a day. Fleetingly, I thought about ditching the rest of my classes, and then I remembered that I had practice after school. Claudia didn't care if we were knocking on death's door; you didn't miss cheer practice.

The lunch bell rang, and I winced. Pressing my fingers to my temples, I tried to shut out the snapshot of images that had been flashing behind my eyes most of the day. I was starting to wonder if I was going nutty, or if Elena had done more than just heal me, like a hex.

I still had to thank her—or curse her. I was undecided.

Scanning the sea of people, I looked for a girl dressed in all black with purple spiked hair. Now was as good a time as any to get it over with. And if I was lucky, maybe she would give me answers for the blank spots that eluded me. Not that I expected her to be obliging. It wasn't in her nature. If anyone could be persuaded to the dark side, my bet was on her.

I spotted her at one of the far lunch tables, and my heart plummeted. Clearly it must have shown in my face.

"What is going on with you?" Claudia asked, coming up behind me in line. "You skipped out on me last night at the Halloween party, and now you look like death."

I gave her dry look. "Thanks, Claudia. Remind me never to call you to talk me off a ledge."

She shrugged and bumped my shoulder. "If you're dumb enough to get yourself up there, you can get yourself down."

Mental note: Do not ask Claudia for advice. She'll make you feel like crapola.

I slumped into one of the round tables and twisted the top off my water. My appetite had vanished, and I was feeling bitchy. "Thanks for the solid advice. And nothing is wrong. I'm just feeling out of it."

"Does it have anything to do with that?" She indicated with a nod to where I'd seen Elena with none other than Seth.

I hadn't been able to tear my eyes off them since I'd stepped

111 | P a g e

into the cafeteria. They were cozying up to each other over a plate of fries. Elena had one leg swung over the top of his, and she was dangling a fry in front of his mouth. Our eyes clashed from across the crowded room, and she smirked.

I was going to vomit.

And I couldn't pinpoint why.

I squeezed the bottle of water in my hand, plastic crunching under impact as a slow burn of animosity flickered inside me.

"I am going to take that as a yes," Claudia muttered.

"That bitch," I said, looking to Claudia who was watching me curiously.

"I don't get it, Katia. If you want Seth, why don't you just go get him." She popped a seedless grape into her mouth. Claudia thought everything was at her fingertips, including boys.

This was hard to admit. I played with the cap from the water bottle. "Believe it or not, I did."

"And…" she prompted, hating to be left dangling.

I sighed. "And he wasn't interested in me."

"He what?" she shrieked and then glanced at Seth, studying him. "Hmm, he must be gay."

"Claudia," I grumbled, my lips twitching.

"What?" she replied innocently when she was anything but. "Look, I am going to be straight with you. I know guys. I know how they think, what they want. I have two brothers, so it's like second nature to me. And I am telling you, no matter what comes out of Seth's edible lips, he wants you."

I rolled her words in my head. "Maybe, but it looks a little late now."

She pursed her lips. "Girl, it is never too late. Fact. He couldn't be any less into that blood-sucking vampire chick if he tried. Any minute he is going to remove her leg from his. She is suffocating him." Claudia sat back, and I propped on my elbows as we both watched, waiting.

Sure as shit, Seth nudged her leg and leaned as far back in his chair as possible. Elena scowled.

Claudia grinned, completely pleased with her guy-intuition, and popped another grape. "Told ya."

I had to hand it to her; that had been pretty impressive. But I couldn't dwell on it for long, because the damn black spot in my head was nagging me and our next classes were about to begin.

"Don't be late for practice today," she warned, flipping her dark hair as she stood up from the table.

I rolled my eyes. "Whatever you say, warden."

She walked backwards, grinning. "You know it. I am going to be on you like stink on shit."

Lovely.

***

I arrived at practice right on schedule, to Claudia's delight, and thank God, because when Harper walked in five minutes later Claudia started busting her chops.

Jeesh, and I thought I was having a heinous day.

"Listen up, bitches." Claudia's voice boomed through the gymnasium. "Our first game was a freaking debacle." Her blue eyes found mine, and she gave me a pointed look that said it was entirely my fault.

I shrunk.

"We are not leaving tonight until we have performed this routine flawlessly. Got it?"

There were a bunch of grumbles and groans from the squad. I wanted to crawl under the bleachers. Cassandra bumped into me as we got into our points. "Nice job," she mumbled under her breath.

Clearly everyone on the team was pissed at me. I stood there wide-eyed and red-cheeked, wishing this day would come to an end. I was ready to throw my pom poms in.

Claudia cued the music and counted down the first steps. Mindlessly, I fell into the moves, but my heart just wasn't feeling it. Not ten minutes into our grueling practice and I already couldn't stop thinking about Seth, seeing his devastatingly handsome face. God, I was Seth crazed. I needed to find a way to purge myself of him, or something. He was interfering in every aspect of my life without even trying.

Yet I couldn't stop seeing his eyes, the color of dark pines, his lazy grin and how it transformed his face. He could go from harsh and cold to irresistible and charming in two seconds flat, with just a curve of his lips. Don't even get me started on his mouth. Heaven help me.

Then like a cloud had been lifted from my vision, the memories of last night unfolded in my head, a tumbling of pictures. From the circle, to Elena's contempt, to the magickal blue flames and how Seth's face was revealed in the smoke after I dropped a piece of my hair into the spell—it all came back in a rush.

I stumbled.

Seth.

Seth was mine.

He was the piece of me I was missing—my starsoul.

I jerked back to the present, standing still while the others kicked and clapped around me. My lungs hurt, and my body went numb.

Damn him. It only took a heartbeat for me to figure out what Seth had done. He had messed with my memories. I could hear Zeke's voice in my head, casting a spell to make me forget. It had Seth's signature oozing all over it. Just like the pompous ass to think he had the right to take something so sacred from me. What gave him that right?

He was going to pay.

Bursting with uncontained rage, I stormed off, leaving a trail of murmurs behind me. Scooping my gym bag from the bleachers, I shoved through the double doors, letting them slam behind me.

"Katia!" Claudia yelled. "What the hell?"

But I was already gone. I was probably going to be booted from the team, but right now, I didn't care.

Seth Nightingale was in for a shock if he thought he was going to get away with this. Well, his brilliant plan was about to backfire in his face.

The engine of my car revved to life, and the tires squealed as I slammed my foot on the gas. I swung into Eddy's parking lot and double-parked. Marching, the door flew open and I glared at my target, spitting mad. He was writing up a receipt for a customer, but I was past the point of logic. The smile he had for the little lady faded when he caught sight of me. I tried to ignore how incredible he looked in faded, ripped jeans, and an oil stained T-shirt.

Yumotastic.

Focus.

I had a purpose here, and it wasn't to check out how fabulous Seth's butt looked in jeans, but it was an extraordinary sight nonetheless. He handed the lady her receipt, and I barely bit my tongue long enough for her to walk through the exit when I pounced.

"How dare you?" I spat.

He cocked his head. "I'm not following. What exactly are you pissed at me for?"

"You had my memory wiped." My voice was tight and flaming.

He didn't deny it. "Kats, what the hell is wrong with you?"

"How could you, Seth?"

Nothing. He just stared at me, looking stunned.

His silence only fueled my fire. "I swear to God, I am going to rip out your tongue if you don't say something." My tone got louder, louder, and louder.

I should have been prepared for him to do something extreme. The next thing I knew, he was in front of me and I was being hoisted in the air. With a whoosh of air, I was slung over his shoulder. "Seth," I rumbled. "Put. Me. Down."

He ignored me.

Time for phase two. I made a scene. We hadn't yet left the shop, so I pounded my fists on his back, wiggling in his hold, making it difficult for him to keep his grasp. He was a lot stronger than I'd bargained for. The muscles in his arms bunched, and I made no headway. He just barreled through the office and out the back door like I was a sack of sugar, not to mention I was still in uniform, which meant the whole shop got a nice view of my red spankies.

So I bit his arm.

This time I got a reaction. He jerked and dropped me to my feet. I wasn't prepared for the jarring impact. "Why you little hellcat…" His jaw clenched.

I radiated anger. "What right do you have to be mad at me? You are the one who stole something from me."

He leaned against the building and folded his arms in that I-don't-give-a-rat-ass stance. "Technically, it was Zeke."

I was seconds away from screaming in frustration. "You can shove your technicalities up your ass. You were the one who ordered him to do it." I poked him in the chest.

He shrugged. "And…"

"And you tried to make me forget that you and I are…are…" I couldn't even say the words.

"Starbound," he supplied, and I hated him for it. How could he be so calm when I was losing my shit?

"Why would you do that? I mean, I get you don't want me—"

His whole demeanor changed. Gone was the offhanded I-don't-give-two-shits and in its place was something dark and scary. "You don't know jack about what I want, Kats."

He circled me, and I was forced to take a step back. "I know that you are the world's biggest A-hole."

"That isn't breaking news, honey," he said with a wicked grin.

I narrowed my eyes. "Don't call me that."

His brow arched. "What do you want me to call you? According to the fates, you're mine." The way he spoke sounded possessive, which only confused me more.

He wanted me. He didn't want me. I wished he would just make up his mind.

My heart started hammering in my chest. "The fates have a seriously sick sense of humor."

There was liquid fire in his green eyes to match mine. "You're telling me."

"And last I saw, Elena was draping herself all over you. Isn't that just peachy?" I added sarcastically.

Deep bottle-green eyes held mine. "Jealous?"

No.

Hell yes.

Fine. My whole body was laced with dark jealousy. "Not in this life."

"Since when did you become a liar? His voice had lowered into a zone I recognized as dangerous. "Anyway, it's none of your business." He stepped toward me.

None of my business? Okay, so we weren't a couple, we hadn't even ever been on a date, but in reality, we were a hell of a lot more than that. He was, in a better sense, my soul mate—the one chosen for me by the fates. That made it my business. Our lives, our futures were intertwined whether he liked it or not. "Since you took it upon yourself to use magick on me. What do you want from me, Seth? If you don't want me, then why go to the trouble to make me forget?"

He had somehow managed to box me against the side of the brick building with his body. Tingles radiated through me at his close proximity. With a gleam of defiance and danger, he ran the back of his hand down my cheek. "It doesn't really matter what I want."

My chest rose and fell in heavy breathing. "I hate you." Even as the words left my mouth, they felt weak.

The air surrounding us was electrifying. "That's just it, Kats. You and I both know that hate isn't what you feel for me."

I shoved at his chest, nowhere else to go. "Screw off, Seth."

"The crap that comes out of your pretty mouth never fails to amaze me." His eyes shifted to my lips.

I tried not to melt into a puddle at his feet. "Bite me."

"With pleasure." He gave me another wicked grin, a slow curving of lips that erased some of the harshness from his face and replaced it with a devastating hotness.

Holy crap.

I didn't know whether to slap him across the cheek or kiss his mouth. "Stay away from me," I warned, afraid I was going to do both.

His eyes snapped back to mine. "Easier said than done."

That was it. I'd reached my boiling point. If I didn't leave right then, I was going to do something utterly stupid and regrettable. My nails dug into my hands as I clenched them in frustration and desire. How the hell could he make me feel both at the same time?

I clung to my last thread of sanity and pivoted on my heel. My hair soared through the space between us, and my middle finger saluted him. It was *my* signature move.

How had that gone so horribly wrong? How had I gone from hating him to wanting him in a blink?

Damn Seth Nightingale.

Chapter 11

Seth

Shit. On. A. Brick.

Kat remembered.

Not only had she remembered, but she had me twisted in knots. Closing my eyes, I sunk against the brick building, needing all the support I could get. My body was craving her, exuding with the need for her presence.

Balling my fists, I was going to wipe Zeke's face with the floor, and that was before I let him explain how the hell this had happened. If he had duped me, he was going to get a black eye. Forget that we were friends—this was Kat's life at stake.

I ran an unsteady hand through my already ragged and tousled hair. Christ, she drove me bonkers in both maddening and needful ways.

Kat had not left mere minutes ago when I heard the bells

from inside the shop chime. The last thing I wanted was to deal with people, not now, but my job had other ideas. So much for hiding outside, I still had a job to do, at least for another hour.

Pasting a false smile on my face, I pushed through the back door and glanced up. *Just freaking great.* Today was just my lucky day. Everyone wanted a piece of me. I groaned internally when I saw Kat's mom waiting in the small lobby of the shop.

My smile fell. "Hello, Mrs. Montgomery. Can I help you with something?"

She was so refined, giving me a glimpse of the woman Kat would become. Her blue eyes, almost like her daughter's, were warm and inviting. "Did I just see Katia?" she asked.

Busted. "Yes. She successfully told me to jump off a bridge."

Kat's mom's eyes twinkled, reminding me of Kat, spunky and full of fire. "That sounds like my Katia. Do you have a minute, Seth? I know you are at work…"

What a day this was turning out to be. Two Montgomery women in one day, this was surely going to be a trying experience. I had yet to pull myself together after going round one with Kat, and then her mom came waltzing in. "Sure. Is everything okay?"

She folded her hands on the counter, bracelets on her wrist jingling together. "I hope so. Katia seems to be going through some rough patches lately. I've noticed that she hasn't been herself."

"And you thought I might have something to do with it," I responded, folding my arms.

"Do you, Seth?" Straight and direct like her daughter.

"Honestly, I don't know," I admitted softly. "Things have gotten…messy between us the last few weeks." There really wasn't a simple way to explain what was going on between Kat and me. And I was even less comfortable telling her mom. "I don't know how it happened. I don't know what changed this year."

She tapped a finger on the counter, contemplating. "So you've noticed that she is different?"

I nodded. "I've noticed. She is starting to put the pieces together."

"Is there something we should know about, Seth? Have you and Katia—"

I avoided her eyes. This was a nixie who could detect a lie a mile away. "No. Nothing like that. We had a small hiccup on All Hallows' Eve, but I took care of it, though she is persistent and very resilient. I am not sure how much longer we can keep her in the dark."

Pride crossed her expression. "That sounds like her. There isn't a puzzle she can't solve. It was naïve of us to think that we could protect her from this."

I wasn't going to argue with that. From the get go, I wanted to tell her and had almost spilled the beans at least a gazillion times over the years. Then someone would dangle her life in front of me and the idea no longer felt safe.

"I know how much you care about her, Seth, and I am so sorry that things couldn't be different. I want my daughter to find happiness. It breaks my heart knowing that she will never have the kind of love she deserves." Regret crinkled at the corner of her eyes.

She will never have me, I thought to myself. I am the only one who could love Kat the way she was meant to be loved. Her mom knew it. I knew it. And now Kat knew it. It filled me with all-consuming jealousy thinking of her with someone who wasn't me. But what choice did I have?

Knowing Kat, it was only a matter of time before she did something reckless now that she knew what Zeke and I had done. I needed to get to her first and fix this. For both our sakes. "Me too," I whispered. Sorrow and remorse mirrored in both our faces.

"I don't know anyone with your strength, and I haven't said it enough…but thank you, Seth, for keeping her alive. For thinking of her first. I won't ever forget this." Her eyes misted with fresh tears.

"I would never do anything to jeopardize her future. That hasn't changed." I scuffed my foot on the worn-out red carpet.

"Watch yourself, Seth. When my daughter wants something, she won't give up, and I can see that she has her sights set on you.

I don't envy you. Not. One. Bit."

"I can handle Kat." I sounded a lot more confident than I felt.

A small smile curled on her lips. "I have to believe that one day you will both find happiness. Take care, Seth."

She breezed out of the shop, a bouquet of lavenders lingering. I closed my eyes and squeezed the bridge of my nose with my thumb and index finger. I had a complex relationship with Kat's parents. Every so often they would pay me a visit just to make sure I was keeping my end of the deal. At one time, we had all been in agreement, including my parents, on what was best for the Kat and me. I didn't know if they'd ever found out that Kat and I used to sneak around to see each other, before things got hairy. My guess was they had, but it had been harmless then.

Harmless until there was desire.

Lately, everyone was on edge. Between her parents and mine, I felt the weight of the world. It was bulldozing me. There was this unspoken sense of foreboding among us, like they all thought she and I were doomed. Goners. Dead meat.

I had to believe that somehow, someway, Kat and I were stronger than all the others. We were going to pull through this and live a merry life. Just not together. We would each go off to college, move on with our lives, and try to forget the other and the curse that hung over our heads.

It was nice to have dreams.

Because the truth was, I couldn't envision a life without Kat in it.

I had once tried the whole dating scene. It had ended badly. My parents had harped me about moving on. Kat had just starting seeing some d-bag, and they thought it would be a great opportunity to explore *other options*. Meaning other people. The thing was, I already knew there would be no one else for me…so what was the point?

However, I got tired of the endless badgering and started seeing Missy Hastings. I always thought Kat would be my first kiss, funny how things never worked out like we imagined. Missy was a fun girl. She had a great sense of humor, an infectious laugh, and we had a blast together. The problem was, she was like a friend, a cool chick to hang out with.

Our first kiss had been extremely awkward, and I still cringed when I thought about it. In the end though, it had been destined to fail before it really ever had the chance to bloom.

Kat came between us, which was ironic since she was the girl I'd been trying to forget, but using Missy to do just that was mean, low, and selfish. I ended up hurting someone who I had come to really like.

Missy told me that I was obsessed with Kat. Called me plenty of colorful names and dumped my sorry butt. Apparently, I had done a shitty job hiding my feelings. It had been harder then. The feelings were still newly developed and fresh. All I could think about was Kat. All I had wanted was Kat

As much as it sucked to lose a friend like Missy, I had felt such relief. I hadn't learned to build a defense against my yearning for Kat, but luckily I was a quick learner. Missy still gave me the stink-eye every time we saw each other.

I headed home that night feeling dejected and bogged down with an excess of despair. It was one of those days where I didn't want to give two-shits about the curse. I didn't want to fight what I was feeling. What I wanted was just one day without the curse whispering in my ear, and the opportunity to spend a whole day with Kat, a day where I could be free, without restraint.

Clicking on the TV, I dialed Zeke's number after I'd shut myself in my room. He answered in his surfer-boy tone on the third ring. "It didn't work, Zeke." There was a long pause as if he was trying to process what I was talking about, so I figured I'd better enlighten him. "You are either losing your touch or you just plain suck," I said.

"Real funny, man," Zeke answered, thinking I was full of BS.

Pulling off my grungy shirt, I tossed it in the hamper and stretched on the bed. It felt good to be off my feet. "I'm serious. It didn't work. She remembered everything."

"Are you sure?" Zeke asked, full of disbelief.

Oh yeah, I was sure. "There's no mistaking. Kat got her

memory back, and I got the claw marks to prove it. She is on a bitch roll." I closed my eyes, seeing flashes of Kat.

"Oh shit."

He could say that again. I ran my fingers through my scraggly hair. I needed a shower. "Her first victim was me. How long do you think it will take her to figure out it was your spell, if she hasn't already? She damn well knows that I can't do it. You're next on her list, Zeke…and watch out; she's lethal," I warned. Not because he needed it, but because it was fun.

I could hear him pacing the floor. "I don't understand," he stated, conflicted. "There is no way on holy ground that spell shouldn't have worked."

I switched hands, holding the phone to my other ear. "Well, Zeke, I hate to break it to you, but you've lost your mojo."

"The hell I have," he defended. "I'm telling you, Seth, there has to be another reason it didn't work, and it's not my mojo."

"Fucking curse," I swore. It was the only logical explanation.

"Yep. Couldn't have said it better," he added. "Do you really think it is the curse interfering?" he asked.

"I don't have a clue, but I am not ruling it out, and it is just like something I would expect from a curse. Twist the rules of the game." I was aggravated beyond belief.

"What are you going to do?"

Wrong question. "You mean what are *you* going to do," I

stressed.

"Seth, you can't be serious," he argued, leaping to what I was implying. He knew me well.

"Zeke, this time…you make it stick. Her life depends on it," I stressed, trying to make him understand how monumentally important this was.

He sighed heavily, his reluctance loud and clear. "Yeah, yeah. I got it. No pressure, right? I don't like it, but I got it."

"Thanks man. I owe you."

"You owe me for life," he responded, not happy, but he would do it nonetheless. Zeke was a great friend.

I stared at the ceiling. "Maybe, but only if Kat lives."

Chapter 12

Katia

I was completely turned up inside regarding what happened with Seth and me, which was sort of a pattern that we had going. It felt like my stomach had been scrambled. At least I knew why I had this irrevocable pull toward him. What should have been a joyous, heart-stopping discovery was turning out to be an epic fiasco.

Neither of my parents was home when I walked through the door, just Collins, and she was exactly what I needed. Girl time with my little sis. I plopped down on the couch next to her, sinking into the cushions.

She looked at me from the corner of her eye, long lashes shading her hazel eyes. "What, no hot date or raving party?" she asked.

"I do more than party, Collins. And it's a weekday." However, that had never stopped me before. I couldn't blame her for the attitude. I also hadn't been the greatest big sister. It sucked just now realizing how much time I had wasted on stupid and useless things.

"Whatever," she replied, turning attention back to the boob tube.

"Why are you here?" I asked, thinking she normally hung out after school sneaking around with Seth's little sister.

"Duh. I live here." She had her coffee-colored hair pulled back into a side ponytail, curls in wild disorder.

I rolled my eyes. Why had I thought some sisterly love was what I needed? "Mom and Dad still have no clue you guys are friends?"

She blew a giant grape bubble with her wad of gum, and I stuck my finger in it, popping the purple balloon in her face. Picking sticky remnants of gum off her face, she said, "Zlitch. We are so much more pro than you and Seth ever were."

"Is that so?"

She shifted on the couch, hugging her knees to her chest. I could see that there was something bothering those cat-like eyes. "What's going on, Katia? Why is everyone acting so weird?"

I angled my head toward her, straightening up. "What do you mean?"

She rolled her eyes. "How can you be so oblivious? You. Mom. Dad. Seth. And Mya's parents." She listed off the involved parties.

I still had no clue what she was implying, but if there was one thing I'd learned, it was you didn't discredit little sisters. They heard things their little ears shouldn't, and my sister was the queen of eavesdropping. "I don't know. Tell me why you think something is going on," I prodded.

Her eyes bored into mine, the TV forgotten in the background. "Mya and I think it has something to do with you and Seth."

If she only knew.

She had my full attention now. Was it possible that my sister knew that we were starbound? Did our parents know that we were fated? I chewed on the idea, tapping my chin lightly. "What could it possibly be?" I muttered, thinking about confessing everything to Collins, but I wasn't sure I was ready to talk about it. Not when my heart was still confused and battered.

"Something bad. They are always whispering when they think no one is around. I've heard your name and Seth's too. So has Mya." There was fear in her voice. She was afraid for me.

"Hey, it will be okay. Whatever it is, we'll figure it out, especially if Seth is involved. He won't let anything happen to us." I believed that wholeheartedly. Seth might not want me, but he was an exceptional guy. It was in his nature to protect, even me. Always had been.

She gave me a small, reassuring smile. "I miss you, Katia."

I ruffled her curly ponytail. "Me too, bug."

"I'm glad you're not a bitch anymore," she added, grinning.

My lips curled. "Don't let Mom catch you talking like that."

"I'm a lot smarter than you."

For an eleven year old, I would have to agree. "Oh yeah…"

She snapped her gum with a thoughtful look. "I guess if I can't have Seth, then it's okay if you want him."

My heart lurched then sloshed to my belly. "I'll keep that in mind." I barely got the words out.

"And Katia…"

"Yeah." I glanced up, meeting her big, innocent hazel eyes.

She gave me a grin far beyond her years. "Don't break his heart like the others, or Mya and I will have to hex you."

I gave her a sad grin, doubting that was ever going to happen. Seth would have to care for me to break his heart, and he had been crystal clear about not wanting me.

***

The next day, I arrived at school at an ungodly hour still as twisted up inside as ever. My brain felt like it was going to short-circuit. I think I'd even beaten the teachers to school and that was pathetic, but I wasn't here because I was looking to get some extra credit. I was hoping that I could catch Seth before classes.

We needed to talk.

Not argue. Not play tonsil hockey.

But dear God, the latter sounded much more fun than what I had in mind. He might have said things that had caused me pain, he might have done things that sent a bolt of anger through me, but I still couldn't control my irrational need to see him. It sent a thrill of excitement through me.

Get a hold of yourself, Katia.

I was not some horny teenager.

My knee bounced with nerves, and I nibbled on a cuticle. God, he better not make me wait long. I was sitting on a bench just outside the entrance doors. Overhead was a massive weeping willow blanketing the morning sun and offering privacy—the perfect spot to discuss unusual matters. Was it sad that I knew which entrance he used?

I brushed aside wisps of my hair, trying not to bite my nails and screw up my manicure.

"Hey, Katia, got a minute?"

I looked up at the sound of my name and found myself staring into Zeke's boyish grin. His sky-blue eyes were jam-packed with unease as he shuffled his feet.

I shook my head. "You heard you are on my shitlist, huh?" I said as he finally decided it was safe to take a seat beside me on the marble bench.

His brows lifted. "I figured I would come and accept my

135 | P a g e

punishment before you strike me down when I least expect it."

My lips twitched. I knew that I should have been mad at Zeke, but I just couldn't muster up the effort. First, I was tired of being angry. I seemed to reserve that all for Seth. And second, Zeke was just too damn adorable to be seriously upset with. "Smart move," I replied, letting him know I really wasn't that angry and wouldn't be turning him into a toad anytime soon.

Gazing out into the courtyard, he apologized. "I really am sorry about what happened, about what I did." He laid a hand on mine.

It was warm and nice with just a tiny undertone of magick at his touch. I interlaced my fingers with his and gave his hand a squeeze. "Don't stress, Zeke. I know it wasn't your idea." Okay, so I was totally letting him off the hook, but I couldn't stay mad at a baby-face like his.

Regret shadowed his powder-blue eyes. "Yeah, maybe not, but I am just as much at fault. Still friends?" he asked, giving me a charming and harmless smile.

A shot of warmth climbed up my hand and through my arm. It took me by surprise, and I examined Zeke's hand covering mine. I knew that feeling. It was right there on the tip of my comprehension, and then…it slipped away.

"Katia?"

"Huh?" I replied, my eyes felt glazed over as I met the

confusion on his tan face. What had we been talking about? I couldn't remember.

His brows slammed together, and he kept my hand steady in his. "Are you are okay? You look a little pale."

"I-I'm not sure," I stammered. "My head feels weird. Christ, I hope I am not getting sick. Claudia will probably kick me off the squad if I miss practice."

Speak of the devil. "What is this geek doing here?" Claudia interrupted, coming out of nowhere. She squeezed between Zeke and me, planting her butt down on the bench. Her jean skirt rose up on her thighs, showing a sinful amount of skin.

"Claudia, be nice," I scolded, still feeling fuzzy, and pressed a hand to my temple.

"It's cool," Zeke said, standing up and gathering his books. "My work here is done."

I glanced up. "I'll see you later?"

"Sure," Zeke assured, giving me a smile that looked almost sad. Now what would the happy-go-lucky Zeke be sad about? I weeded through my brain, trying to recall what in the world we had been talking about before Claudia rudely meandered her way between us.

"What were you doing with him?" Claudia asked in a voice mightier than God.

"Nothing. We're friends." I stared after Zeke, picking away at the blank spot. There was this wall in my brain, and I couldn't see past it.

"Since when?"

I rolled my eyes. "Actually I've known Zeke most of my life."

Her eyes checked him over one last time before he disappeared behind closed doors. "He is kinda cute in that dorky way."

I tried not to smile. "You guys would be so adorable together."

She gave me a saucy grin that said she was up to no good. "Yeah, we would."

Seth

Kat.

Only *she* smelled that wonderful, of cherries, summer, and all the things I wanted but could never have.

I think I loved those jeans. Well, at least on Kat, tight in all the right places.

Walking into Ms. Harper's English class behind her, I decided perhaps being this close to her was a very bad idea. She looked over her shoulder at me, eyeing me funnily, like she had something to say but couldn't remember what it was.

Zeke. My lifesaver.

He must have already gotten to her, because I'd been

expecting an icy exterior. Sweet thanks, that boy moved fast.

"Hey, Seth." Her sexy voice washed over me as I struggled to keep from tossing her on one the desks and having my way with her.

I blinked. "Oh, you're talking to me again? Last I checked, you've been giving me the silent treatment since sixth grade." There was nothing I loved more than pissing her off, except for kissing her. It was a fine line. There was just something so distracting about getting under that California tan skin of hers. Not that I wouldn't like to get under more than just her skin.

Would I ever.

I really needed to stop thinking with my hormones. They were going to get us both in a serious shit-ton of trouble.

It was also familiar territory for us—the bantering. At least when we were taking snubs at each other we knew where we stood. It was the blazing gazes that stirred trouble.

Iridescent eyes narrowed and lit up like blue flames. "Kiss my ass, Seth."

And just like that everything was right in the world between Kat and me. I breathed a sigh of relief and took my seat, avoiding those expressive eyes for the remainder of class.

By the time lunch rolled around, I was ready to call it a day. She was driving me freaking bonkers. I watched her from across the common room. Long curls curved around her face, and her eyes were looking at Claudia as she yakked away, yet Kat still looked lost. Biting her lip, I could see the internal clock ticking away in her brain. She was gnawing away at something in that noggin of hers.

"Ugh. Do you ever stop starting at her? It's exhausting." Elena groaned, bumping my shoulder with hers.

"Do you ever stop forcing yourself on me?" I snapped back. Ever since I agreed to her stupid terms, she'd been bugging the shit out of me. Every time I turned around Elena was there, smothering me. I couldn't breathe. She was drowning me, when all I really wanted was to be left alone.

"Nope." She weaved her fingers through my hair. "It is just too much fun."

I jerked away. "Not here."

She lifted a brow. "Why not? Afraid Miss Popularity will see us. Isn't that the point?"

A bolt of anger ricocheted inside me. "You don't know jackshit about Kat."

"Touchy, touchy." She pursed her blood red lips. "I know that you want her, yet you won't accept her. Sounds pretty twisted, Seth."

"Trust me, it's a whole lot more complicated."

"Always is when Katia's involved."

"Ain't that the truth," I grumbled.

She continued like she didn't hear me, turning in the chair so our legs sort of interlocked. "So, what do you want to do this weekend, lover boy?"

Internally I groaned. "I've got to work most of the weekend," I informed her, aggravation in my tone.

Her silver eyes flashed in annoyance. "That job consumes your life. Between your precious kitty Kat and the grease shop, there is time for nothing else."

I couldn't figure out how she was okay with this arrangement. Elena damn well knew that the only feelings I had for her were friendly, and those were starting to dwindle. Her actions as of late were low, even for her standards. Why she wanted to ruin that, taint it with this fake relationship, was beyond my understanding.

In a way, I felt sorry for her. I knew that deep down Elena longed for love and acceptance. She wanted people to see her for who she really was, not a goth-freak. Under all that gunk, there was a really cool girl any guy would be lucky to have.

Just not me.

But then again I couldn't feel too bad; she had entrapped me.

I shrugged and leaned back in the chair with a cocky grin on my face, glad to have an excuse. "Hey, a guy has to earn a living."

She jabbed me in the side. "Be real. You tinker with cars. That hardly constitutes as work." She got this prowess gleam in her eyes that had me on guard. "And maybe I am trying to help you, Seth," she whispered.

Her face was inches from mine, and she pressed up against me. There was nowhere to retreat as she used her body to cut off my means of escape. I knew she was going to kiss me, which was the very last thing I wanted. Clearing my mind, I looked anywhere but at her and her sultry red lips. It wasn't working. What did she mean she was trying to help me?

"Let's spice things up, shall we?" she murmured. There was trouble brewing in her voice, and her eyes glistened with mischief.

The next thing I knew, Elena had her lips on my mine. And it wasn't just any kiss. She went for it full throttle. Her hands cupped the back of my head, trapping my lips with hers, moving softly over mine.

It was a nice kiss, but I didn't feel anything.

It was mechanical.

There was no gut-wrenching punch—no warm fuzzies like the time Kat had kissed me.

Chapter 13

Katia

I was listening to Claudia go on and on about some college guy she had hooked up with on Halloween night while I had been MIA with the circle. I didn't hear a single word she said. My mind had that fogginess blanketing it, and no matter what I did I couldn't clear the cobwebs. It was like an itch I couldn't scratch—like Seth.

I tried to supply the appropriate responses, all while picking away at the black spot in my head. It was like déjà vu. I got the sense that I had been down this path before.

A tingle skirted down my spine, and I looked across the span of the commons. It was filled with a cluster of kids hanging out during lunch, stuffing caffeine and carbs into their bellies. Then my eyes zeroed in on one pair. They were intimately sealed in a smoldering embrace, lips working over each other. Their faces were hidden from me, but I didn't need to see them. My body's reaction told me enough.

All I saw was murderous red.

Starbursts of hot jealousy raced through my blood, spiking with insane rage. "I am going to rip out her ovaries."

"What?" Claudia asked, genuinely confused and taken aback, and then she followed my burning gaze. "Oh." I could hear the smirk in her tone. "Since when is your crush interested in goth-girl?"

"He's not," I growled, suddenly feeling strangled by the scarf I had around my neck. Maybe I could use it to choke Elena.

Claudia had on her bad-girl grin. "Well, by the looks of how far she has her tongue down his throat, I would say that they have been doing a lot more than nothing."

She was so not helping. Before I realized what I was doing, my feet were marching across the common room straight at Elena. I was going to pulverize her. Seth was mine. He was my... Holy shit.

I was struck by the truth of those words. Seth was indeed mine. He was my starsoul. And that asshole had wiped my memories. Again.

I was going to throttle them both, slowly, until their eyes bulged.

How could they do this to me?

It wasn't enough that he kept screwing with my memories; the

144 | P a g e

two of them had to go flaunt their groping, rub it in my face. If Seth hadn't shattered my heart before, the two had just about finished the job.

Neither of them heard me coming, not until I snarled in murder. "What do you think you are doing with Seth?" My nostrils might have flared.

Elena took her sweet time untangling herself from him and each second I envisioned a different way to kill her. Facing me, she kept a hand on his chest. "I think it's pretty obvious what we were doing." She smiled smugly.

"Elena." Seth's voice was dark and low.

I was acting on pure instinct alone and words were just popping out of my mouth. "He's mine. Nothing you can do or say will ever change that."

She arched a brow mockingly, and I wanted to deck her in the nose. "Not from where I stand. He is fair game until you bind yourself to him, which you haven't. Starbound or not, Seth's with me," she hissed under her breath.

Seth just stood there like a statue with his mouth hanging open.

My jaw started to throb as I clenched it in fury. "We'll see about that." The next thing I knew, I was sailing through the air as I launched myself at Elena.

She squealed in surprise as we tumbled to the floor. It was a good thing it was carpeted, but the impact of the fall was still harsh. We landed on our sides, facing each other, and she went straight for my hair and yanked. A total bitch move, considering she had a boy cut and it was impossible to grip her black spikes. My head snapped back. Luckily I outweighed her, and my legs were like pythons. Thank you, Claudia, for all those grueling cheerleading practices.

I rolled over, pinning her with my extra twenty pounds. A crowd had started to form, along with the sounds of jeering. Who didn't love a good fight during school? Catfight? Even better. This wasn't my first rodeo. You didn't get to the top of the food chain without taking a few people down along the way.

Before I had a chance to really get my grubs on Elena, arms of steel wrapped around my waist and hoisted me up. "Relax, little spitfire," Seth whispered in my ear.

"Let. Me. Go." I strained unsuccessfully against his bonds, which only increased my angry streak. I didn't want his hands on any part of me. And I wanted them everywhere.

He chuckled softly for my ears alone. "I am not sure that is wise."

I stilled in his arms, not because I'd calmed down, but because a different kind of flame began to spread through my body. Being in his arms suddenly took on a whole new meaning. Awareness seeped into my limps as I went lax, molding my body with his. I knew the nanosecond he felt the change, and I swore I heard him sigh. The warmth of his breath fanned my hair, and I leaned my head back against his chest.

Across from us was Zeke, holding a very wild and uncooperative Elena. He looked like he had his hands full and was enjoying it. With the last ounce of sanity I had left, I pushed against Seth's arms, not expecting them to budge, but he let me go.

The moment my feet hit the ground, I was gone and I didn't look back. I didn't care what they did, or what he had to say. How many times was I going to make an idiot of myself over Seth Nightingale? Right now I needed fresh air, time to clear my head— to think—without the interference of magick.

Hightailing it out of the commons, I headed straight for the double doors of the school exit. A gust of wind tore through the air, kicking my hair up in my face. The heat of adrenaline left my flesh and an arctic chill replaced it. November in Vermillion had blown in like phantoms in the mist. It was too late to wish I had thought to grab a sweater.

"Katia," called a sweet voice behind me.

I let out a long ragged breath I hadn't realized I'd been holding and turned around. "Olivia, this isn't really a good time—"

"I need to tell you something." She was persistent, and the somber color of her purple eyes gave me pause.

"Okay." I pushed the hair out of my face and tried to calm my overtaxed heart.

Olivia did a quick survey of the area to make sure we were alone. "Seth is only with Elena because she forced him."

I angled my head and narrowed my eyes. "What do you mean?"

She pulled me to the side of the brick building, eyes darting all over the place before landing back on my face. "The night you got the concussion, Seth begged Elena to heal you. She refused."

"Figures," I snipped, nothing shocked me anymore.

"But you know Elena. She doesn't do anything out of the goodness of her heart."

I bristled, afraid I knew where this was headed. My heart began to beat rapidly against my ribs.

She barreled forward, determined to get it all off her chest. "Seth was desperate and would have agreed to anything if it made you better."

"Lately I'm not so sure about that." Doubt rose in my eyes.

She shuffled her feet on the concrete path, the sun glinting off her red hair. "It's all a front. Zeke and I both know how Seth *really* feels about you. Elena does, too."

I wasn't going to stand here shivering and argue about Seth's so-called feelings. "So her condition *was* Seth?" There was an astonished bite to my words. Disbelief didn't even cover what I was feeling.

Olivia stuck her hands into the pockets of her skinny jeans and looked at me under tentative lashes, probably assuming I would freak out. "You got it. She would only heal you if Seth agreed to go out with her."

I ran my hands through my hair unsure what else to do with them, when all I really wanted was to hit something. "Un-freaking-believable. What is with everyone lately? Seth has Zeke screwing with my memories. Elena makes the moves on Seth. And I have no idea what is going on."

There was something close to pity reflecting in her eyes. "You're losing me," she said.

I pulled the black and white scarf closer around my neck. A chill had made a permanent home inside my chest, prickling my heart. "Tell me about it. Imagine how I feel."

How could I explain what I barely understood myself? But it was one puzzle I was determined to solve.

Something was going on, and I was going to get to the bottom of it, so help me God.

Chapter 14

Seth

Christ. What a mess.

How the hell did Kat keep getting her memory back?

I had to believe, after the second time, that it was most certainly not Zeke and everything to do with this retched curse. There was the slimmest possibility that Zeke was blowing smoke up my ass and he never actually did the spells accurately, but I trusted Zeke. He knew how dire this situation was and what she meant to me.

Kat tore out of my arms after an impressive body-slam—though in the moment, seeing her hit Elena full-force had made my chest tighten. I didn't have any other choice but to let her go. For one, the staff was making their way through the crowd, and I didn't want Kat to end up with a detention. The two of them might start another royal rumble being shut up together for a

Saturday. Second, it felt way too good having her in my arms, and that was cause for alarm.

The heat from her body was still imprinted on mine, and the desire to go after her was immense. My heart felt heavy as a swift bout of anger rose inside me at the injustice of the cards we'd both been dealt.

This sucked.

Zeke had finally released Elena, who was spitting silver daggers at me.

How the hell had I ended up in this dilemma? Better yet, how was I going to get out of it? I not only had to deal with Kat and her returned memory, I also had a pissed-off healer, who put me on her I'm-going-to-make-your-life-miserable radar.

Shoving my hands through my hair, I knew that the time had come. I had to tell Kat everything; there really wasn't another way around it. Her parents were just going to have to deal with it, because I was done with the games. I was done hurting her for the price of her safety. This was our last year together, and when we parted ways at graduation, I didn't want it to be on bad terms. I wasn't so delusional that I thought we would remain friends after high school. That would have been dreadfully hard, but pleasant to avoid any awkwardness on visits home would be preferable.

What I wouldn't give to use something or someone as a punching bag.

Katia

I had no idea how long I sat in my car just staring out at the rocky formations of South Dakota. Patches of grass grew between the crevices, clashing against the rusty rocks. An hour, maybe two, passed—it didn't really matter, just as long as I was left alone. I played with my magick for a little bit, calling it to the surface, the tingles vibrating at my fingertips. Taking comfort in the feelings it enticed. I didn't really understand my powers. They were somewhat of a mystery to me. What was so great about being freakishly good at puzzles? Right now I wished I had the ability to banish someone to Siberia.

That is where I would send Seth right this second.

I was so unbelievably angry at him. He made me crazy. Everything I'd been brought up to believe about love and starbound was a crock of poop. Seth wasn't supposed to push me away. He was supposed to be ridiculously in love with me. We should have been drawn to each other, captivated, lured to just be near one another. It might not make sense or sound rational, but for the first time I realized what I'd been searching for—Seth.

Being so close to him but just out of my reach had left a hole inside me.

FML.

Love blows.

Glancing at the dashboard clock in my car, I came to the conclusion that sitting here, wallowing in my self-pity, was a waste of time. It gave me no answers, no results, no reprieve from the betrayal and pain I was feeling. School was out and Seth had the day off from Eddy's, which meant that he and shitbrick were probably hanging out somewhere.

I had come out here to the cliffs with the mindset to blow off steam, but I found myself just as tangled and livid as I had been when I decided to play hooky for the rest of the day. If anything, I had stewed in my anger, working myself up into a tizzy. Putting the Jetta into drive, I went on the hunt for the object of my wrath.

I found them chillin' on a dirt road not far from where the clearing was. It was a given that dumb and dumber would be together. Zeke and Seth were as thick as thieves. They were sitting on the back of Seth's truck, looking better for wear, but even on a bad day Seth looked mouthwatering.

His jeans were ripped, and the wind picked up pieces of his dark hair. I tried not to think about how yum-o-tastic he was and focused on getting answers. Zeke looked like a surfer boy on a cool summer night.

They both glanced up at the same time as my little Jetta pulled into view. My sticky palms gripped the steering wheel. Nerves clawed at my belly, and seeing them, I got pissed off all over again. I was anxious to learn what they were hiding, and being edgy made me mad. They'd better have an extraordinary reason for why the two of them conspired and took my memories twice. The circle I had once been a part of would have never used magick on each other—not in harm—not for kicks—not to besmirch.

I shut the car door behind me and tucked my windblown hair behind my ears. They both eyed me warily, feet dangling off the end of the truck bed. Smart boys.

"Uh-oh," I heard Zeke mumble under his breath. "Dude, you are in serious shit."

Seth popped him in the leg.

I marched up to the truck, driven by stress and anger, not a pleasant combination. "Get ready to check his vital signs," I said to Zeke.

"Why?" Zeke asked, brows raised.

I thought it was pretty obvious. "'Cuz I am going to kill him."

Zeke laughed.

Seth frowned. "This isn't funny."

"The hell it isn't," Zeke replied with sparkling blue eyes.

I put my hands on my hips and gave Zeke a dry glare. "I wouldn't be laughing; you cast the spell."

Zeke's smile fell. "Right. I forgot that teeny, tiny detail."

"Lucky for you, I didn't," Seth told him. "If am I going down, then so are you, my friend."

Zeke looked from me to Seth and shook his golden head. "I

am not sure how close of friends we are going to be after this."

I was tired of their stalling banter. "As much as I hate to break up the bromance, I am still very much pissed."

Seth jumped off the bed of the truck, all six foot two of him towered in front of me. "Kats, it was for your own good."

If I had a penny for every time someone has said that to me. Craning my neck, I looked up at him. "Twice! Twice, Seth. You care so much that you had Zeke wipe my memories twice?"

He scratched the back of his head. "Well, when you say it like that it sounds bad."

Zeke snickered.

"Zeke!" we both bellowed in unison.

"Gives us a minute, would you, Zeke?" I demanded more than asked. "I am not taking any chances of you messing with my mind a third time. I'll deal with you later."

He leaped down and stopped where I stood. "Katia, you have to know that I would never hurt you." There was a plea in his soft eyes.

"Maybe," I conceded. "Right now I am not sure of anything, least of all who my friends are."

Hurt crossed his face. "I really am sorry. I never should have listened to the jackass. Don't go too hard on him. He had damn good reasons. Whatever comes out of his mouth, I am telling you that he cares about you."

I stood my ground, masking my emotions, which were pinging all over the place. "I find that hard to believe right now, Zeke."

He snuck a quick glance out of the corner of his eye at Seth, who was now leaning on the side of his black truck. "I swear it on a blood oath, on the moon goddess. He loves you, Katia. Like honest to God loves you, and he would do anything to protect you."

It was much harder to hide the doubt and surprise from my face, or deny that my heart was pounding in triple-time. I angled my head. "Protect me from what?" I whispered, because it seemed like Zeke didn't want Seth to hear us.

"It's not for me to say, and he is already going to kick my ass to China for saying this much."

"Well, someone better start talking," I grumbled.

He tossed me a brief grin. "That bastard has no idea how lucky he is to have you. You're one badass chick."

My lips twitched. "Thanks, I think."

"Anytime. Oh and, Katia." He smirked and raised his hand like a boy scout. "I promise never to play in your head again."

"I'm holding you to that, Zeke."

He took off toward his Impala, and I waited for the purr of the engine before I turned to Seth.

"So I am guessing it is my turn," he said, eyeing me.

I strolled right up and socked him in the gut. He made an *oomph* noise in the back of his throat, but I didn't get the doubled-over results I was looking for. It was disappointing

"I guess I deserve that." There was just the slightest touch of amusement in his voice.

"You guess?" I shrilled.

"Can we talk about this rationally?" he tried to reason.

Then before I could object, he had his hands on my waist, lifting me up on the back of this truck. I tried to not notice the muscles that flexed in his arms. The truck bounced under his weight as he heaved himself up beside me. I let out a long irritated sigh. "What's going on, Seth?"

He scratched his chin. "I don't even know where to begin."

My eyes narrowed.

He held up both of his hands, and a twinkle lit his green eyes. "Just don't hit me again."

I felt the corner of my mouth lift, dissipating some of my anger. "Well, at least you are admitting that something *is* going on."

"You have no idea," he said after a few moments.

"I will if you tell me."

Seth was quiet, his shoulders unnaturally tense. "I was really hoping I would never have to."

I shifted on the metal bed, turning toward him with my body.

"Why?" I asked heatedly. "I don't understand. Is it because of what we are to each other? *Starbound.*

A breeze blew through, messing his already tousled dark hair. "That's part of it. A big part of it," he admitted.

"How long have you known that we are—" My insides were tight. Just thinking about what he was to me made me go mushy and starry-eyed.

The setting sun gleamed on his striking features—the curve of his jaw with tiny stubbles, the exotic color of his eyes. All of him seemed more intense and dangerous out here in the middle of nowhere. "Forever."

My breath caught.

"I grew up with the forewarnings of the curse. Instead of nursery rhymes, I got stories of our families' curse."

"Curse," I echoed. This was definitely going to go to a dark place. Pressure squeezed in my lungs.

"We're cursed," he stated matter-of-factly.

I didn't know what to say. What he was suggesting sounded so farfetched. And why wasn't he having a meltdown? I was on the verge of a full-on freak-out. *Cursed?* But I was a nixie, and I knew better than to think the impossible wasn't possible. I might be ticked off at Seth, but I knew he didn't lie. Not about something this gargantuan.

"Do you remember the first time we saw each other?" he

asked.

A smile tugged at my lips. "How could I forget?"

"We were four, and I saw you playing in the park with these big curls bouncing as you raced across the monkey bars. I knew who you were before you told me your name. I felt it in my blood. It recognized you as mine. And I thought to myself, *That's the girl who is going to kill me? She's not that scary.*" He chuckled under his breath. "Little did I know…"

I met his eyes, my heart warming at the memory. "I told you my name and you pushed me down. You told me you hated me and to stay away from you."

His eyes smiled, crinkling in the corners. "I did. I was scared of you. And then every day I went to the park to see if you would show up. On the days you came, I watched you from inside the wooden fort. Even at four I was drawn to you. Eventually I realized that you were just a girl, and it wasn't your fault any more than it was mine that you were born a Montgomery."

"So this curse…it's because of our bloodlines?" I asked, trying to follow the dotted lines.

He nodded, a glint of regret reflecting in eyes darker than the bottom of the sea. "It only happens once a century. One of each line is born, destined to repeat history. The curse prevents us from being together. As long as we don't complete the sacred vow the curse stays dormant, but if we do…and the curse is activated…it will kill you."

I felt like I'd been dropped kicked in the gut, and then kicked again when I was down. On a loud gasp, I hugged my stomach. He was talking about our deaths, and all I could think was, *did that mean that Seth really did want me?* Even years ago, when I thought he was the biggest asshole on the planet, had that been to protect me? Was that why we had drifted apart? A handful of unanswered questions tumbled through my head.

His fingers were under my chin, lifting my face. Eyes like liquid emeralds stared at me with powerful emotion. "I won't let that happen, Kats. Not to you. I refuse to watch you die."

Heat zipped through my veins. A crack of lightning struck the sky behind us. We sat thigh to thigh, his hand now cupping my cheek. The thrill of his touch was far stronger than anything I'd ever felt before.

"You have the most amazing eyes. They remind me of starlight." His voice was soft and seductive.

I swallowed, and my legs stopped swinging. "What are we going to do, Seth?" I asked, my voice barely a whisper.

He broke down the details that surrounded the curse, filling me in on the origin. I listened to the seductive lull of his voice. It didn't matter that he was talking about our deaths, or how we had to be careful and keep our distance. His voice was hypnotic, pulling me. His hand fell away from my cheek while he was reciting the curse word for word, and I immediately missed the contact. It ended with, "There is nothing we can do, Kats. It is set in stone, written in the stars; the curse is unbreakable."

I had to fight back tears of frustration and injustice. This curse had nothing to do with Seth and me, yet we were the ones who had to pay the ultimate price. Staring down at our feet, I swallowed the lump of emotions clogging my throat. There was one question that was chopping at the back of my head. "I-Is the curse the reason you pushed me away?"

He made a sound of guttural pain, and my hand was captured by his. "Can you honestly look at me and believe that I don't want you? That I ever didn't want you? It literally tore me up inside." His finger began to trace lazy patterns on the inside of my palm.

Holy hotness times infinity.

I chewed my lip as I tried to stop my heart from going into cardiac arrest. "Seth…" I couldn't believe what I was about to say, but my tongue was flapping before I could second guess myself. "Hold me? Just once. If I can't ever have you, I think I deserve one night with you."

Oh. My. God. Did I really just ask him to spend the night with me?

His dark eyes widened. I didn't think he was expecting that, but then he shook his head. "We can't risk it."

I wanted to be able to remember what it felt like to be in his arms. The way he smelled in twilight. The sense of completion I'd only be able to have with him. "Are you saying that you won't be able to control yourself for one night?" I was taunting him. Sometimes to get what you want, you had to play dirty. Plus, Seth owed me; he had manipulated my memories.

No hesitation. "That is exactly what I am saying."

Sweet baby Jesus. "Oh." How was a girl supposed to respond to that? Yeah, I didn't have anything intelligent.

"What can we possibly gain by what we can never have? I can't. Having you in my arms, even for a little bit, would haunt me for the rest of my life. It's bad enough that I still taste your lips when I close my eyes—when I dream."

That made two of us. I knew that his kisses were intoxicating, and I wanted to savor them one last time. I needed to make sure my memory and the effects of the alcohol hadn't dulled how earth-shattering I remembered his lips to be. It was all in the name of science. "Aren't you curious what it would be like between us?" I asked, holding his gaze with mine.

His jaw ticked with a firm willpower that apparently I just didn't have. "I want you alive more than I want to satisfy my curiosity. Don't ask this of me, Kats."

Okay, so talking about me dying was sort of a heated moment buzz-kill, but I figured I might as well take it a step further and go for the plunge. I was feeling reckless. "If I did ask you…would you deny me?"

His eyes seared, flashing with heat and eventually lingered on my lips. I held my breath. An electric current ran between us as we sat facing each other on the back of his truck, suspended in a flicker of uncertainty. Then he let out a heavy sigh and looked away, staring off into the distance. "I would deny you nothing. I can't."

Oh mercy, that was so worth the plunge. My heart soared, somersaulting off a cliff. I squeezed my eyes closed, struggling with indecision. My heart was begging me to take the leap, and my head knew that Seth would regret it afterward if I pushed.

I hopped off his truck and glanced up. The sky was gloomy behind him, and the darkness brought a chill. "I need to talk to my parents."

He nodded, watching me with the saddest lush eyes I'd ever seen. My legs felt like Jell-O as I began to walk to my car. The winds howled in the distance, and my heart was crumbling with each step away from Seth.

"Kats!" he called.

I turned around and found myself engulfed in his arms. His scent surrounded me, woodsy and serenely bewitching. I clung to him and drank in the feeling of his golden warmth. For one blinding moment, I imagined in perfect clarity what it would be like to be with Seth. I craved it.

His arms tightened around me, and I could feel the struggle in his body, whether he should pull me closer or push me away. In the end, I made the decision, stepping out of his arms. It was the hardest thing I'd ever done. Well, almost, walking away was just as hard when every inch of my body was screaming to run back into his embrace.

Tears washed over my cheeks.

Chapter 15

Katia

I walked through my front door like a zombie. There was an ominous shadow that followed me home. Every block I thought about whipping the car around and making my way full throttle back to him, even though I was sure he was on his way home as well.

What a day.

What a wave of information.

What a sack of shit.

It was almost too much to handle in one day, especially after having my mind muddled with, getting in a catfight, finding my soul mate, and having my heart broken.

All in a day's work.

It was tiresome, and I was exhausted.

But I wasn't done yet.

No matter how beat I was, there were still two people I had to confront—my parents. Sure it could have waited for another day, but hell, I figured why not, I was on a roll. Truthfully I didn't think I could wait. They owed me an explanation. Not only had they lied to me and kept the truth from me, they had also taken away my ability to decide what Seth and I could have been.

My whole relationship with him felt cheated somehow, because we were always sneaking around. Now that I knew why our families kept us apart, I had to wonder why my parents had even taken the chance and had kids. Sure there was a 50/50 chance of having a boy. Then there would be nothing to stress over, yet here we were…

I found them both in the kitchen, Dad on the laptop and Mom doing the dishes—without magick. I had missed dinner, but I knew there would be a plate of leftovers waiting for me in the fridge. No matter how much I felt deceived, I knew my parents loved me and in their own way, like Seth, they were protecting me.

"Hey, stranger," Dad said as I slumped into a seat beside him. There was a soft touch of grey at his temples.

I chewed on a nail, trying to decide what the best route was. "Do you have a minute? I need to ask you something."

"This sounds serious." Mom shut off the water and dried her hands. I knew that she would be testing the air to get a read on my feelings. She was intuitive to emotions—that was her gift.

"It is," I admitted still in sort of a numb state. I waited until they were both seated at the family dining table. Where did I begin? "I talked to Seth Nightingale tonight." That should get things going.

Dad immediately began the same lecture. "Now, Katia, you know you are not—"

Mom laid a hand on his arm, silencing him. "Oh, honey, I am so sorry." Her eyes glistened with tears.

"So it's true." I half expected, half hoped that it was all a big fat lie and Seth was just being a jerk. I expected to feel something, but I felt nothing.

Mom nodded. "Very much so." She clung to Dad's hand across the table, and he squeezed her fingers in encouragement.

Seeing the two of them, I realized Seth and I would never have that, at least not together. I could only hope that I could find someone who would complement me, but that meant giving up that all-consuming, rock-you-to-the-core kind of love. "Why didn't you ever tell me?" The words came out harsher than I'd intended.

They looked at each other, but it was Mom who spoke. "I can't believe you didn't find out sooner, but I guess I have Seth to thank for that. Eighteen years ago, when I found out that Seth's mom, Ashley, was also pregnant, we both knew that our worst nightmare had come true. The offspring of both a Montgomery and a Nightingale born in the same year happens only once in a century, and you and Seth were going to be victims of a curse we couldn't control or break. It was maddening, terrifying, and we were all desperate.

"Shortly after the two of you were both born, the four of us got together and came up with a plan. It wasn't foolproof, but we had to cling to something. We are sorry we lied to you, kept you in the dark, but, Katia, never once have I regretted having you, just the curse that looms over your future."

"I can't believe this is real," I said full of disbelief, and I slid lower in the chair. I didn't have the willpower to hold myself up anymore.

Mom was apparently the spokesperson or maybe it was because Dad looked pale as a ghost. "I am sorry. If I could take the pain away, I would. A hundred times over. And I know Seth feels the same. If he could spare you from hurting, there isn't anything he wouldn't do, or hasn't done."

Was that supposed to make me feel better? Knowing, that for years Seth has suffered the responsibility of this curse alone? "God, it's not fair," I cried.

"No, it's not," she agreed.

"So you don't really hate Seth or his family?" I asked, thinking my whole childhood had been based on lies.

She shook her honey-colored hair. "No. I actually adore Seth."

That made it ten times worse. "I think I need to go lie down." Nothing could make this gut-stabbing pain any less severe. I felt as if I was being carved from the inside out. So many emotions, I didn't know how to separate them, to deal with them. Love, pain, fear, sorrow, and the list went on.

There wasn't anything left to say, so they just watched me with somber eyes as I walked out of the kitchen with my head hung low and fresh tears stinging my eyes.

My bedroom was my sanctuary.

I ran my hands over the length of the old carved wood dresser that had been polished to a gleam. It felt like silk under my fingertips and was ages old, a part of my family history—a history that now haunted me. It had been a gift from my grandmother. There was magick in the ancient wood. I could feel it pulse under my touch.

With my eyes shimmering with tears, I lit the pillar candles on the dresser, and the room filled with the aroma of beeswax, tangy smoke, and vanilla. The beaded curtains blew lightly from the night's gentle breeze, chiming like music. As a little girl, the sound made me think of ancient castles in Wales. Moonbeams reflected off the colored crystals, casting an array of mystical colors on the floor. It was like being in the middle of a rainbow after a rainfall and Mother Earth rejoiced.

Tossing aside my jeans, I slipped on a pair of sweats and

collapsed onto the bed. Cries afflicted my shuddering body, and I fell asleep to the song of wind chimes, the sweet smell of vanilla, and a broken heart. And I dreamt of spiders.

Seth

They said it was supposed to get easier after I turned eighteen. Well, I was months shy of adulthood and...they lied. I knew it was only going to get harder and harder to deny my love for Kat, fighting every day not to be with her. I knew it wouldn't be so easy for us. There was nothing easy about not being able to love Kat.

I lay down on the bed of my truck, listening to the crunching of her tires as she drove away. Twinkling stars dotted overhead in a pattern of diamonds in the sky. Her scent lingered in the air, faerie roses and cherry blossoms, and my heart collapsed.

Now that I had nothing to hide, no secrets left to protect, I thought I would feel free, not this chest-crushing pain. That one blinding moment with her wrapped in my arms, I hadn't wanted to let go. It felt like it was going to be the last time, and the misery in her eyes cut me like a knife, worse than anything the curse could do to me.

Closing my eyes, I let the moonlight spill over my face and the autumn breeze cool my skin. Imagining her in my arms was so simple, her head buried against my chest, the steady beating of her heart with mine. I'd never understand how someone could damn the future, let alone their own blood—their kin.

I could only pray to the stars for so long without receiving any answers.

Going home that night wasn't the sense of relief I'd expected. There were no secrets or lies between us, but it didn't change the rules. She was just as untouchable as she had been in the sixth grade.

I heard Mom's laugh from the family room as I dragged my butt home. It was late. She was curled up on the couch with Snickers, our cat, and a sleeping Mya at her feet. My little sister looked peaceful, but I knew how much of a nuisance that angelic face could be. So much mischief and trouble gleamed behind her fey green eyes and dark silky hair. I knew all too well that she and Kat's little sister were grand schemers.

"Why so glum?" Mom whispered, careful not to disturb Mya.

I sunk into one of the recliners, taking comfort in being home with family. "Kat knows."

Her eyes went wide. "Oh crap."

"You can say that again."

"I should call Miranda." She started shuffling on the end table for her cell phone.

I kicked off my shoes. "I am pretty sure Kat has already talked to her parents."

She paused in her search and studied me with eyes as green as mine. "Seth, how are you holding up?"

I leaned back into the chair and linked my hands behind my head. "A week ago, I would have said just peachy. Tonight I feel like I've been hit by a wrecking ball."

The soft glow of the dim table lamp picked up blue highlights in her black hair. "That bad, huh?"

I closed my eyes. "The pits."

"I can honestly say that I am relieved. It has gone on for far too long." She suddenly sounded as if she had aged ten years.

Maybe we both had. "Yeah, I guess. It still blows."

"I know you want to protect her, Seth, but I think you've done just about all you can do. It's time for Katia to be able to make her own decision about what's best for her," she said.

She was probably right, but I had been doing it for so long, it was like losing my left arm. I didn't know what else to do if I wasn't trying to keep her safe.

"This burden isn't yours alone to shelter. Let her help you," she told me.

Kat help me? Was she crazy? I couldn't even be in the same room with her without wanting to attack her with my mouth. Probably best I kept that erotic detail to myself. I doubted Mom wanted to hear how I had constant impure thoughts when Kat walked into the room.

Before I knew it, I was snoring logs.

And I dreamed of spiders.

Chapter 16

Seth

I had no freaking idea how I got out of bed the next day and made it to school. It was all a big blur to me, until I saw Kat. She was waiting on the side of the brick building of Vermillion high, hugging a book.

She looked amazing. It might have been totally piggish of me to say, but she looked bangin'. The teal cardigan deepened the silvery blue in her eyes, and those damn jeans hugged every curve she possibly had. I literally salivated on sight, a testament to my lack of sleep.

Damn spiders.

Let it go on record, I hate spiders.

It was the way my body reacted that made me put an end to this. "Kats, we can't keep doing this to each other. I know you are still processing, but I think it would be best if we kept our distance...for now."

She bit her lip and tucked wild curls behind her ears. Those were her nervous habits, and they were such a damn turn on—so not helping my hands-off policy. My fingers were itching to dive into her silky hair. I stuffed them into the back pockets of my jeans, just in case they got any funny ideas.

"I know," she said softly, her eyes directed on mine.

Then she caught me off guard. I never knew what she was going to do. She could have slapped me. She could have kicked me in the junk. Or she could have...

Stood up on her tiptoes and pressed her lips lightly to mine. They were as soft as July peaches in the height of summer. A surge of shock bolted through my system, and my hands automatically went to her hips, keeping her close to me. I marveled in the feeling of her body pressed against mine. When Kat kissed, she went full in, no holding back.

Unfortunately, she ended the kiss too soon. I wanted to devour her. Looking up at me, tears shone in her eyes. "I think I love you," she murmured breathily against my lips.

The world disappeared around me like the eye of a storm. There was only her and me and those three words I never thought I would hear her say. Didn't think I deserved to hear after all that I had put her through lately. And now that she had...I couldn't catch my breath. I couldn't think. And I sure as hell couldn't just let her walk away.

Not this time.

But while I was still trying to stable my pulse and gain control of my emotions, she stepped out of my arms. My fists clenched at my sides. "W-wait," I said discombobulated.

"See you around, Seth," she whispered and walked through the doors.

I was struck dumb. The sounds around me came swooping back in a rush of irritating noise. People were all around me, shoving, pushing, getting ready for classes, but I was drowning in the aftermath of a tsunami. I just stood there, feet planted, wondering what the hell had just happened.

Katia

The following days, we went about ignoring each other, pretending that nothing existed between us, trying to forget that last sweet kiss. It took a toll on both of us. There weren't any steaming exchanges…What was the point? There weren't any more heated fights…No fight was left. There weren't any more snarky comments between passing periods…Why bother?

There was just a cloud of unbelievable sorrow that hung over our heads. And spiders. I don't know what the deal was with the eight-legged-furry-skin-crawling creatures, but every time I closed my eyes at night, their beady black eyes were there to greet me. Or more like freak me out.

I went through the motions of school, cheer, and home without really knowing what I was doing. I was on autopilot. Honestly, I never felt more inhuman than those first few weeks, learning to deal.

It did not get easier with time. Whoever said that was bogus. Time had not healed my wounds or my heart. Maybe if I wasn't forced to see Seth every day or if we didn't live in the same town, it might have been different.

But I seriously doubted it.

Days turned to weeks. I had no freaking clue how or where we found the strength to continue day in and day out not together. No kissing. No touching. No hugging. I can't tell you the number of times in a day I really needed to be in Seth's arms. Some days it felt like only he could rid me of this violent emptiness that had settled inside me.

We both went through the motions of life, but neither of us was really living.

I didn't know how Seth had gone years with the knowledge of what we were and kept away. He was a much stronger a person than I. It was hard to describe, and really, I don't know why it had taken me so long to acknowledge the feelings I had for him. Why had I not admitted it sooner? Had I, and just pretended otherwise? Had my social climb and ambition to be popular masked those feelings?

It didn't really matter now. I couldn't change what had come to pass, but that undeniable attraction pulled me daily, as if the curse was working against us, teasing us to take the bait and give in to what we desired. Normally finding your starsoul was a treasured and rare gift. It was blissful, like walking in the clouds. A time of discovery, sharing magick with someone you loved, trusted, and honored. What made a starsoul different was the binding of souls, flesh, spirit, and love through magick. It was a ceremony of old charms and sacred vows shared by both. Nixies naturally want to share magick with those they love, and the starbound spell was probably as ancient as this curse.

To occupy my time I began to more than just dabble in oils and dried herbs. My craft and magick were the only things that kept me from going batshit crazy. I began to exercise the power that lay dormant in my veins, trying to figure out what made it tick, what made it surge, and what made it sing.

Setting aside the bowl, I looked through the bottles lining my dresser for the right oil to mix with the crushed rose petals. My room was the one place lately that I felt any peace. Frowning, I plucked up two oils, trying to decide between them. Moonglow or mandarin?

I heard a creak behind me as I put the last droplet of ingredients into the glass bottle. Looking over my shoulder, Collins was leaning in the doorway, watching me. "You've gotten better. It doesn't smell like crap on a stick."

I rolled my eyes. "Here, try this." I dabbed a drop of my newest concoction on each of her wrists.

She lifted her wrists and sniffed cautiously. "Hmm. This is really pretty. It's light and floral with just a hint of…mandarin?"

I nodded, pleased with her detection.

Smiling, she walked into my room and plopped herself on my bed. Blonde curls like mine spilled out of her ponytail. "So are you going to tell me what is going on?"

For someone who was only eleven, she was awfully perceptive. It was annoying. "I'm not sure that I should. And I am guessing you probably already know half of it."

"Well, Mya and I have been comparing notes. We heard something about a curse, which we assume involves you and Seth." Lines of worry ceased her heart-shaped face.

Putting down the glass bottle, I sat beside her on the bed. "It's not a big deal. Seth and I have come to an understanding. We aren't going to let anything happen to either of us."

"So you really are…cursed?"

I twiddled my fingers in my lap. "Afraid so. It's complicated." She gave me her "I'm not a baby" glare. I sighed and gave her the gist of the curse that plagued me.

She tucked her legs underneath her. "Wow. That is some

serious pile of poop."

I couldn't have summed it up better. The corner of my mouth curved. "Tell me about it." Leave it to Collins to put it all in perspective for me. She might be a pain in my ass, but I loved her, probably like most big sisters.

And somehow through this tragedy, we grew closer. Before I was always too busy with boys, parties, and cheerleading to really spend any quality sister time with Collins. Now I made the time. Hanging out with her and Mya proved to be quite entertaining. They were so darn carefree, and they made so much trouble for themselves.

I lost count of the number of things those two set on fire, made disappear, or caused to explode. More than once I was sure the fire or police department would surround us, guns blazing. I don't know how they got away with half the crap they did, and if our parents or even Seth's found out, well their butts would be grass.

Collins was the only bright star in my otherwise gray world.

***

Then of course there was the college tour, and let me tell you, Claudia was more interested in dorm parties and frat boys than she was in the college itself and what it could possibly offer for our blossoming futures.

Go figure.

I had completely forgotten about the weekend trip Claudia, Harper, and I had planned months ago to visit the University of South Dakota. Now it was too late to back out. The last thing I wanted to do was slap on my false smile and fake happiness, but then again, maybe it would be good for me. Who was I kidding? A weekend with Claudia and Harper on a college campus was a recipe for disaster.

However, I could use a retreat…a distraction.

I needed to get the hell out of Dodge—stat.

Away from Seth. Away from the daily reminders of all that I couldn't have. Away from the enticement he tempted me with constantly.

A girl only had so much strength, and I wasn't the kind of girl that was used to denying herself anything.

Good grief. I was arguing with myself, and it was making my head hurt.

They did have a stellar cheerleading squad, which was ultimately the only requirement Claudia cared about. It would give me a slice of what life was going to be like after high school. Once Seth left for Europe, and I was stuck here. Alone. I needed to explore my options.

Well then, it was settled. *USD, here we come.*

The three of us packed inside my Jetta—no easy feat. Three girls on an overnight stay, Claudia packed more makeup than clothes, Harper more shoes than Rodeo Drive, and well I packed more secrets than the CIA.

Mom stood on the porch waving us off, and Collins gave me a wink.

Oh Lord, I hope I come back in one piece.

Actually, I would have loved to come back refreshed, renewed, and restored. I wanted to put this love affliction I had for Seth behind me. Was that possible in just a weekend? God, I hoped so.

The University was actually in Vermillion, surrounded by beautiful countryside, not that any of us noticed. Claudia was too busy channel surfing and checking the silkiness of her long straight hair. Harper spent more than half the ride with her head in the front seat; heaven forbid she missed our riveting conversation about hot frat boys, being college roomies, and what color bra we were wearing.

There really wasn't a need for an overnight campus visit, but Claudia insisted that we needed the full-on experience. If I hadn't felt so off and down in the dumps lately, I would have opted out. But who the heck knew? Maybe a weekend with my besties was what the doctor ordered.

The college itself was a combination of old and new. Some of the buildings looked like they were built in the 1800's, and then there were the more sophisticated structures made entirely of glass.

It was overwhelming to think that next year I could be a student at this massive school.

"Girl's, we have officially arrived," Claudia announced as I parked the car. "Let's go leave our stamp on college life and show these frat boys what they are in store for next year."

Oh goodness.

"Come on, let's get this over with," I grumbled, pulling my bag from the trunk.

"Katia, don't be a debby downer. We are just getting started," Claudia said, slapping my butt. Her dark hair was pulled into a high ponytail, swishing with her movements.

I jumped and scowled in her general direction.

"It will be a guaranteed riot," Harper added, the sun glinting off her blonde highlights.

As if that was going to make this trip better.

We toured the campus, the classes, and the dorms, all while Claudia was making snide comments under her breath. She could be such a monster when she wanted to be. Harper and I exchanged glances of exasperation. There was no fun in anything I did anymore. Once Claudia's antics had been humorous and exciting. Now I found them immature and insensitive.

Eyes brimming with mischief, Claudia grinned at Harper and me. "Alright, ladies. Let's make this a night these boys will never forget."

I rolled my eyes.

My dress was too tight. My mascara was clumpy. And my feet were already killing me. If I never wore another pair of uncomfortable heels again, it would be a godsend.

Trailing in Claudia's shadow, Harper and I followed her inside the Sigma Omega house. There were large Greek letters decorating the outside and inside of the house. Had the music not been blaring, had there not been some drunken guy bumping into me, who then tried to grind on me, I just might have appreciated the beauty of the fraternity.

At another time I would have been all over the sorority life. Kinship. Sisterhood. Socializing. Those were all things that had been important to me, but now...none of it held the same importance. I wanted different things from life. My craft, family, love.

Drunk Guy gave me a lopsided grin, sloshing his beer over the rim of his cup. He had a dopy cuteness about him. Wavy brown hair, soft chocolate eyes...and then he belched *hello*.

Gross.

I shoved Swivel Hips off me and went in search of a quiet corner where I could disappear.

Twirling the red solo cup in my hand, I nibbled on my lip, wishing I was with Seth. My party days were behind me. I couldn't stop my mind from drifting to him, wondering for the zillionth time what he was doing at this exact moment. Was he as lonely as I was? Did he think of me? Maybe he was with Zeke, or worse, Elena.

The thought brought tight pangs to my chest. Picturing Seth with Elena immediately filled me with white-hot jealousy. I downed the contents of my glass in an attempt to rid myself of the atrocious images.

I really wanted to see him, even if it was only for a minute. I would even settle for just hearing the sound of his silky voice.

Drunk dialing was always a bad idea.

Chapter 17

Seth

A month went by.

And another.

Then another.

Three months since Kat had found out the truth. Three of the longest, most agonizing months of my life.

The holidays came and went. Snow dusted the South Dakota plains. There was nothing friendly about South Dakota winters. And Kat and I continued to ignore each other. When one of us walked into a room, the other turned a blind eye—though my body was hyper-aware of her every move. I never felt more alive than when we were together. Even while giving her the cold shoulder, a piece of me thrived on her presence.

So consequently I was moody, grouchy, and an overall asshole to be around. My family gave me space, Zeke tried to pull me out of my constant state of grump, and Eddy put my butt to work. He said that if I was going to bite everyone's head off, then I could take my aggression out on the cars. I was deemed unfit to deal with customers until I cleaned up my attitude.

It had been three months, and I was still confined to the garage.

I could tell that Eddy was worried about me—my parents and Mya too—but there was nothing anyone could do. The small amount of spare time I did have, I spent with Zeke pouring over any ancient books of spells, magick, and curses I could get my hands on. I knew others had tried to break the binds of the curse, but I felt like I had to do something. This was a different age, a different century, and one with more technology than the nixies of the old could have ever fathomed.

I was praying to every god and goddess possible that there might be a loophole or a new spell that would break us from the curse of death. It was a long shot, but I would do just about anything to be able to have more than I had now. Oh, I definitely wanted Kat more than I wanted life itself, but at this point, I would take the smallest sliver of hope.

But I was also prepared to fail.

Hey, I was a realist, and my heart could only splinter so many times in this life. People dealt with pain in their own ways; it just so happened I became the biggest dick of the century, and

Kat…she became the girl I used to remember. The one I fell in love with in sixth grade. That in itself was like shoving a knife into any open wound and throwing salt on it.

It burned like a mother trucker.

She still hung out with Claudia and Harper, but I could see the things she used to hold important slipping away. I was glad to see a renewed friendship between Zeke, Olivia, and Kat. She needed good people like them surrounding her, and as far as I was concerned, there weren't two better people than Zeke and Olivia.

The weekend Kat left with Bimbo One and Bimbo Two was the longest day and a half of my life. I swear the winds howled in mourning. Pacing like a caged animal, I had to stop myself multiple times from jumping into my car and racing after her. There was this sudden caveman inside me that roared to the surface and wanted to drag her back home by her hair, beat my chest, and scream *mine*.

If I felt like this with her leaving for a weekend, what would it be like to put an ocean between us?

"Are you going to pout the entire weekend?" Zeke asked, casting his pole into the lake.

I glared at him from my side of the boat, contemplating rocking his grandpa's pontoon and spilling him into the murky waters. Fishing wasn't really my thing, but I'd been a shitty friend recently, and I felt like I owed Zeke, so here I was, floating on the

Vermillion lake, freezing my ass off. The water lapped against the boat, occasionally sloshing icy H2O in my face.

We were having unseasonably warm weather for this time of the year. The lake never froze, and the weathermen were blaming it on global warming. But I knew better. There was something brewing in the air, something dark, sinister, and frightening lingering in the shadows of Vermillion. Waiting…

I wasn't the only one who felt it. Everyone was on edge. Olivia and Elena had both mentioned something to me about the shift in the winds.

"I can't believe I let you drag me out here," I grumbled not for the first time. A shiver gripped my body.

It was official, Zeke was crazy. We were the only damn boat stupid enough to be out on the lake. The fish were biting, but only for Zeke, and I was pretty sure he'd charmed his pole. I wouldn't put it past him. I cursed as Zeke hooked another walleye, and I threw my pole into the water.

Zeke laughed. "You're a sorry excuse for a fisherman, you know that?"

I watched the fishing rod sink. "Maybe, but I'll kick your butt in nixiecraft every day of the week."

He shook his head. "Show off."

"Are we done? You have enough fish to feed a small country." I looked into a bucket of slimy fish.

He smirked at me. "Yeah, you can help me clean them."

"Don't hold your breath." I thought about throwing a handful of wormy bait in his face for even suggesting it.

"Do you ever think about dating?" Zeke asked. "It might take your mind off other things…"

Meaning Kat.

Elena had just recently started talking to me again after the whole Kat-Elena fight, and I was pretty sure I couldn't handle the drama of a relationship. I didn't think there was a girl out there who would understand my obsession to keep Kat safe, or the complexity of our non-existent relationship. They would just think I was some kind of stalker freak.

The boat rocked as he took a seat. "We could double date," Zeke dangled as if it was an incentive.

Dating was the furthest thing from my mind. "Thanks, Zeke, but I just can't right now."

He slapped me on the back, rocking the boat again. "If you change your mind, I'm here for you."

I smirked, the first smile of the day. They were rare these last few months. "I bet you are."

By the time I got home, it was well after midnight. I tried to push my body past the point of exhaustion. It had yet to work, betrayed by rampant thoughts and profound unfairness. I couldn't sleep, and I had been making pictures out of the shadows on the ceiling cast by the moonlight when my phone buzzed. The sight of Kat's number at one in the morning was alarming. My fingers fumbled with the buttons.

"Kats? What's wrong?"

"Hmm. I love the sound of your voice. It makes my belly feel all fuzzy inside," she said in a languid tone that was both sexy and sleepy.

The corners of my mouth twitched. "Oh yeah. What else do you love?" I didn't know what I was thinking, flirting like this. I told myself it was harmless. She was miles away, but obviously she and I were tuned into the same wavelength.

For a moment, I didn't think she was going to answer, and then she sighed. "Your eyes. Your stupid grin. Your lips. I love all of you."

I swallowed. *Shit.* This was going to blow up in my face. I should have hung up. I never should have answered her call. I should...

Stop everything and pick her up.

My pulse hammered in every part of my body. I squeezed my eyes shut, fighting to control the swift wave of desire that hit me.

"Seth?"

"Yeah," I replied huskily.

"I miss you so much."

I groaned. "Kats. You're killing me."

"Good." I could hear the smile in her voice, and I pictured the dimples I knew would be on either side of her cheeks. "I just wanted you to know. Night."

I listened to the click of the phone as she hung up. Clenching the phone in my hand, I lay on my bed and swore. There was no way I was going to sleep tonight. Not after that stimulating, unexpected call from Kat.

***

Everything seemed to be going fairly smooth considering the circumstances, which were anything but ideal. We were over halfway through our senior year and graduation was creeping up around the corner.

Then Kat changed the rules.

Leave it to a girl to mess up the plan.

Katia

It was Valentine's Day, and I was feeling like a lonely loser. While all the girls on the squad talked about their plans with their boyfriends, I got looks of pity.

Me.

They didn't have the slightest clue what love was. What they had with their lame boyfriends wasn't even a quarter of what I should have had with Seth. He wasn't just a teenage crush or my first love.

He was my epic love.

My starbound.

A piece of me that I could never have.

I wanted to tell them to take their pom poms and shove 'em. Yeah, I wasn't feeling very lovey-dovey at the moment. I was bitter and mad. If I saw another pink heart, cupid arrow, or red rose, I was going to vomit.

No, I was probably going to start breaking shit.

Three months had gone by without so much as a *hi*. We avoided eye contact because it was too painful. Just being in the same classroom with Seth made my heart bleed. It got to the point where I thought about talking to my dean about switching teachers.

But today of all days, I just wanted what I couldn't have.

Seth.

One day.

And that set a plan in motion...

A stupid plan that, at the time, sounded brilliant and just what the psychologist ordered. Of course, there were always consequences for our actions.

I just didn't realize how enormous mine would be.

***

"Mandatory meeting at my house on Saturday, bitches. And, girls, bring your pom poms, 'cuz it's going to get rowdy," Claudia announced at the beginning of practice.

God hates me.

She stood in front of the squad with a bright smile and her hands on her hips. "First up, strap on your harnesses, ladies, because we're going to the top of the pyramid today."

Goody gumdrops.

She was evil.

That meant I got to be the needle on top of the haystack. Reluctantly I waited as the bottom row took position. This group of girls used to be everything to me; now I felt nothing. Around me there was unity, giggling, and team spirit, but I never felt less a part of the group as I did this year.

And they noticed.

If it wasn't for Claudia and Harper, I would have been singled out completely.

One by one the human pyramid took shape until I was the last piece. Placing a foot on the shoulder of one girl and the back of another, I made my delicate climb to the top. Then steadying my feet equal lengths apart, I centered myself, fighting for poise, and stood up with my arms in the air.

Claudia clapped below. "Perfect. Don't break form."

I don't know what happened. Maybe my foot slipped. Maybe one of the girls below lost her balance, but the next thing I knew I was free-falling through the air. It wasn't until my butt hit the mats under me in a breath-stealing force that I even realized I had fallen.

My eyes closed, and I groaned. When I opened them again, there were a dozen faces hovering over me. Their lips were moving, but I couldn't hear anything except for the sound of the ocean, like when you put a seashell to your ear.

I just lay there. Taking inventory of my aches and pains, I verified that most of my body was in working order and I hadn't busted anything.

"Holy crap. Are you okay?" Claudia asked, squatting down beside me.

I blinked. "I just fell like nine feet. I'm not okay," I groaned.

Claudia's lips thinned. "Fine. I'll give you a hall pass, but…just this once."

Really? Oh, how gracious of her.

For the remainder of practice I sat on the sidelines and took the opportunity to send Seth a text. It was all part of the brilliant Valentine scheme I was brewing. I was playing with fire, but it was the first excitement I'd felt in months.

I guess being dropped from the top of a pyramid and having the wind knocked out of me somehow made me realize that I didn't want to live my life safe. I wanted to *live.* I wanted to take chances, experience love in ways I never dreamed possible.

I wanted Seth.

The gym cleared out after practice, but I hung back, lingering.

Nervously I nibbled on my manicure while I waited for Seth. The waiting game totally sucked. I had asked him to meet me after practice, and I finally sent the last girl's scrawny butt packing. Now I was a bundle of nerves. Time seemed to stand still as I listened to the clock tick each passing second.

I was just about to pick up my phone and chew him out for making me wait, when every nerve ending in my body went erratic. It was like being jolted by a livewire. I glanced to the double doors and watched him saunter in. My heart back-flipped.

Holy mackerel.

"You wanted to talk to me." The sound of his dark voice had my mind floating.

In just a minute, I thought. *First, I need to drink up the sight of you.* And it probably wasn't the time to mention that talking was the furthest thing from my mind. How could he look so sinful and so sweet at the same time? How could tattered jeans and black T-shirts be so damn knock-me-over sexy?

He looked me over from head to toe in slow blissful torture, before landing back on my face with green eyes so dark they almost looked black.

Sweet wicked moonbeams.

I was going to need to be revived before the *fun* even began.

Before my heart stopped fluttering, I did what I had longed to do every day for the last three months—I threw myself into his arms. He caught me around the waist, and I wasted not a spare moment. Under half-closed lashes, I closed the distance between us, planting my lips on his. My fingers dug into hair as black as the wintery night, and I sighed in sheer paradise. Our bodies pressed together, and I felt him soften into me. His fingers tightened on my hips, pulling me closer against him.

All the tension left me as his lips moved hungrily over mine. It had only taken a simple taste for things to escalate. We had essentially been starve-crazed for one another.

I never wanted to stop kissing him.

Seth

A flash of heat rippled through me. The scent of her brought me to my knees, and you can imagine what the taste of her did. She had taken me completely aback when she launched into my arms without so much as a word.

Her arms were wound around my neck as I breathed her in, her lips warm against mine. She sent my senses buzzing. When the kiss ended, she kept our faces near, pulling back just slightly.

"What was that for?" I asked softly and confused.

"Because it's Valentine's Day and the only thing I wanted was this," she replied with a smile that lit her entire heart-shaped face.

I stared at her mouth, captivated by her dimples. "Good enough for me," I murmured. *We aren't done. Not by a long shot*, I thought crushing a kiss to her cherry lips.

My arms tightened around her, tangling more than just limbs and tongues. I could feel a surge of magick summoning in my blood. I couldn't stop. Pressing her into the white block walls, I trapped her with my body, her soft exquisiteness brushing up against me. She moaned as I changed angles, and she melted in my arms. Gently, I kissed her dimples, the dip of her neck, her satin skin. Soft words of love tumbled from my lips, and my blood sang. I never thought I was the kind of guy to murmur sweet nothings, but I guess it took the right kind of girl.

My hands trailed from her waist to her hips, going farther south until my fingers grazed bare skin—her thigh. She was still in the cheerleading uniform, and a growl escaped from some deep recessed part of me that was driven wild by her.

Grabbing the back of her thigh, I lifted her leg, wrapping it around me. I was on the verge of bursting out of my skin, or maybe it was just my pants. Either way, I was seconds from ripping this skimpy getup off Kat's perfect body.

My mouth was still engaged in a seductive dance with hers. I clenched a fist of cotton from the bottom of her shirt, pushing it up. In between kisses I murmured her name, over and over. There was only one goal running through my foggy mind. I inched the shirt higher, exposing her flat belly. Just a little bit more—

"Seth!"

I swear to God that better be a horrible trick of my head, because if Zeke was really here, I was going to go apeshit on him. Pushing all thoughts of Zeke aside, I sucked the tender spot of her lobe and felt her shiver. I whispered her name.

"Seth, stop!" Zeke yelled. "What are you doing? Are you freaking insane?"

I blinked. That sounded so real. So close. I angled my head to the side, breathing heavily, keeping my arms wrapped around Kat. I wasn't letting go just yet, not when my entire my body was humming. I spotted Zeke, and he was very much not a figment of my imagination. Annoyance flashed in my eyes. "What the hell is wrong with you?" I cursed. Kat's heart was pounding against my chest, and she buried her head into my shoulder. I almost lost it when I felt her lick my neck.

"*Me?*" Zeke screeched. "Christ, Seth. You just said the sacred vow."

"What?" I must have heard him wrong. He was talking so goddamn fast.

"How far did you go? Did you—tell me you didn't complete the starbound?" he rambled on like a lunatic.

I narrowed my eyes, as it finally sunk in what he was saying. Tingles of magick were coursing through my veins. There was no denying that I had called upon magick; static tendrils danced in the air. I stiffened in her arms.

No! No! No!

Did I just issue our death sentence?

Full-on panic set in.

Oh. My. Freaking. God.

Had I really said the words that would make me solely hers?

I had been helpless to stop it. I wasn't even conscious of what I had been saying, let alone that I was also using magick. This was a fuck up of epic proportions. Had Kat? Had she in turn said the vow as well? Had we doomed ourselves over one kiss?

Quickly, I glanced down at the beauty still in my arms. Her curls were in disarray and half-lidded eyes clouded with part desire, part confusion. Taking her wrists, I flipped them over to the inside, looking for the binding marks—five stars that made up a five-pointed star. I sighed and sagged against the wall in relief—nothing but flawless skin. Glancing up, I realized that we weren't out of the woods yet. She looked up at me with love shinning in her incandescent blue eyes, and I could see the words on the tip of her tongue—our end before our beginning. I put a finger to her lips, silencing her. "Don't you dare, Kats. You can't. It will kill us."

She blinked.

And I watched as comprehension shed the misty lining of desire. Then, her eyes widened.

I untangled myself from her, putting much needed distance between us. It was slightly easier to breathe when I couldn't smell her summery scent. More than anything I wanted a happy ending for Kat, without or without me—I wanted her alive.

Chapter 18

Katia

"Seth?" I didn't know what was going on. Why was Zeke here? And why did I feel so funny inside?

I mean I knew that Seth's kisses packed quite a punch, but this was a whole new level of hotness—it was amazificent. His body stiffened against mine, and his eyes cleared. Then suddenly he moved, leaving me to lean on the wall for support. I missed his warmth instantly.

"Kats, tell me you didn't." Seth ran a ragged hand through his dark hair. There was a desperate plea in his tone that was laced with real fear.

"Didn't do what?" I asked, looking from a worried Zeke to a freaked-out Seth.

Zeke stepped forward because clearly Seth was having issues forming coherent sentences. His blue eyes looked at me soberly, their normal light-heartedness gone. "Did you call upon magick?"

I gave him a strange look. "No." He had interrupted what was singlehandedly the most mind-blowing experience of my life and scared me half to death, just to ask me if I'd used magick? "What gives, Zeke?"

"You didn't hear what he said?" Zeke arched a brow.

"Seth?" Had he said something? I remembered him whispering my name, and—

I gasped.

Oh shit. Oh God. Oh shit.

Zeke gave me a knowing look. Seth had his fingers stuffed in his hair, and I noticed for the first time that he had some marks on the inside of his right wrist. I swallowed a coal-sized lump that formed in my throat at the sight of the five-stars imprinted on Seth's skin.

I was going to puke.

They were marks I'd never seen and never thought I'd see. Starbound. Forged by love, ancient magick, and free will. It made it all so very real glimpsing the tiny black stars on his wrist. Then there was the blooming of warmth that burst in my chest. Seth had pledged himself to me. He loved me, was in love with me.

Though, at this moment, I was the only one who looked happy about it. Knuckleheads One and Two both looked like they were going to blow a gasket.

"Do you feel any different?" Zeke asked, studying me.

I looked over his shoulder at Seth and nodded. "Yeah, I guess." There was this glowing inside me, an aftermath of magick and something else…

Zeke shook his head. "The two of you can't be left alone for five minutes," he complained.

My cheeks flamed. He probably had a valid point. I knew I should have been out-of-my-flipping-mind scared, but I was secretly happy—ecstatic. It was like I was carrying a piece of Seth with me for the rest of my life. What girl in her right mind wouldn't want a piece of Seth Nightingale?

I came to the conclusion that the only person with their head on straight was Zeke. What would we do without him? Seth and I couldn't be trusted to be alone, especially now. The pull to him would have intensified. It was the natural order of things. The starbound demanded a union from both parties, and it wouldn't quiet this roaring need inside me until we had. Already I could sense the demand inside of me, and when I met his eyes across the gym, heaven help me, I weakened.

Seth and I were in a whole ocean of hot water.

Oh God. I shuddered to think. Everything could have ended tonight, on Valentine's Day. We came within a thread's width to activating the curse of death. If Zeke hadn't shown up…

Now that I thought about it, what was he doing here? "Why

are you here, Zeke?"

He shrugged. "Seth asked me to chaperon. I was a little late getting to the party."

I'd say. "You needed back up?" I shot Seth a dirty look. How quickly my feelings could go from dewy-eyed to peeved.

He gave me one-sided grin. "You're lethal."

No one could argue with that.

Sensing what could turn into a lover's spat, Zeke cut in. "Now what?" he asked, like any of us had a clue.

We stood there staring at one another, me still with my back to the wall, Zeke between Seth and me, and Seth as far from me as he could get. I tried not to be irritated, but it was hard when mere minutes ago he'd had his hands all over me.

It was Seth who finally spoke. "First off, we don't tell our parents." He turned to Zeke. "Got that?"

Zeke held both his hands up in the air. "Why are you looking at me?"

Seth gave him a droll glare. "Because you have a mouth bigger than Kat's wardrobe. Hell, my little sister can keep better secrets than you."

"I am totally offended." Zeke pretended to be hurt, putting a hand to his chest. "You're lucky you're my best friend."

"Too bad you can't wipe your own memory."

"Funny," Zeke added dryly. "What the hell do you see in him

again, Katia?"

I glared at both of them in exasperation. "Can you guys just smooch and makeup already?" This was serious.

Seth's eyes met mine. "First, we wait and see if anything happens. I think we might be in for a few unsightly surprises, but since the link is only one-side, we should be okay. I hope."

"That's your grand plan?" Zeke asked sarcastically.

Seth rolled his eyes. "No, genius. We need to break the curse."

Zeke smirked. "That's more like it. You think it can be done?"

Determination rolled off Seth. "I haven't the slightest idea. Others have tried and flopped—epically. And I am not holding out hope that we will succeed where others have failed, but I can't just sit around twiddling my thumbs while we wait for the curse to consume us. The least we can do until graduation is figure out a disenchantment, anything to release the hold it has on Kat and me."

"Cool. I'm in," Zeke said, grinning. If I didn't know better, I'd say he sounded like was looking forward to the challenge.

Me?

I'd been silent during the whole exchange, and I really wasn't sure that we stood a snowball's chance in hell, but...

Sky-blue and emerald eyes looked my way, waiting. "Sure, why the heck not?" Especially if it meant more time spent with Seth.

Geez, I was just hoping to live to see eighteen.

"Yes!" Zeke hissed. His embarrassing happy dance was rudely interrupted. Someone didn't like what had gone down here tonight, and they were making their disapproval clear.

The ground began to quake, and the gym floor trembled under my sneakers, followed by a cracking sound that echoed throughout the large gymnasium. Bracing myself on the wall for support, I looked over my head and gasped. Large, jagged splinters cut across the ceiling, pieces snapping off and freefalling like spears around me.

Oh. My. God.

We were all going to die, crushed by tons upon tons of drywall and roof shingles. Not exactly an ideal way to go.

Seth reached me in two strides, shielding me with his body as debris and plaster began to tumble upon us. I squeezed my eyes shut and buried my head into his chest, holding onto him, taking small comfort in his embrace. Fear snaked inside my stomach, coiling around my heart. If this was it, then there was nowhere else I wanted to be than in Seth's arms.

I clung to him as chaos rained from above.

Then I felt a surge of magick that shimmered from Seth and knew he was conjuring something of his own.

Pandemonium erupted around us, and the noise thundered in my ears. The sounds were unimaginable, groaning, creaking, booming. I was sheltered from the destruction, not knowing whether the ceiling was going to collapse on us. All I could do was pray it would end soon and we would all be in one piece.

The curse's temper-tantrum had probably only lasted minutes, but in the midst of danger it had felt like hours. None of us budged when the ground finally stilled and it ceased pouring drywall on us.

"Are you hurt?" Seth whispered in my ear.

I shook my head and got the courage to peer over Seth's shoulder, the dust was beginning to settle. Zeke was beside us shaking the white ceiling powder from his hair and wiping the gunk off his face.

"A riot shield? Dude that is so badass," Zeke said, grinning like an idiot at Seth.

I could only conclude that this had something to do with the stupid clear plastic-like-thing over our heads. Only guys.

Seth lips twitched even while his eyes were still wary. "It was the first thing I could think of."

He had summoned a riot whatca-ma-thingy to protect us. Was I supposed to be impressed?

"So, when do we start kicking this curse's ass?" If Zeke could be a smartass, then he was definitely okay.

I let out one long breath I'd been holding just as Seth stepped back, shoving his hands in the back pockets of his jeans. There was a cut along his cheek and on his forearm. Immediately, I reached out to touch his cheek, wishing I had the power to heal, as Elena did.

He wore a deep scowl, eyes scanning the rubbish, and winched. "The sooner the better. We need to get out of here before it all decides to crash down on us."

I coughed. Dust littered the air, but through the smog, I got a good look at the gym. The bleachers, barely visible, were covered with so much crap. It didn't look like we were going to be holding basketball games in here any time soon. That got a huge hooray from me. "I couldn't agree more," I mumbled, wrapping my arms around myself.

Seth held out a hand and helped me over a pile of broken ceiling tiles. I hissed, my leg buckled, and pain shot up my thigh. It was just my luck that a piece of shrapnel had embedded itself in my leg.

Seth bent down. "Looks like you got a nasty cut." And the next thing I knew, tears were stinging my eyes. He had pulled out the sharp hunk of metal without so much as a warning.

I bit my lip…hard. There was a trail of blood running down my leg. "Jeesh, thanks for the heads up."

The corners of his mouth tipped. I tried not to think about the tingles coursing through me when his fingers grasped mine. We meandered our way through the garbage, and I only managed to trip once. I might have done so deliberately, playing up my injury a tad just so I could feel Seth's hands on me again.

Totally devious, but hey, sometimes a girl has to play dirty to get what she wants.

And I so wanted Seth.

That might be the starbound talking, though it hardly mattered. Even after having my life threatened, which probably should have given me the red warning light, I liked to break rules. I could still feel his light inside me, and I clung to it as a beacon of hope.

When we reached the door leading outside, it was barricaded with trash. Seth pushed his way through, kicking what he could out of the path. He shoved down on the bar and then put his shoulder to it with the force of his weight. The door squeaked, not really nudging. It took two more tries before we saw the first crack of a dull light.

The sky was grey, blanketed with dark thick clouds. I gulped my first breath of fresh air, tasting a heavy dampness like after a storm. My nose burned from the kick-up of so much dirt and dust.

Zeke shook his entire body, spraying me with a shower of tiny white particles.

"Hey," I complained, trying to dust what I could off my clothes. I needed more than just a shower. Maybe I could run myself through a carwash. I winced as my hand touched a scrape on my leg.

For someone who had almost gotten pulverized, Zeke was in good spirits. Too good. I actually thought he might have enjoyed getting the crap scared out of him. That boy had serious thrill-seeking issues. "So what's the plan, because I am so ready for some payback?" Zeke asked with more enthusiasm than was necessary right now.

I plucked a piece of plaster from my hair. "Could you just give us a sec to be thankful we're not dead?"

A moment of silence elapsed, which was all Zeke could handle. "Okay, game plan?"

Shaking my hair out, I growled in aggravation. "This isn't a game, Zeke."

Seth peered up at the formidable sky. "He's right, Kats." His voice was crestfallen and tired. "We need a plan, like now. This thing is getting angrier and us ignoring it, ignoring each other, isn't helping. We are only pissing if off. So let's do something." He punched the last sentence with renewed fire.

I didn't know how he found the strength. It was like working with a bunch of testosterone junkies. "Fine," I relented.

The two of them stood outside the school building, eyeing the destruction and scratching their heads. It was clear that I was going to have to be the one to come up with a devisable plan.

"I think we should go back in time," I suggested. They both

looked at me like I was speaking Greek.

"Did you hit your head?" Zeke said.

I rolled my eyes. "Not literally, you dope. I was thinking a spell, with the circle. Maybe we can get the scoop about what really happened to our families and uncover some answers."

"And how do purpose we do that?" Zeke asked.

"With a really kickass spell."

They both gave me blank stares.

I sighed. "Okay, fine. I don't know any kickass spells, but there has got to be something in all the boxes of old literature, journals, and spell books my family has kept. It is a starting point."

The duo shrugged, and Seth stared off at the incoming trucks and flashing lights. "It's probably a one in a million chance, but what other choice do we have?" he grumbled.

Sirens sounded in the distance. I grinned, which might have seemed misplaced considering the circumstances, but I didn't regret what had happened in the gym between Seth and me, at least not yet. There was this glowing light inside of me that I recognized as the aftermath of Seth sharing magick with me and giving me more than he ever bargained for—a vow of magick that bound him to me forever. For the first time all year, I felt a purpose. I felt alive again after living months in gloom.

And this meant I got to spend more time with Seth.

I was a glutton for death.

Chapter 19

Seth

It was the most bizarre feeling stepping inside Kat's house, like walking into no-man's zone. Both of her parents were at work, which made me nervous, but I brought Zeke along as a safeguard—not that it was exactly reassuring.

The events in the gym plagued my mind 25-8. When I thought about what I had done, I couldn't help but berate myself. So stupid. One kiss and I was throwing myself at her mercy, binding myself to only her. If I had wanted a chance at a normal life, I had just squashed it to smithereens on one kiss.

But good God almighty, what a kiss. I take it all back. It might have very well been worth the risk, and given the chance, I'd probably do it again. And again.

Ugh.

Apparently I was nowhere near as smart or cunning as I

thought I was. But Kat…she was something else. Just knowing that ribbons of my magick now ran in her blood gave me goose bumps. Seeing the five-stars on my wrist gave me chills and, at the same time, made my heart swell.

There was a warmth of welcoming that lived in the Montgomery house. From inside the doorway, Kat sent me a jaw-dropping grin that could cure any ailment that might plague me. She was halfway down the stairs with a hand resting on the white banister. Her curls were piled in a messy knot, and dimples dotted either side of her lips. Hiding the intense feelings that were boomeranging in my chest was harder since my astronomical screw-up.

Collins held open the door, staring between Kat and me suspiciously. "I thought you guys were cursed. And what is this bonehead doing with you, Seth?" She nodded to Zeke beside me, and my lips twitched.

Zeke glanced over his shoulder to Kat. "I see where she gets her sunny disposition."

I nudged Zeke in the side, reminding him to play nice. She was only eleven, after all, but he did have a point. Attitude ran deep in the Montgomery bloodline.

Collins crossed her arms and gave Zeke the stink eye.

"Hey, Collins," I greeted as she shut the door behind us.

She sent me a cheeky grin, almost nearly as devastating as her older sister's, with cute matching dimples. "Hiya, Seth."

"How come he gets the royal treatment?" Zeke asked, feigning outrage.

Collins sent him a sour smile. "'Cuz he is like family."

Zeke put a hand to his heart, amping up on the charm. "What am I, chopped liver?"

Kat's little sister was a handful. She rolled her eyes. "You're a dork."

He dropped the act. "Coming from someone who still watches Sponge Bob," Zeke commented, lifting a brow to the TV in the other room.

A small smile broke out on Collins's lips. "Sponge Bob is the shit."

Zeke coughed, trying to cover up a laugh.

Kat rolled her eyes.

And I smirked.

"Alright, you two, put down the gloves. We have work to do," Kat cut in before any more crossing of words.

Zeke groaned. "All work and no play makes Katia a dull—"

"Zeke," Seth and I both said in a unison warning.

"Are you guys going to complete each other's sentences next?" Zeke was in rare form today.

Collins snickered from the couch, as the three of us climbed the stairs. Kat and I ignored him, but Zeke winked at Collins before we disappeared to the second floor.

"Just a warning," Kat said, looking back over her shoulder. "The attic isn't pretty. Actually, I avoid it at all cost. Gives me the willies."

"Oh great," Zeke mumbled as he opened the door that led to the third floor—the attic. "It's like *Night of the Living Dead* in here."

"I warned you," she said, following carefully behind him.

"Zeke, grow some balls and get in there." I couldn't be tempted by Kat's backside for much longer, or her scent. Through the musk and dirt, I could smell her sweet shampoo and the cherry blossoms that followed her everywhere.

"Wow, don't you guys have a Swiffer or something?" Zeke said, swiping at a cobweb with his hand.

"And displace all my eight-legged friends? I'd rather they stay up here and out of my room." She shivered.

He angled his head. "Good point. Might I suggest Merry Maid?"

If we couldn't take a few measly spiders, how the heck were we going to destroy an ancient curse cast out of desperation and high emotions?

Katia

Glued to Zeke's back, I stepped over the threshold. I'd be damned if one of those webs fell in my hair. It would be lost forever, tangled in my curls. "No one ever comes up here, you dingleberry."

Zeke's eyes twinkled. "God, I've missed you, Katia, and that mouth."

I rolled my eyes.

"Watch it," Seth growled behind me.

"Note to self: Never mention Katia's mouth in Seth's presence," Zeke mumbled to himself, taking out another monstrous looking web.

I smiled, trying not to get overly distracted by Seth's alluring presence behind me. "You're my hero, Zeke."

He guffawed. "If my spider killing skills impress you, you should see my—"

"Zeke!" growled Seth. "Just get us to the boxes in the back."

"Jeesh, someone has their tighty-whiteys in a wad."

Seth's brows were pulled together. "Just cut the wisecracks and open a book."

"God, now you sound like my mom."

Seth exhaled, and I couldn't help but smile. It felt like I was caught in the middle of an episode of Scooby-doo. I guess that made me Daphne.

We poured through thick bound books with fragile papers, discolored and aged. Handwritten script we could barely read with foreign symbols, many none of us knew how to decipher. The pages smelled musky, but the knowledge between the pages was rich and vast. Yet nothing we learned was what we were looking for, what we needed.

Discouraged didn't come close to describe what I was feeling. This sucked.

My neck had a cramp and my back was strained from scouring books all day in my dust-ball of an attic. Collins had brought us a pitcher of lemonade, but I think she had ulterior motives, like snooping. We had been at it for hours. Although we hadn't found squat that was worth any value to our cause, I'd literally had the best time. Seth and Zeke had me rolling on the dingy old floorboards, laughing like a hyena.

It was refreshing, therapeutic, and damn fun. Who would have thought?

Rubbing the back of my neck, Seth stretched out his long legs beside me and let out a groan. His thigh brushed against mine, and heat zinged up my leg. The temperature in my body skyrocketed. "We should probably call it night," he suggested, eyes on me.

"What, you scared of the dark?" Zeke teased, his head in a book, unaware of the electric shock that charged the air.

Before the sharp comeback I knew was on the tip of Seth's tongue ever came to fruition, a brown leather book fell to my feet. It clattered to the floor with a thump. It was so quiet you could hear a fly karate chop the silky thread of a spider web.

Bending down, I picked up the book that literally sang in my grasp like the Holy Grail of spell books. It hummed under my fingertips. The relic Celtic symbol on the cover glowed like the moon as I ran my fingers over the three oval loops encircled in a larger one.

This was it.

The one we'd been searching for.

The three of us held our breaths as I opened to the first page. A surge of power bolted down my hands. I half expected the book to levitate in the air, pages flipping on their own until it landed on the spell we needed. I guess that was too much to hope for, and far too easy.

Instead the curse decided to pay us all another visit. And it was nearly as pleasant as the last one. A tiny tapping clattered onto the hardwood floors. My gaze lifted, meeting Seth's and Zeke's. Seth angled his head, listening. Then I felt something brush my arm. Not going to lie, I was afraid to look.

It was my nightmares come true.

A hairy spider the size of a quarter was talking a stroll down my forearm. Not even a gag could have stopped the scream from erupting. It ripped from my lungs. I had no sooner opened my mouth when Seth flicked his wrist, casting a spell that flung that *thing* off me.

All those creepy dreams I had about spiders suddenly became

a reality.

I barely had time to breathe or do a wiggly heeble-jeebie dance in my seat when the sound of splitting wood punctured through the close quarters. The three of us froze, afraid to move. My stomach was in my throat with the unexpected noise. I latched onto Seth's gaze right before shit hit the fan.

A wooden beam fell from the exposed frame of the roof, smashing it with a force strong enough to knock me on my ass. I hit the tattered floorboards with breath-stealing impact. Seth and Zeke hadn't faired much better, but none of us had time to react or brace ourselves. I was going to have a bitch of a bruise tomorrow, on my butt nonetheless and probably a few other places I couldn't yet feel.

The beam landed with a crash that shook the entire house from top to bottom, which caused an aftershock of miscellaneous shit to break. The noise echoed in some warped glass-shattering fireworks display. It was a deafening sound that I thought was never going to end, but that wasn't the only thing to fall on us.

Spiders. They were everywhere, dropping down on us like an epidemic.

I squealed, my arms instinctually covering my head. Seth crawled to me and encompassed me in the safety of his arms.

Wasn't that a catch-22?

I felt safe and secure in the same arms that would ultimately be my death.

Bullshit of epic portions.

A rainfall of dust bunnies, debris, woodchips, and, my personal favorite, spiders continued to tumble around us. Seth's grip tightened, shielding me with his body. The curse—it felt angry. Seth and I were almost eighteen and had come so close to completing the starbound. It was raging to be let loose, to steal what it felt was rightfully its—our lives.

Each time we stopped from fulfilling our fates, the curse was going to lash out until it got what it wanted. Each time we came closer to finding a way to break the power it had over us, it would find a way to hurt us.

When the ringing in my ears finally stopped, all I could think was *Collins*.

Chapter 20

Katia

"Your ancestor has a sick sense of humor. Someone needs a chill pill," Zeke yelled at the curse. I doubted it could hear us, or cared. The curse had caused its destruction.

I pushed at Seth's chest so he'd let me up, but he wasn't easily moved. "Collins. Seth, I have to find Collins."

My words penetrated the haze of protection shimmering in his eyes. Right now, Seth was only thinking about my safety, but I had a little sister downstairs, alone and probably afraid, that I was responsible for.

"We'll find her," Seth assured.

Suddenly, the three of us were in action. Seth rolled off me, scattering a group of eight-legged beasts, and jumped to his feet. He held a hand out for me, tugging me up. I refused to look at the floor, because I was sure I would puke—or pass out. Zeke was already in motion. As swiftly as possible, we made our way through the clutter and the critters crawling about to find that the attic door was blocked.

"Of fricking course," I grumbled. Couldn't I get a break here?

Seth and Zeke attacked the piled-up crap, kicking and throwing what they could out of our way. "Screw this," Seth swore. A second later, he gave a swoop of his hand and the air radiated with magick. Following the movement of his arm, the rubble was tossed to the side, leaving a clear path to our only way out.

"Whoa. Now you're talking," Zeke said with a grin of approval.

"Let's just get out of here before round three decides to descend upon us," Seth mumbled, swinging out the door.

I couldn't have agreed more and rushed down the stairwell. On shaky legs, I prayed my house was still standing and Collins was safe. If this skank-ass-curse had harmed a hair on my sister's head…

It was one thing to come after me, but when you messed with my sister, well that brought out seven different colors of crazy in me.

I ran down two flights of stairs in record time, screaming Collins's name. It wasn't any where near as horrible as I had imagined. Items had been knocked off shelves, off the walls, but the house was still intact. And...no creepy-crawly spiders—thank goodness.

"Katia." Collins's voice quivered.

I exhaled as I saw her head pop up from under the table. There were tears in her eyes, but she was okay. "Collins," I said in relief.

She crawled out and launched herself into my arms. "What was that? An earthquake?" she whispered, her voice muffled by my tight embrace.

"Thank God, you're alright." I pulled her away at arm's length, taking a good look at her. No scratches, no blood.

Her owl-sized eyes looked up at me. "By the look on your face, I take it that it wasn't an earthquake."

I shook my head.

"The curse?" she asked softly.

She was too wise for her age. "Yeah."

"What did you guys do?" Her eyes narrowed, looking back and forth between Seth and me.

Zeke snickered.

I rolled my eyes. "Nothing that warranted our house being shaken off the ground." I tucked a strand of hair behind her ear. "You're sure you're okay?"

She nodded. "But Mom and Dad are going to have a shit-fit when they see this house."

It was on the tip of my tongue to tell her to watch her language, but then I realized she was right. How was I going to explain this mess? I eyed the house. "That is why, little sister, you and I are going to clean house."

"I didn't make this mess," she argued.

"Well, Mom and Dad don't know that. Come on, it will be fun."

"You have a warped sense of fun. Why don't you have Seth and Zeke help you?"

I turned behind me, looking at Trouble One and Trouble Two. "Because, they were just leaving," I said, scooting them to the front door.

"We need to talk later," Seth whispered.

I nodded, and then remembered what we had found. "The book…" I murmured. My eyes filled with disappointment as I realized we had left the book in the attic, probably buried under a ton of spiders with grotesque furry legs.

A sneaky grin slipped across Zeke's lips as he held up the leather bound book.

I couldn't help but return his smile. "Zeke, you are the best." I was so relieved that I didn't have to step foot in that room again. Eventually I would have to tell my parents about our new bug infestation, or hope the spiders left on their own. That seemed unlikely.

"That's what I've been telling you guys."

Seth tugged Zeke out the door by the back of his shirt. "I'll call you later."

My heart skipped.

It was time to make a little magick of our own. Good thing I had Collins. She was sensational at levitation.

***

Elena shoved a handful of popcorn in her mouth. "Okay, does somebody want to tell me why we are really here? And don't give me that crap about hanging out and watching a movie. If this is some lame excuse to get Katia and me to get along, then you guys are going to be sadly disappointed—"

"Elena, shut up for a minute," Zeke said in exasperation.

She gave him the one-finger salute from her seat on one of the recliners in Olivia's house.

Classic Elena.

Seth was beside me on the couch, which probably totally burned Elena's butt. Good. "Shockingly, this isn't about you," I snapped.

She glared at me with silver blades. "No. It is always about *you.*"

I had no argument, because it *was* about me. Well, Seth and me.

"Ladies, retract the claws. We have a spell to plan," Zeke

interrupted before I jumped out of my seat and strangled her.

Olivia's parents were gone for the night. So we had arranged a powwow with the circle that hopefully wouldn't end in some kind of disaster. I wasn't sure there was any place that was safe, but we had to try to find some answers. That was if Elena and I didn't kill each other first.

Seth began to fill Elena and Olivia in on our plan to use a spell to find out the origin of the curse. Why it was conjured to begin with. With the why and the how, maybe, just maybe, we could find a way to stop the inevitable from happening. I, of course, shouldn't have expected Elena to cooperate.

"You want to cast a powerful spell against a curse that's centuries old? Brilliant. Are you guys insane?" Elena asked, looking at Seth and Zeke with discontent.

In the back of all our minds, we might be thinking the same thing, but the difference was the rest of us had the decorum to keep our opinions to ourselves. Elena didn't operate that way. She was tacky, but we needed to play nice. For now. "Look, together we are stronger. Once we figure this out and complete the spell, then we can go back to pretending that we hate each other."

"Oh, I am not pretending."

"Whatever," I said sharply.

"I'd rather stab myself with a spork than help you," Elena spat.

Yeah. I got that loud and clear. I gritted my teeth, on the verge of tearing her a new butthole. My jaw was throbbing from the pressure. Seth snuck a sideway glance at me. Poor Olivia. I really didn't want to bloody her carpet, but my fist was itching to pop Elena in the mouth. She wouldn't be so quick to shoot down our only hope then.

Seth leaned forward, catching Elena's eye. "Fighting amongst ourselves is only going to hurt the circle. This is something we need to do, and we can't do it without you, Elena." If anyone was going to convince the she-devil, it was Seth, as much as I hated to admit it. I was jealous that she had feelings for Seth. We might not be able to be together, but in my heart, he was mine.

Elena's grimace flickered, and I knew that Seth would be able to chip her down. That was if my mouth didn't blow it. "Let me guess, it was *her* idea?" Elena asked.

Seth shook his head. A strand of dark hair fell forward onto his face. "Not quite. It was mine."

"Just freaking great. It gets better. I should have known. Tell me why I should waste an ounce of my magick on you?" Elena snapped.

Last night I had scoured every spell in that book until the page literally jumped out at me. The words on that aged paper shimmered and came to life. It was all the confirmation I needed that this was the one we had been looking for.

I returned Elena's glare with one of my own. It was time to pull out the big guns. "Because I know that you care about Seth in your own twisted way," I replied.

Everyone in the room paused.

Awkward.

Elena chewed on her blood-red lip, and for the first time I saw something other than contempt in her eyes. Mention Seth and it was hook, line, and sinker. "I am going to regret this," she complained.

Seth exhaled. "So are we all in agreement to do the spell?" he asked.

"Hell yes," Zeke said.

Olivia nodded, giving me a small smile. "Of course."

All eyes turned to Elena. "Fine, but I'm not bringing anyone back from the dead, so this spell better be da bomb. I so don't want to be part of some suicide group spell."

It was settled then. On the next new moon, we would gather in the clearing and, with the combined power of the circle, cast a spell to bend time and space. We were in over our heads. Seth and I looked at each other, mimicking the same sense of fear laced with hope. I could feel his unease swirling inside me.

Our little interlude didn't go unnoticed. "Now that we have all doomed ourselves, I'm outta of here. Text me the deets. See you lame-os." Elena sauntered out of the room. The melody of chains clinking together on her pants followed her, and a few minutes later the front door slammed shut.

"Well, that went better than expected," Zeke grumbled, staring after Elena and wrinkling his nose.

Olivia got to her feet, brushing her long red hair off her shoulder. "How about that movie?" she asked, trying to make the downer ambiance less obvious. Bless her sweet soul. I knew how much she wanted the circle to be how it used to be. Fun. Trustworthy. Unified. Unbreakable friendship. Truthfully, deep down, I wanted that too. I didn't want to be at constant odds with Elena. But I didn't have a clue how to reach her. How did I patch this broken friendship?

Maybe if I actually lived through this curse, I would try to find a way. Right now I could only think about getting through the next few weeks.

"Tell me you got something bone-chilling? I want to be scared shitless," Zeke said, getting up to make more popcorn.

I had enough scary crap in my real life. There was no real need inside me to watch more on the TV, but I also understood that Zeke was trying to rekindle the group nights we used to have. And it was always a cheesy horror film. Elena and Zeke loved them.

Shocker.

They were gruesome buddies.

"Coke or Pepsi?" Zeke yelled from the kitchen.

"I better help him," Olivia said, closing the tray to the Blu-ray player.

And that left Seth and me. Alone.

Oh boy. Sparks were going to fly.

I shifted on the couch we shared, turning toward him, searching for something to say. We hadn't been alone since that day in the gym. The day Seth had said the words that linked him to me forever—our spirits and our souls. Just what the curse wanted.

My eyes were drawn to his wrist, and to the five stars gracing his skin. I wanted to touch them, feel the quickening of his pulse dance under my fingertips. "What did it feel like?" My voice was soft as I reached out, lightly tracing the star pattern.

As predicted, embers ignited on contact. It still caught me off guard. I looked up at Seth. The green flecks of his eyes deepened, and my chest squeezed tightly. A flood of feelings burst inside me.

"It's hard to explain. There is a sense of exhilaration inside me, and relief."

I arched my brow.

"For so long, I've been trying to prevent this from happening." He looked down at the marks on the inside of his wrist. "It's weird not having to fight that feeling anymore. I sort of feel lost without it. That internal struggle has been such a part of me it's like I am missing an arm. On the other side, if we never find a way to break the curse, I have to try to find a way to move forward. Without you. I don't know how that's possible…"

I didn't want it to be possible. I had to believe this was going to work, or I was going to drive myself nutty with anxiety. "If things were different—" I was asking questions for which the answers might taunt me for a lifetime, but I couldn't stop myself.

He gave me a level gaze. "Kats, you know that this bond wouldn't be one-sided. I wouldn't let you out of my sight. Make no mistake, I want you."

Those were the kind of words that made a girl risk her life for love. Tingles frolicked throughout my body, and I leaned forward, captivated by his voice. I wasn't really thinking, other than there was too much space between us.

Olivia and Zeke chose that moment to walk back in, arms loaded with drinks and bowls of popcorn. Their lighthearted banter filled the room, snapping us both out of our steaming gaze.

We sprang apart.

I picked at the burgundy fuzz on the armrest of the couch, trying to get my rapidly beating heart under control. If either of them noticed the electric vibe bouncing from our side of the room, they did a good job masking their suspicions. I kept my eyes averted from Seth.

Olivia killed the lights, engulfing us in darkness. The munching of popcorn and the fizzing of carbonation occupied the silence as we snuggled in and waited for the movie to begin. I sunk into the cushions, wondering how I was going to get through the next two hours without jumping Seth.

It didn't look good.

He weakened my resolve. Over buttery popcorn, I could smell the sinful scent of Seth. Earthy. Fresh. Woodsy. It was driving me hormonally bonkers. My cheeks flushed, and I wrapped my hands around the cool can of soda. I was ready to slap it on my forehead.

To distract myself from the fine specimen lounging next to me, I tried to think about anything but his lips. Soft. Moist. Sweet. Memorable. I snuck a tiny sideways peek. He was nibbling on his bottom lip.

Epic fail.

I groaned under my breath.

The movie wasn't much of a diversion. I couldn't lose myself in the plot and the characters, not when my mind was constantly straying to Seth. To make matters worse…I nearly fell out of my seat when I felt the first charged touch.

He fingers stroked the back of my hand, making me shiver. In the dark, my senses heightened and every nerve ending in my body was amplified. A simple movie with friends was turning into one of the most erotic nights of my life, all thanks to the guy sitting so close to me, but it wasn't enough.

I edged nearer to him on the couch, needing to feel his heat fused with mine. The urge to touch him even in the most innocent way, like thigh to thigh, was too much for me to ignore. It wasn't long before the innocent flirting did nothing to satisfy this burning need inside me.

"I need more popcorn," Seth mumbled in the middle of the movie, pushing up from the couch and exiting into the hallway.

I really shouldn't. I knew that I was only seeking trouble, but my body and my heart were screaming for five minutes alone with Seth. A minute went by. Then two. And I finally made my move. Olivia was gripping the edge of the armrest as the girl onscreen was cornered by a guy with a wicked looking machete. Zeke was beside Olivia with his eyes glued to the screen, stuffing his mouth blindly with popcorn.

"I'm going to use the bathroom," I murmured, sneaking out of the room unnoticed. It was almost too easy. Heading down the hallway toward the kitchen, I listened for Seth.

Before I got to the light at the end of the hall, a hand weaved through mine, tugging me to the side. My back hit the wall, and Seth's body was pressed up against mine, boxing me in. Not that I minded in the least. Glancing up, his eyes flashed in the dark corner. I rose up on my toes, lacing my hands behind his neck. My breath hitched, and I tilted my chin to kiss him, meeting him halfway.

He didn't hesitate.

"Just this once," he whispered against my lips.

I nodded, agreeing to anything as long as he didn't stop kissing me, touching me. It was a long and languid kiss, one I could savor for days. Hopefully the memory would sustain me for years. His hands were everywhere, but at the same time, it wasn't enough. That seemed to be the theme of the day.

Smoothing down the sides of my stomach, his hands rested low on my hips. I doubted there would be another stolen moment as perfect as this. I let myself get swooped away by his silky kisses, which was a big no-no.

If I lost my head, I lost my life. Being cursed sucked llama balls.

His tongue swept across mine, and I felt the sparks of magick radiate from him. Now that he was tied to me it would be as natural as breathing to share magick. The burden or resistance rested within me. I sucked at denying myself pretty much anything. I was used to getting what I wanted, but not today.

Why did it always feel so good to have something forbidden? It tasted sweeter. Felt more decadent. *I love you*, I whispered inside my head. At least I thought it was all in my head.

Chapter 21

Seth

I pulled away as the first signs of magick surged through my blood and looked down at Kat's flushed face. Her eyes were bright with longing, and her lips were petal pink. I dropped my forehead to hers, taking the time to let the scent of her imprint on my senses. She smelled like a faerie garden—sun-kissed dust and pixie roses.

I rubbed my hands down arms sheen and soft, afraid she would disappear if I blinked. Being with Kat was like a fantasy. "We should get back," I murmured.

She nodded, keeping her eyes fastened on mine.

Brushing back the hair from her cheeks, warmth cascaded through me. We both lingered, knowing that these moments were far and few between.

She stepped out of my arms, and I watched her disappear around the corner. My forehead hit the wall, and I clenched my fists. An overwhelming urge to pull her back into the shadows bombarded me.

I was able to slip back into the room and take my seat beside Kat, but our little interlude hadn't gone unnoticed, as we had hoped. Zeke caught my eye, lifting his brow. I gave a slight shake of my head, letting him know there was nothing to worry over. Kat's life wasn't doomed yet.

When the movie finally ended, I think we were all a little surprised that the evening had gone without a hitch. No curse activity trying to ruin our fun. It was just the kind of normal I needed. Sneaking around with Kat had been an added bonus.

"Next time, I'll bring the party favors," Zeke said, grinning and finishing the last of his Pepsi.

Olivia rolled her violet eyes and smacked him. "Hey. There is nothing wrong with the classics. Not everyone needs booze to have a good time, you know. Just ask Kat and Seth."

Oh snap. She did not just call us out for making out in her hallway.

Kat grinned, dimples winking in the dark.

I followed her home, just to make sure there were no mishaps lurking in the night. You never knew which block the curse was hiding around, or when it would strike next. I was taking no chances, not with the new moon just a few days away. As soon as she slipped inside, I hit the gas on my truck and headed home. The whole way, I felt like I was living a dream, floating.

I went straight for my room, my bed never looking so inviting. Leaving the lights off, I fell onto the mattress face up, kicking my shoes off at the end of the bed. The last week had been a constant state of chaos. There wasn't a day that went by that this curse didn't torment us somehow. It was so close to being unleashed, it all but tasted freedom and the lives it would claim.

Just as my head hit the pillow, with the taste of Kat still on my lips, *her* voice oozed through my brain like green slime—the curse. And then, in just one heartbeat, my night went to crap.

The sleek voice of the curse slithered, filling my head with thoughts and ideas that weren't mine. Unprepared and caught off guard, she easily manipulated the images that weren't real. Memories of Kat and me together—happy and in love. Snapshots of a future that had never been a possibility.

A porch swing on a spring night.

Our wedding.

The honeymoon we would never have.

Growing old with the family we made.

In one of the fake memories, I caught a quick glimpse of Kat's wrist, seeing the five tiny stars dotting her skin. Even knowing that it wasn't real, my heart swelled, because I so wanted it to be real. Damn curse.

I hated the feelings it enticed, torturing me. It was that dire want that sparked my bitter anger, flaring it to a potent level that tasted like blood in the back of my throat. Or maybe it *was* blood—my blood.

Rage coated my insides, and I didn't care one way or the other what *she* did to me, just as long as Kat was safe. On either side of me, my hands clenched, fighting the stream of magick the curse weaved like a demented seamstress. I wanted her out of my head—out of our lives.

She felt my defiance, searing my head with a blinding pain that had my ears ringing. Behind my eyes, she stamped quick flashes of enlarged spiders with fangs as large as daggers. They dripped with sticky venom that would fry my brain. I grabbed the sides of my head. The curse wasn't going to cease fire, not when Kat and I had grown closer and still resisted our natural need to bond. We threatened her.

And she was wiggin' out.

The worst part, I knew that Kat would be able to sense my distress. I didn't want her doing something stupid, which was a given. She only thought with her emotions, making her reckless and impulsive. I needed to end this hold the curse had over me before I found Kat in my bedroom.

Holy smokes.

That was exactly what I didn't need, and just what the curse was hoping for. Kat and me behind closed doors with a bed a foot away. Total formula for tragedy…or freaking bliss.

If the curse wanted to push me around, I was just going to have to push back. She wasn't the only one with a few charms up her sleeve. I called forth a little spell Zeke had taught me long ago for blocking unwanted visitors poking around in the mind. Tingles radiated through my veins, but no matter how much energy I poured into the spell, the curse clung in my head like ivy.

Until finally, with no warning, when I was on the verge of exhaustion, the images just stopped. I lay staring at the ceiling, taking in a sharp jagged breath. It was hard to breathe. Immense pressure sat on my chest, and it took me a moment to realize I wasn't breathing.

I forced myself to exhale, and then inhale, long, deep, even breaths. It was actually harder than it sounded. Whatever voodoo she had worked on me, it was screwing with my respiratory system.

With a not-so-steady hand, I ran it through my hair. And as if Kat knew that I needed her, my phone buzzed. It was kismet.

A text message from hers truly flashed on the screen. **What the hell are you doing? Trying to give me an ulcer?**

My head might be feeling like it had been clunked with an axe, but Kat could still bring a smirk to my lips. Wincing, I replied, **Keep your panties on. It was nothing.**

Well, that sure didn't feel like nothing. I thought my heart was going to spring nails and rip its way out of my

chest.

Funny.

Who's being funny? She shot back.

I was afraid to tell her the truth. I didn't want her to get upset
or worried. We had enough on our minds with the approaching
new moon and our own conjuration. **It was just a bad dream.**

**Hmm. You better not be holding out on me, Seth
Nightingale. I will roast your bum if I find out you are lying.**
The fact that she was suspicious was just more proof that things
between us were changing. Good, bad, it didn't really matter, not
when neither had a happy outcome.

Duly noted.

Okay. BTW, I miss you.

Damn.

And just like that she could make my heart trip and make me
feel like a douchebag all at the same time. Skills, Kat had skills.
There were so many things I wanted to say. I typed "I love you"
and then erased the words that were in my heart. Instead I said,
Goodnight, little Kats.

I'm not little anymore, Seth.

Didn't I know it.

I never had a problem with sleep before, but insomnia had set
in. My thoughts ran wild, thinking about all the dangerous things
that had happened over the last few weeks. The curse had amped

up the ante—big time. Whatever it was that we were doing, she was infuriated. The further we dug and plotted, the more hazardous our lives became, but none of us was willing to give up.

Not yet.

***

Katia

I chewed on the end of my purple nails, contemplating. Seth and I didn't have to sneak around any longer to see each other, yet that didn't mean it still didn't feel naughty telling Mom where I was going. It was the first time, though, that we would be alone, and it had taken some severe convincing to get Seth to agree.

I was bursting with excitement and anticipation.

The new moon was tomorrow night, and the preparations would begin. The spell might be a complete bust, but it might be the piece we needed to take down a curse that had destroyed our families for decades. A curse that has interfered with fate too many times. The pros outweighed the cons.

Butterflies fluttered in my belly. I had spent three days chipping away Seth's icy resistance. It took one lonely tear to finally get Seth to cave as he brushed aside the tear on my cheek with the pad of his thumb. All I asked for was one day. Just him and me hanging out—normal stuff. No pressure. No walls. No curse. Just us.

We were about to embark on a powerful spell that would take us on a very risky journey; the least he could do was spend a few hours with me. The future was uncertain. Why waste the here and now?

Then there was also the motivating factor of possibly stealing another kiss...or five. Ever since Olivia's, I had a one-track mind. Seth's lips. Seth's lips. Seth's lips. I felt like *he* had me under a spell as well.

It was becoming redonkulous.

On the flip side, I needed something to remember before we decided to cast a power spell. But right now, I had to get past Mom.

Ugh.

"And where are you off to?" she asked, seeing the stupid enormous grin that wouldn't leave my lips. I wouldn't have been surprised if there were stars twinkling in my eyes as well.

"To meet Seth," I answered, coming down the stairs.

"Hmm," she said, pursing her lips. That was her not-so-subtle way of letting me know she thought that was a bad idea, but not even her hesitation could damper my elation.

"Don't worry. Nothing is going to happen. We are just hanging out." I swiped my handbag from the end of the banister, and started digging for my car keys in the bottomless pit that was my bag.

"Katia, I know that you think you can handle spending time with Seth, and maybe you can, but I don't want you to underestimate the magnetic pull that lies between the two of you. It is a force that goes beyond the natural order of the universe."

Did everyone think we were destined to fail? To die?

I felt like our parents were just waiting around for what they thought was the inevitable. It put a small hiccup in my mood. I wasn't ready to give up what I had just found. Imagine if they knew that Seth had already said the sacred vow, that we had already sealed half of the dooming curse. It would only reinforce how catastrophic it was for me to be alone with Seth.

"I know. We'll be careful. I promise," I said, my hand already opening the front door.

We met at the clearing, lounging on a quilt my grandmother had made me as a child. Pieces of my childhood were sewn into each square patch. When she had given it to me, she told me that the thread was woven with magick. I had believed it then, and lying next to Seth, I believed it now.

Nothing bad would happen to me today. Not with Seth beside me, and my grandma's protection.

He stared up at the cloudless blue sky, and I stared at him. The trees were still naked with just the tiniest green buds, except for the towering pines and the needles that littered the ground.

"Why did I let you talk me into this?" Seth asked, pushing a curly wisp off my face.

My skin glowed at his touch. "Because you miss my sparkling personality."

He arched a brow. "Is that so? And it wouldn't possibly be that you crave affection?"

Hell yeah it was, but he didn't need me to stroke his ego any. His dark head was already filled with too much.

"Hmm, that is a hard point to argue since you bound yourself to me. I would say, though, that it is you who craves me."

I watched as his green eyes darkened. "What am I going to do with you?"

"I can think of a few things."

"I just bet, and all of them will get us in trouble. More importantly, get *you* in trouble."

"Not all of them," I said, trying to sound offended. "We could try a little experiment." I gave him my irresistible smile. Flirting with Seth was the most fun I'd had in a very long time. It was spontaneous, effortless, and entertaining. I enjoyed seeing the many sides of Seth, and the different glint in his eyes that went with them.

His eyes latched onto mine. "I know what you are thinking, and I am going to say no."

I lay on my stomach, playing with the blades of grass. "What's the harm now? You already gave yourself to me."

He snorted. "You *would* think like that."

I angled my head toward him, looking down at his face, all sharp angles. "You have no idea what I am thinking." I leaned in closer.

"Oh yeah, I think I have a pretty damn good idea what's running through your head," he said, dark and seductive, our lips nearly touching.

We were both playing with fire, testing how far we could lean over the edge of the cliff, not exactly smart, but oh so rewarding. "I'll show you."

I kissed him.

Heat poured from his lips, and I simply closed my eyes, losing myself in the warmth of the moment. Somehow I always ended up in his lap. He flipped me around so that I was under him. His body pressed into mine, and I sunk into his embrace. My arms slid up his chest, wrapping around his neck and keeping him close. One of his hands framed my face. The other was at the bottom of my shirt, inching it higher. Neither of us was ready to let the other go anytime soon, which was fine by me.

His hand tightened at my hip, deepening the kiss, and tangling more than just our bodies. A light drizzle began to sprinkle from the sky, falling heavier with each kiss, but we couldn't have cared less. It felt glorious; he felt glorious. Our bodies were so hot I was surprised that the rain didn't sizzle off our skin. His touch was magnetizing, as I sighed-slash-moaned against his lips.

With impatient hands, he worked his way one-handed up under my shirt, and I sucked in a breath at the feel of his fingers on my skin. I placed a kiss at the hollow of his neck, oblivious to the storm stirring around us. Then the sky opened up and cracked with a deafening roar. It was the final straw that got our attention. We both jumped, but Seth kept his arms securely around me, holding me tight.

We couldn't believe what we saw. The sky had turned an ugly shade of dark grey, draped in moving storm clouds. A tree beside us erupted into sweltering flames. Wide-eyed, I was about to go into cardiac arrest, and I couldn't decide if it was Seth or the burning tree that had my heart stopping. Burying my head in his chest, I inhaled the scent of him before it all turned to swirling shit.

Thunder and lightning joined the downpour, but the flaming tree only raged on, impervious to the rain. He pulled me to my feet. We stood for a moment, staring at the roaring fire that licked the limbs of a tree.

Seth dragged a hand through his ragged hair. "Remind me never to agree to any of your so-called *experiments* again."

I whacked him on the arm. "Shut up."

He tugged me to his chest. "This is just an omen of things to come, Kats. We've opened a floodgate, and the curse is nipping at our heels."

"Does everything have to be so bleak between us?"

He frowned. "Bleak is an understatement."

My shirt was plastered to my body. My jeans were suction cupped to my thighs, and I was probably going to have to cut them off me. In short, I was miserable.

Seth pushed the wet hair off of his face. "We better take cover before it decides to hit us next. I'd really prefer not to get struck by lightning."

I nodded as he took my hand. Another round of angry light crashed across the sky. Soaked to the bone and shivering we retreated to the safety of his truck. My hair was stuck to my face. Seth shook his head, spraying drops of water at me. "Hey," I complained.

He grinned like a total shithead, looking absolutely adorably drenched. How the hell does he pull that off? "I should probably get you home."

My heart cartwheeled. I wasn't yet ready to let him go, especially when we spent so little time together. Stupid curse. It was like a sinkhole, sucking away all the sands of time.

He dropped me off at my house and gave me one lingering sullen kiss goodbye. I ran like the wind through the house, up the stairs, and into my room. The second I shut the door, I picked up the phone and waiting for Seth's voice to answer.

"Hey. Did something happen?" he asked, concern lacing his dark tone.

"No. I just needed to hear your voice." I fumbled with the phone as I stripped off my wet clothes, discarding them where they fell.

"Kats," he said my name sternly. "This isn't helping. We have to stop. Already we are too deep, too attached."

You can say that again.

He had spoken the sacred vow, bounding his heart solely to me. For Seth, even if we never found a way to break the curse, he could never truly love fully, but I was still free to do so. Just the thought, however, filled my chest with needlepoint pangs.

I sighed, plunking down on my bed in nothing but my undergarments. My room felt gloomy, missing the usual rainbows that scattered over the floor and ceiling. No sun. No rainbows. "I know. It's just…bullshit. I can't stop thinking about you, about what will happen tomorrow night, what we might learn."

The radio was playing softly in the background through the phone. "Tell me about it. It is all I've thought about since we found the book."

I turned on my side, fiddling with the tassels at the end of a pillow. "Do you think it will work?"

"I don't want you to get your hopes too high." He exhaled a long uneven breath. "I won't be able to handle your disappointment."

Or his own. That was what he didn't say. "So maybe we don't break the spell. It doesn't have to be the end of us."

"You know it does. It is not a matter of *if*, Kats. It is a matter of *when*. We both are going to have to accept the fact that there is a stronger possibility that our futures are different...apart." He struggled to get out the words.

Talk about a buzz kill.

Chapter 22

Katia

Elena was the last to arrive at the clearing. Her studded nose ring glinted off the moonbeams, and her midnight hair shone under the starlight as she stepped through the dark evergreens. Needles snapped lightly under her buckled boots. "By the worried look on your faces, I am guessing you thought I would bail. You guys suck."

None of us denied her accusation. It was true. For the last twenty minutes we had been pacing, biting our nails, kicking rocks, and for every minute that ticked by, the pit in my stomach grew.

Elena was lucky that we needed her, because I wanted to jab her in the eye socket.

For the kind of spell were we going to conjure, we needed a complete circle. Without Elena, the four of us wouldn't have enough power to ensure our safety. And even with the full circle, it wasn't fool proof. Something still could go wrong.

Gulp.

I did not want anything to happen to them, not because of me.

Seth had come straight from work. His jeans were ripped and streaked with grease, and the smells of oil mingled with his woodsy scent. It made my sensory system have a freak-out moment. I tried to keep a straight face, but I might have closed my eyes for just a few seconds and enjoyed the warmth that came with his proximity. It literally glowed inside me.

Even Elena with her shit-o-rama attitude couldn't diminish that light. But I knew a darkness that could.

"Let's just get this show on the road," Zeke wisely suggested.

Elena had her eyes locked on Seth. "She doesn't deserve you," she said to him as she passed by.

I spun around, my curls flying in the air around me. My target—Elena. I took one step after her before an arm wrapped around my waist, restraining me. My back hit Seth's chest.

"Let it go," he murmured in my ear.

His silky voice tickling the nape of my neck immediately extinguished my anger and started a different kind of fire. My muscles went lax in his arms. "You can let me go now."

I felt his lips curl against my hair. "I'm not quite ready yet."

I rested the back of my head on his chest. "Your timing

sucks."

He chuckled, and the sound made my heart feel about a thousand pounds lighter. "The story of our lives." He kept an arm around my shoulder, guiding us toward the circle.

Olivia and I lit the large white pillar candles strategically placed around the stone circle. Above us the shadowy branches arched in a canopy, and the shady new moon was a beacon of a fresh start. Kneeing, I placed the ancient book in front of me. A pulsation of impatience emitted from the cracked and crinkled leather bindings. Unable to resist, I ran my hand over the pewter symbol that was branded on the cover.

Scents of lavender, vanilla, and sage wafted in the air. I inhaled deeply to calm my irregular beating heart. We needed to trust in the circle. In our magick. In each other. Easier said than done.

Olivia's violet eyes were huge.

Elena blended with the darkness, except for her pale face. She looked like she was going to throw up.

Seth's troubled green eyes were zeroed in on me, like he was afraid I would disappear.

And Zeke, well, he was the exception. The expression of excitement made me shake my head. What a weirdo.

Me, I was a freaking mess.

As I opened the book to the spell I had marked off, a hum

traveled through my blood. My fingers might have trembled slightly, because I knew that it was time. *Here goes nothing.*

I looked at each of member of the circle. Seth to my right. Olivia next to him. Then Elena and Zeke on my left. My stomach twisted, but I took a deep breath. "I call upon the new moon, to break the threads of time not spun. Space and universes collide, let our spirit take flight and soar, to the past that links to mine. Show me here; show me now. As I will, so mote it be."

A wind kicked up, picking up pieces of hair off my neck and blowing them forward in my face. The wind grew, whistling, and the candles around the circle flickered, forming shadows on our faces. The milky moon was still high and bathing us in its soft glow. Seconds ticked by, turning into minutes, leaving me wondering if I had screwed something up. Nothing seemed different or out of place. I felt the same, no surge of magick as I'd expected.

Then the air stood still. Not a peep out of the woods surrounding us, not even a twitch. Silence stretched out as I waited for that pivotal moment when the spell kicked in, sweeping us to another time, another place.

Again nothing happened. Disappointment weighed heavily inside me. Just as I was about to suggest we try the spell again, crapola broke out.

"Are you sure that was even a spell?" Elena asked.

Through clamped teeth I ground out, "Can you cry underwater?"

"Guys, focus," Olivia said.

"Errr, this is going well," Zeke said.

"*This* is pathetic," Elena said with a huff. "Give me the damn book."

"Like hell." I clutched the book to my chest.

"It is obvious you don't know what you are doing. Let an experienced nixie handle the difficult spells," Elena said with an air of superiority.

"Um, guys." Olivia's voice quivered.

I was on the verge of decking Elena. "Experienced my skinny ass. You don't know which end of a pixie stick to tear. If you recall, *I* was the one who found the book."

Elena's eyes were practically spitting fire. "The only thing you are experienced in is which jock you are going to bang this week."

I gasped.

"Guys, something is happening," Olivia said with concern.

"She's right," Seth said.

"Of course I'm right," Elena and I both answered.

Suddenly, the air around me turned cold, and a chill trickled down my spine. A dense white mist rose up, covering the ground so I couldn't even see my feet. "Are you guys seeing this?"

"Uh-huh," Zeke said, staring at the fog, unmoving.

"We're not blind, Puddy Kat," Elena sneered.

"Christ," Seth muttered. "It's freezing." He rubbed his hands over his arms.

"Toto, I don't think we are in Kansas anymore," Elena mumbled, eyeing me.

I rolled my eyes, getting to my feet. Seth was right beside me. We stepped outside the circle side by side. His body was on alert, ready for the unexpected. There were whispers coming from the edge of the woods, too quiet to make out what they were saying.

My boot snapped on a twig, vibrating through the forest like a canon. I followed the voices carried by the wind, but the winds played tricks. Every time I thought I was going in the right direction, the voices would move. I glanced behind me just to make sure I wasn't crazy.

Seth gave me a WTF look, his brows drawn together.

Before I reached the edge of the clearing, a figure emerged, followed swiftly by another with longer angry strides. Two women. The second woman's flowing dress ate up the ground after the one with hair just like mine, but lengthier. I was taken aback at the similarilties between me and this woman. They were both dressed in shimmery fabrics that would make any fashion designer want to get their hands on. Moi included. I'd never seen anything like it, and the shapes of the gowns—stunning. Sexy cutouts that played peek-a-boo drew the eye.

There was a ghostly quality to the two new guests. And I noticed for the first time since the change in the air that the glade looked different. It was the wrong season. Trees were flourished with vibrant green leaves—thick and dancing. Wildflowers, nightshade, and mandrake were in full boom, popping in bold colors against tall blades of grass. Along with a few other flowers I'd never seen, but would love to get my grubs on.

A whoosh came over me as the one with raven hair walked almost right through me. She would have if Seth hadn't pulled me out of the way. I heard Olivia gasp behind us. My eyes met Seth's, warning me to be more cautious.

There were no words I could find to best describe what had just happened, or the creepy feeling that settled in my gut. It was like an echo of a memory.

The older woman with long raven hair and yellow eyes flung a spell at the young clone of me that had her jerking around to face the older one. She joined him in the middle of our circle, oblivious to the number of eyes that were on them. "Arachne. You will do wise to not turn your back on me a second time." It was a terrifying voice, one that turned my blood to ice and gave me goose bumps. I had a sneaking suspicion that this scary woman was the creator of the curse.

"Crazy there has your eyes, Katia," Elena jeered, just as captivated as I was by the scene in front of us.

Seth put a finger to his lips, signaling for her to keep her big trap shut. I couldn't have agreed more and gave her my you-will-pay-for-that-later look. It was pretty darn effective.

Regardless, I didn't think the apparitions could hear us. That would cause a ripple in time or something—not good. But it was better to be safe than sorry and keep our lips sealed.

Arachne's eyes were pools of sadness. A gentle wind swirled through her silvery-white hair as she confronted the other woman. "Isa, you know that we never wanted to hurt you. Avery cares for you."

Isa sneered. "I guess when I found the two of you together he was showing me how much he cared."

"We were going to tell you. He is my starsoul, Isa. What would you have us do?" Arachne pleaded, her eyes begging for Isa to understand.

"Rot in Hell." Isa spat the words with such violent hate. Her body shuddered. "You knew how I felt about Avery. You never gave us a chance. You just swooped in and took what had been mine and, in the process, stomped all over my heart." Isa suddenly seemed to tower over the petite Arachne.

"I would gladly take your pain. Isa, you have been a sister to me, a mentor, my best friend." The gut-retching despair in Arachne's voice cut straight through me, slashing like knifes.

Isa gave a cold, humorless smile. "*And* that is the worst part of your betrayal. I took you in when no one else would have you. I taught you to be a skillful warrior. You were a sister to me. I curse you, Arachne. Your soul be damned. You took my heart, and I will have yours—Avery's too." She held her hands palm up on either side of her, magick sparkling from the fingertips in a display of power I'd never witnessed.

There was a uniformed sense of wonder from my circle. Isa was a badass, not the kind of nixie I would ever rumble with. She was also letting pain and hurt rule her gift—a deadly combo.

Archane's shoulders slumped. She looked so lost, and Isa just kept pounding on her like a human punching bag. "Look." She flipped over her wrist. "These marks prove that he could never love you as you wanted him to. Please, don't do this, Isa. It isn't his fault. You are right. I should have stayed away. I should have resisted his charms." It was evident how deep Archane's love was for Avery that she would all but fall to her knees in regret and say anything to save him.

"A little too late. Nothing will save you and your lover now. I will ensure that no blood of yours will ever love a Nightingale again. Not as long as it is within my power," she said in a lethally calm voice that made the hairs on the back of my neck stand up.

A surge of energy shot from her fingers. The curse, a visible glimmer of purple smoke, rushed toward me fast, and fear churned my insides. I knew it wasn't possible for it to hit me, as it wasn't really here but in spirit, yet it didn't change the fact that the sight put me in a terrified daze.

Arachne's eyes widened, and it was her voice that snapped me back. "No!" she yelled. "Isa."

But it was too late.

She never even tried to defend herself. The great warrior was rocked with a jarring impact, stumbling as the force of the spell slammed into her. It weaved around her slender body like ribbon, choking her with its power.

Instinctively I jerked.

Olivia had tears in her eyes.

Zeke dug his fingers into his hair.

Even Elena had a reaction, in her own way.

My hand went to my mouth. "Oh God."

"My sentiments exactly," Seth said from behind me, laying a hand on my hip. It was a small comfort, but just what I needed.

I blinked.

The mist. The lush green. The smell of summer. It was all gone.

I was on my knees, my hands spread out over the pages of the book, trembling. Lifting my head, I looked at the others who were clearly as shaken as I was. It wasn't just what we had seen; the return to the present felt like it had sucked the life out of me. I was drained.

Seconds ago we had been walking around, witnessing a harsh past, and now sitting in our circle, it was like none of it had taken place. We stared at each other, needing clarification that we had all had the same experience, that it had been real.

Elena broke it down best. "That was the worst trip of my life," she muttered, rubbing her hands up and down her arms. Her silver eyes were as big as saucers.

I couldn't have agreed more. A permanent chill had taken up residency inside me.

"Christ. Why do these things always have the worst aftershocks?" Zeke groaned, rubbing the sides of his temples.

Olivia was ghostly white.

Elena stood up, brushing dirt from her knees and scowled at me. "You seriously have a messed up family, and I see boyfriend stealing is in your genes."

I didn't have the energy to cross words with her, so I just gave her the stink eye. At least we were all safe and mostly of sound mind—Elena, in my book, was still batshit crazy. I ran a hand over my face, wiping a cold sweat from my brow. This little trip down ancestry lane had shaken me more than I wanted to admit.

"Hey, you okay?" Seth asked me, nudging me gently with his shoulder.

Was I? "I don't know. Not really," I admitted.

"Let's get out of here."

I nodded.

There was no reason to stay and linger. The spell had worked. It had done its job, but we were no closer to breaking the curse than we had been before.

Fuck.

Chapter 23

Katia

I could feel myself tumbling down a long tunnel of depression. It came out of nowhere. After the spell, I thought I would be okay—that I was strong enough—that my love for Seth would see me through the worst of times. But I was wrong.

Horribly wrong.

Love…was a joke.

Love wasn't going to save me.

Save us.

There was nothing that could. No spell. No trick. No charm. It was stupid and naïve of me to think that there was something we could do. Who were we but a bunch of teenagers with minimal magickal experience? Our circle had been formed from boredom, curiosity, and friendship. It wasn't meant to test the spiritual bounds outside of our realm.

My despair crashed inside me, crumbling me to the point that I didn't care what happened. What was the point of living a life without love? Without happiness? Without Seth? I had always been dramatic, and my emotions ruled so many of my decisions. Seth had all the control and determination. I acted on pure feelings, whatever was in the heat of the moment.

The next week was nothing but a blur. The spell and seeing the woman who ruined my life could have never happened—it was that insignificant. Didn't help that I went through the motions of living like a zombie. I was too busy being stuck inside my own head, trying to work through the reality that Seth and I had to go our separate ways. Graduation was tiptoeing around the corner, but the curse was upon us and always would be.

I couldn't ask him to continue on as we had, tempting our lives.

But before we moved on, I needed to say goodbye. A proper goodbye. I only hoped he wouldn't make it any more difficult than it already was.

Seth

Kat's dimples were my downfall.

She stood in the doorway with a smile that made my knees buckle, and I knew she was up to no good. There didn't appear to be anything *sick* about her, and she most definitely was not knocking on Death's door. I didn't know what kind of game she was playing, but I had seriously been worried, heart-jumping-out-of-my-chest worried. Rushing over here in the middle of the night, I had nearly caused a multi-car pileup.

I knew that she had been having a hard time lately, skipping school more days than she actually went. And then I got the text a little bit after 11:00 pm...

Leaning in the doorway, I crossed my legs. "What is going on?"

She put her finger to her lips, indicating for me to be quiet.

My brow shot up.

Grabbing a handful of my hoodie, she tugged me inside the silent, sleeping house, and against my better judgment I let her. Kat was up to something, but it was the first time I'd seen her smile so brightly. I didn't have it in me to diminish her gleaming grin.

"My parents are asleep," she whispered.

I sent her a look, telling her I thought this was a very bad idea. She ignored me, lacing our fingers, and led me upstairs. What kind of shenanigan was she up to? The door to her bedroom softly clicked behind us followed by the turning of the lock. Now I knew I was in trouble.

Kat and I alone in a bedroom was bad news.

And really hot.

My eyes narrowed. "You better have a damn good reason for sneaking me into your room."

She gave me another devastating smile. At this rate, I was going to be putty in her hands. "Don't be mad. I needed to see you," she informed.

Mad? I wasn't sure mad was what I was feeling, but I knew that if I didn't leave, I was going to do something insane, like attack her with my mouth. All of her.

A stream of moonlight broke through sheer white curtains that billowed with a gentle breeze. In the center of the room was a big old bed with ancient carvings on the headboard. Something Celtic would have been my guess. Beautiful and lyrical.

Her room was cluttered with a rainbow of colored crystals and bottles. They hung from a thin wire in front of each window, casting shadowy rainbows on the ceiling, the walls, and the floor. It was as breathtaking as Kat herself. The scent of her was in every nook and cranny of the room, a mix of cherry blossoms, faerie roses, and ancient magick.

I tried not to get swept away by it, by her. She had been absent from life the last week, and I wanted to soak up the sight of her even though my head knew it would only lead to suffering. "You know that we shouldn't be here alone."

She pushed off the frame of her bed undeterred by my prickly tone. "I was afraid you would say no, and I really needed to see you in person."

I folded my arms, appearing bored and at the same time trying to tell my body to relax. "You're right. I would have said no."

A smug look crossed her expression.

"Well, I'm here now…"

She inhaled, taking a step toward me with purpose and determination. "So I see." She slid her hands into the back pockets of her jeans, rocking back on her heels. "I need to ask you something, but before you shoot me down, just think about it. Please?"

I angled my head, trying to ignore the jump in my pulse. "My instincts tell me to say no now, before I even hear what you have to say." My eyes darkened.

She ran a hand through her tangled curls. "Seth," she groaned.

I smirked. Hearing my name on her glossy lips was intoxicating.

"This isn't a joke. Spend the night with me?"

The air was sucked out of my lungs. That had not been what I had been expecting, and she took me by surprise for the second time.

"Just sleep," she rushed, pleading her case before I ran out the door. Too bad she misread the look in my eyes. My shock was more because I very much wanted what she asked. "I want to be in your arms," she continued. "I want to feel safe for one night without the nightmares."

I bit my lip. She knew how to break through my resolve. Trouble and something else brewed in her silvery eyes. It was the something else that had my body coming alive.

She took another step toward me. "How many more times am I going to have to say goodbye to you? It seems like that is all we do. I am just asking for one night, and then we can go back to how things used to be."

I think we both knew that if I stayed, there was no going back. Below the aggravation in her face, there was something impish in her voice. I understood her frustration, and a warning went off inside me. We needed to create distance, as she implied. I got that. Hell I endorsed the idea...or I used.

Before I had sealed my fate to hers.

Now the idea of being separated seized me with dread. "Just sleep. No funny business." I stepped closer, watching her eyes widen, and tucked a curl behind her ear. I was feeling dangerous.

She rolled her eyes, but the enormous grin betrayed her. "Yes, Daddy."

I gave her a dry look. "Funny." I couldn't believe I was agreeing to this harebrained idea.

She walked backwards toward the bed, her hand in mine, pulling me along the way. I dragged my feet out of habit. When she crawled into the spacious bed, I got in beside her, the mattress squeaking under our combined weight. My eyes never left hers. Burrowing her head into the crock of my arm, she nestled against me.

It was torture. And I loved every second.

Her little pink and white heart boxers were distracting me, showing off her golden legs. I tried to keep my mind off them by losing my fingers in her hair. It didn't work. Silky strands fell onto my shoulder, spilling over my chest.

She rubbed her cheek against mine. "Why is this so hard? Why does it have to be so wrong to want you?" she whispered, her voice so soft I almost wasn't sure I'd heard her correctly.

I dropped my hands to my sides, knowing if touched her any longer, I wouldn't be able to stop. My hands fisted until my knuckles throbbed. She asked the same questions I asked myself a million times. My throat felt like it was going to collapse, because I knew she was right. I forced a smile, trying to sound lighthearted. "In a few years, some other guy will sweep you off your feet. You won't even remember me." The words felt like sandpaper in my mouth.

She tilted her face up, resting her chin on my chest, eyes bright. "What bullcrap. You know that's a lie. I know it's a lie. That is not how this works. Besides, I don't want any of them to be my first, Seth. I want you."

Holy Virgin Mary.

This was definitely a dangerous topic. We were supposed to be keeping things simple, not complicated them more. A tremor rippled down my body, my resolve weakening. "Kats, are you telling me that you and Matt never..."

She shook her head, wisps of curls falling on her face. "No. We didn't. Why is it so hard to believe that I'm a virgin?" she barked back, her eyes narrowing, and really, I couldn't blame her. I, of all people, shouldn't have assumed.

Shit.

Of course I dug myself deeper trying to recover from my blunder. "I don't know. It's just that you are so..."

"So what?" she snapped.

"Christ, Kats. Are you going to make me spell it out for you? Beautiful. There I said it. You know you're gorgeous. And I just figured since you and Matt went out for so long..." I couldn't fathom anyone not wanting her the way I wanted her.

Right now.

She was killing me.

The only thought that kept me from kissing her just then was that her parents were down the hall. She snuggled back into my arms, and I pulled her close, loving that I was surrounded by everything that was Kat. I was positive that neither of us would sleep a wink. Surprisingly, that wasn't the case.

Katia

Seth thought I was beautiful. It was the last thought I had before I dozed off, engulfed in his warm embrace. Maybe I already knew he thought I was beautiful, but I'd never heard it from *him*. It was so unbelievably different coming from Seth's mouth. And dear God, I wanted to hear him say it again. And again.

In my dream, that was exactly what he did. It wasn't the first fantasy I had involving Seth. Trust me, I'd had plenty, but it was the most vivid one to date. In my dreams I could be whoever I wanted, even the sexy, cool girl who wanted to seduce the jaw-dropping Seth.

A warm hand stole across my belly, landing just under my breast. In feather touches, the pad of his thumb rubbed in circles. I turned into the body beside me and brushed my lips over his neck just below the ear. "Seth," I murmured.

"Hmm," he mumbled.

"Kiss me." I was ready for him to go where no man had gone before. In my dreams, obviously.

"Kats," he said in a half groan, half moan, burying his face in my hair.

My hands framed his cheeks, feeling the tiny stubbles. "I love you, Seth, and I know you love me, too."

I waited for his response. My blood was singing, my body aching.

"Kat..." He growled, a deep, sensual growl that had my blood tingling.

I played dirty, brushing up against him. Dark forest green eyes pinned me, and I could see his resolve diminishing. He entwined our fingers, and from the look in his eyes, wild goblins couldn't have stopped us. I lifted his wrist to my lips and placed a gentle kiss over the five stars, flicking my tongue over his racing pulse.

He sucked in a breath.

Letting go of my fingers, his hands gripped my waist. There was a glowing heat in his eyes as we gazed at each other, spellbound. Couldn't he feel how much I needed him, needed this? I wanted him to kiss me more than I wanted to live.

And my wish was granted. Well, the kissing part.

My head dipped, our lips meeting in a deep, drugging kiss. Nothing tame and just what I wanted. A low sound rumbled in the back of his throat, and his fingers tightened at my waist, pulling our bodies together. The blood in my veins pumped hot at just one of his kisses.

God above, please don't let him stop. I swear I will kill him.

My fingers curled into his dark hair, loving the texture and the sensation of his body. We had somehow switched positions so I was underneath him. There was desperation as we clung to one another, but there was also tenderness. He sipped on my lower lip, and I purred at the bottom of my throat.

I was afraid that if we stopped kissing even for a second, I would wake up, and that would suck. Our lips locked together, and I moved, needing to feel the lines of his hard body against the softness of mine. Wrapping a slender leg around his waist, my gut twisted with desire. Having Seth roam from my mouth to my neck to my shoulder and every place in between bewitched me.

Sneaking my fingers under his shirt, I pushed the material up and over his head. My heart pounded in my ears as I gawked at his chest. He looked like he had been dipped in sunshine. Lines of muscle were etched down the sides of his stomach, trailed by a dusting of dark curls that disappeared behind his boxers. I traced that line with a fingertip, watching the muscles quiver. Somewhere in my mind I knew that I was testing the boundaries. Did I dare? Nope. This was a fantasy and all's fair in love and dreams.

He rolled, taking me with him.

Oh hell yes.

I felt his fingers grasp the hem of my shirt, and I straddled him, lifting my arms in the air. He discarded my shirt next to his on the floor, leaving me in my red bra. Green eyes blazed into mine as his hands tenderly swept down my arms to my sides and settled at my hips. But they didn't linger for long. He fumbled with my waistline, making my breath catch each time he brushed my bare skin. Somehow I wiggled out of my boxer shorts, kicking them off the bed.

Sweet baby Jesus. This was really happening.

To keep things fair, I unsnapped his jeans and tugged down the zipper. He took over, quickly shedding himself of his jeans. My eyes were drawn to the line of hair that disappeared into a V beneath his boxers. I traced the ripples of muscle, watching them jump under my touch. He sucked in a breath, and I gave him a sexy half grin.

His eyes deepened at the sight of my dimples. Power. It was immensely empowering knowing that I could affect him so. And then I was the one being swept away as he kissed me again, the heat from our bare skin sparking between us. Each touch, each reaction brought on a wave of new feelings—intense. I ran my tongue along the bottom of his lip, feeling him shudder.

He blew my mind in ways I couldn't even imagine. There was no time to think—only feel. The mattress groaned under our weight as we rolled, limbs intertwined, but we were so lost in each other that we wouldn't have heard an ambulance if it had driven through my room.

"I need to kiss you," he murmured.

"You are," I whispered against his lips.

He broke away. "No, I need to kiss your body."

Yes. Yes. Oh. God. Yes. "Oh." Um…did I even need to think about that? "What are you waiting for?" I managed to say, and I don't even know how I was able to articulate the words.

He chuckled against my skin, and I sunk my fingers into his dark hair. With the first touch of his soft lips to my stomach I nearly jumped off the bed. His tongue teased the charm dangling at my belly button. I bit my lip as he licked a circle around the hoop, and I gripped his shoulders.

Good thing this was a fantasy and consequences weren't an issue, because nature had a way of pushing us together. In dreams we no longer denied that force—it would be unnatural if we had. And what Seth and I were doing was anything but unnatural.

Through the magick we created together, our remaining articles of clothes slipped off. Lying skin to skin felt like a sensory overload. He was gentle, sweet, and whispered all the right words. It was me that was unable to bite my tongue. I was the one who spoke too soon. I was the one who wasn't strong enough.

Go figure.

I was the emotional, reckless one.

Raining a path of kisses along his jaw, I thought I might have murmured that I loved him between kisses—multiple times, but I couldn't be sure. And before I even realized what I was saying, words were tumbling from my mouth. "Freely I give, what's mine to give, if our souls were meant to be. Our paths merged by flesh, heart, soul, spirit, and magick. I bind thee." Then I captured his lips with mine, sealing my vow with all the love pouring from me.

That's what it would be like to utter the starsoul to Seth. My head fell back as I felt the buzzing of magick tingle through my veins—his and mine. Everything about me was alight, and my senses were going haywire. There was this building inside me, begging and begging for release. Accompanying it were tendrils of pure, silky, vibrant magick.

In that moment, it was enthralling—hypnotic—and so was the act of being with him. His body fit mine in a way that I knew not another guy ever would. And yeah, the initial pain was there, but he made me forget about it, distracted me with searing, smoldering kisses, and the things he could do with his fingers made me blush. We came together not only in flesh, love, and spirit but in magick as well. Being connected with someone intimately was a joy so great it was euphoric. Sharing magick at the same time was…erotic. Alluring. Seductive.

Afterwards, I lay glowing in his arms. I swore my skin shone brighter than a glowworm on a hot summer night. Stretching out beside him, I felt like a cat after a long nap. My limbs were relaxed and my body tired, but in a really good way.

My head rested on his chest, drawing mindless doodles on his stomach. Slowly my heart rate returned to normal, but that was where normal stopped. We weren't connected anymore, but he was still a piece of me. I could feel a mishmash of emotions whirling. There was something different about me, but I couldn't pinpoint what, not when I was still basking in the radiance of having just been with Seth. My mind was too clouded from the afterglow.

And I didn't want anything to tarnish this dream. I wanted to capture it in a mason jar and release it whenever I needed a reminder that life could be beautiful, breathtaking, and enticing. The whole night seemed so impossible that I wanted to pinch myself.

"God, this dream is too good to be true." I turned to my side, eyes closed.

"Tell me about it," Seth mumbled.

What? That was strange. Did Seth just admit that he was dreaming as well?

My eyes popped open.

"Shit," Seth cursed, holding my wrist in the air. His body stiffened.

And I realized that none of it had been a dream. We had just burned up the sheets. We had done the freaky-deaky with my parents down the hall. I had said...

I caught a glimpse of the five black stars on the inside of my wrist. The room suddenly spun in dizzy rainbows as I realized what I had just done.

I had activated the curse.

Chapter 24

Seth

I stopped breathing. The black tiny stars on the inside of her wrist started to swirl together as my vision blurred. I thought I might black out or have a mental breakdown. My eyes clashed with Kat's, and I watched her face go from flushed to ghostly white. My stomach plummeted as I realized what that humming was inside my blood. It was Kat—more specifically Kat's magick. A string of F-bombs went off in my head. At least I thought they were inside my head.

"I'm sorry, Seth. Oh God, I am so sorry. I thought I was dreaming. I didn't know what I was doing." Tears rolled down her cheeks, streaking her face.

The horror of what we had done shattered my heart into a gazillion, jagged fragments. What did I say? I wanted to offer her comfort, but at the same time I didn't know how. My arms were wrapped around her, and I held her tight. Fat tears pricked her eyes. "Hey, shh. It's going to be okay." I wiped the tears from her cheeks, wishing more than anything that I could see her dimples instead of her tears. Nothing was ever going to be okay again.

"Not. True. Seth." She sobbed.

Something inside me snapped. I couldn't stare down into those tear-drenched eyes another second. Everything was so intense. Her grief. Her fear. My dread. My anger. It wasn't my first rodeo, but *it* had been Kat's, and I was livid that the curse had taken that from her, too. That it had screwed up her first time. Darkened it. The damn curse was going to take everything from us, and that was bullshit of epic proportions.

I jumped out of bed, noticing the soft rays of sunlight just beginning to rise, and threw on my jeans. This was probably the jerkiest move I'd ever made, but I had to get out of her room. Out of her house. Grabbing my wadded shirt from the floor, I put my arms through the sleeves. "I need some air," I mumbled, slipping the cotton material over my head.

She sat up on the bed, gaping at me with gut-stabbing sad eyes and an open mouth. I never felt so helpless in my entire life. What did she expect me to do? Cuddle her? I couldn't—not now. Not with the turbulent storm churning inside me. I was hanging on by a thread.

"Seth?" she squeaked. A sob shook her bare shoulders.

I braced a hand on the doorframe, unable to meet her gaze. "I can't, Kats." And then I turned and raced down the stairs. The sound of her weeping followed me outside. I wasn't sure I would ever be able to get it out of my head. I was living a nightmare.

I got outside without being detected by the parentals. It was early, and I assumed they were still in bed. That would have been all kinds of awkward considering… The air was lukewarm, but it could do nothing to chase the cold that had made an everlasting home inside me. Looking up at the partly dark, partly sunny sky, I didn't know whether to scream or rage. How could this have happened?

The curse was activated, and I could hear it laughing in my head. *I've got you in my clutches now*, it sneered.

Sliding behind the steering wheel, I thundered the engine to life and hit the gas. I made it two blocks before I had to pull over. My hands shook. My heart was thrashing against my chest. With an all-consuming frenzy, I slammed my hands down onto the steering wheel. I gripped it until my knuckles turned white.

I was numb.

In my numbness, I drove. And drove. No destination in mind, just as much space and distance as I could put between Kat and me. But no matter how far and how long I drove, that suffocating feeling never left. The pressure in my chest never let up. If anything, it got worse.

I dialed her number so many times and hung up that the keys were worn and beginning to fade. There wasn't enough groveling or apologies in the universe to make up for how I had reacted. Kat had just issued our death sentences, but there was no way I would let her become consumed with guilt. This whole damn thing was my fault.

If I had been stronger…

If I hadn't already bound myself to her…

If. If. If. I was drowning in ifs.

***

The next morning rolled around.

I never thought the sun would come up. Last night I had not slept a wink. How could I? My mind raced with thoughts of Kat dying—of the curse whispering, gloating in my ear. I spent the whole night staring at the inside of my wrist, poised on edge. I barely blinked, afraid I would miss *it*.

The curse had been activated, I didn't doubt that, but we didn't know the timeframe at which it would devour her. Did she have a month, a week, a day, or God forbid…hours? The only thing I was sure of was that the marks that linked us together would disappear. When Kat left this realm, the connection we had forged would dissolve. I knew that as soon as those black stars faded, Kat would too.

I couldn't take my eyes off them.

STARBOUND

By the time I arrived at school, I was a total basket case. My eyes searched for Kat, needing to see her, speak to her before classes started. I might get all tongue-tied trying to apologize for acting like an ass, but I had to try to make her understand. It wasn't her. It wasn't what we did. It was the thought of losing her that had me losing my cool.

In my search for Kat, Zeke found me instead. "What's wrong? You look like utter shit," he stated. Just like my best friend to not beat around the mulberry bush.

I gave him a drool look. "If you had the kind of last thirty-six hours I had, you would look like hell, too."

He twirled a pencil between his fingers. "The curse?"

"Worse."

"How much worse can it get?"

I lifted a brow.

The pencil clattered to the floor. "You didn't?"

Silence.

His fingers dived into his already messy blond hair. "Jesus Christ, Seth. What happened?"

My head hit the white wall behind me with a thump. "Things got out of hand," I said with my eyes closed.

Zeke joined me on the wall, his book bag slipping off his shoulders as he processed the news. "How is she?" he finally asked.

Goose bumps prickled at the back of my neck, and I felt my magick hum to the surface, flowing through my blood. Opening my eyes, I saw her, and for the first time since I had left her house, I was able to breathe easier. "See for yourself."

Kat strolled down the hall, looking like a burst of sunshine. Her glossy curls bounced on her shoulders, and a small smile touched the corner of her lips at something Claudia said. The need to go to her steamrolled me.

"Um, I hate to state the obvious…but Katia looks damn good for someone who is dying." Zeke said the exact thing I was thinking.

I scowled. "I know. It's freaking me out."

"What gives?"

His guess was as good as mine. "Beats me," I muttered.

Katia

I still couldn't believe that Seth had left me with no explanation, just an "I can't" and *poof* he was gone, while I bawled my eyes out for the next hour. Collins had wandered into my room, and I knew that I needed to pull my shit together for her, or she would spaz. I didn't want to worry her, not yet.

What was the point?

So far nothing had happened. I felt the same. Actually, I felt like a freaking rock star, but I wasn't getting my hopes up. I didn't want to go about this curse naïve and like an asshat. Fool me once, shame on me. Fool me twice...oops, I'm dead.

Later that night, when I found myself alone, the tears started again. How could I have been so stupid? Why hadn't I listened to Seth? He probably hated me. And really, who could blame him? Hell, he couldn't even stand the sight of me and had left like his butt was on fire. It wasn't just me I had doomed. Seth would eventually wither away and die. That was how this starbound stuff worked. Once I had passed on, his heart, over time, would stop. The elders say that they die of heartbreak.

I would kill Seth.

The thought of Seth dying was like a bullet to my heart.

"Kats." His voice pierced my soul.

I knew he had been staring at me since I turned the corner with Claudia. My entire body came alive, purring with magick. Now that we were starbound it linked our flesh, our hearts, our spirits, our power, and our souls. His presence would always entice some kind of reaction inside me.

I braced myself, before spinning around to face him. "Seth."

He cast a sideways glance at Zeke, who just stood there, gaping at me. "Zeke," Seth mumbled under his breath.

"Oh. Is that supposed to be my cue to leave?" Zeke's sky-blue eyes held mine. "Before I scramble, I just want to tell you that I love you, Katia."

Oh crap. Now he'd done it. Seth had told him. It was written all over Zeke's face. Sadness and grief were pouring off him. I could feel my throat closing, and the last thing I wanted to do today was shed another useless tear. He engulfed me a bear hug. "And now I will go, because Seth's dark scowl is unnerving me. I really don't want a black eye before first period," he said, leaving on a lighter note.

I let out a small, emotion-clogged chuckle. Now alone with Seth, I was afraid to look him in the eye, so I stared at my black wedges. I didn't want to see condemnation in his emerald eyes. I couldn't take it. My heart would crack all over again. And that would just plain suck.

Seth shoved his hands in his pockets. "Kats, look at me."

I shook my head, my hair hiding my face.

His finger curled under my chin, lifting my eyes to his. "I'm sorry. I should never have left like that. I should never have left at all."

I wrinkled my nose. "Why did you?" The question had occupied my mind ever since.

His jaw clenched. "Mostly because I was scared, and extremely pissed off at myself."

"You can't just leave when things get tough." I shifted on my feet. "It was my fault, Seth."

His fingers imprisoned my chin again, keeping my face lifted to his. Reluctantly I glanced up from under my lashes. Lush green eyes held my attention. "Never. We did this together. You and me." He weaved our fingers together, and a blue spark flared on contact.

Words escaped me, and luckily, I didn't have to find any. The bell rang over our heads, and I jumped. His hand tightened in mine, and he gave me a weak smirk.

Maybe we had done this together, but I was the one who pushed. I was the restless one who couldn't just let things be, who always had to have more. It was a hard lesson to learn, and we both were going to pay the ultimate price.

***

A week came and went.

Seth walked on eggshells around me, as if he was afraid I would tumble to my death at any moment. He was driving me up a wall. I just wanted him to treat me like he always had. I was still the same girl; there was just a ticking bomb on my life.

The only upside was he kissed me every chance he got. He held my hand during the passing periods. All the little things normal boyfriends do with their girlfriends. We even went on a date. Stop the presses. A real, bonafide date. It was the sweetest date I'd ever been on.

A night alone in front of his fireplace, eating takeout and talking about anything as long as neither of us mentioned the words *death* and *curse*. I will always remember the way his face looked shadowed in the dark with the flickering flames lighting up his eyes. The smells of firewood and his skin and the sound of his laugh will be tattooed in my memory.

He couldn't have given me a better ending to this life.

It wasn't until the end of the second week that I started to feel the first inklings that something was off. Little things at first, a normal person would chuck it up as a bad day, but I wasn't normal by any standard, not even for a nixie.

Harper was rambling on about something Claudia had said earlier that got under her skin. I swear playing referee for these two was exhausting in itself. Only half listening, I had no idea what Harper was actually bitching about. I mean, I had some serious crap on my mind. Couldn't she see that?

Then I stumbled.

It would have been embarrassing if I had just tripped over my own feet, or something equally as humiliating, but it wasn't. At first I thought nothing of it, but as the day dragged on, so did my body—drag, that is. I started to feel just the tiniest prickle burning inside me. It grew. And grew as the hours passed, weakening me. By ninth period, I was zonked. My eyes could hardly stay open, and I was lightheaded, swaying on my feet. It didn't take a genius to know that the curse was working its magick, zigzagging and picking away at me from the inside. I didn't know how long I had, but with each passing hour—minute—I knew that my days were numbered.

Pressing a hand to my locker to steady myself, I sucked in a long breath, finding my bearings.

I had to tell my parents.

No more long sleeve shirts to hide the marks.

No more lies about feeling just fine.

Just the cold hard truth.

I was dying.

And, as if to solidify the fact, the first black star on my wrist vanished. My heart stopped.

Only four more to go…

Chapter 25

Katia

This curse was kicking my butt from here to kingdom come.

When my parents arrived home from work, I was laying on the couch with drooping eyes, waiting for them. It took most of my strength to keep them open while I waited. Mom took one look at my fading color and she knew, which was sort of was a blessing. At least then I didn't have to form the words. I still got all tongue-tied admitting that I was biting the dust.

I mean, who wouldn't when telling their parents that you were dying?

In my head it had sounded so much simpler.

Me: Mom. Dad. Seth and I might have done something bad. Real bad. You know the talk about the birds and the bees...well, things we a little too far and...

Mom: What!

Dad: Are you insane?

Me: It just happened. We didn't plan it.

Mom: How could you be so reckless?

Unfortunately, inside my head didn't come close to the real thing. Emotions played big factors in making it harder.

"Oh, Katia, tell me you didn't?" Mom pleaded. The fear in her expression made my stomach clench.

I sat up on the couch, tugging the covers up to my chin. Never had I needed my mommy more. My entire body was an iceberg, freezing and unstable. All I could do was nod.

She sunk onto the edge of the couch beside me. Dad's back hit the wall with a stunned expression. I felt like I had disappointed them in the biggest screw up of my life.

Mom's hand shook as she reached out, tucking a stray curl behind my ear. "I'm not even going to ask how." She inhaled deeply, like what she had to say was a struggle for her to get out. I knew the feeling all too well. "Your father and I knew this day might come, but we prayed—" Her voice hitched. "We've had seventeen years to prepare, but it doesn't dull the pain; that's for sure." Her hand covered her heart as if she could stop the pain from slicing it into ribbons.

My father remained speechless propped against the wall. It was the only thing keeping him on his feet. His face looked about as pale as I imagined mine did. I hated that I was causing them grief, and it was only going to get worse. "I'm so sorry," I whispered, tears gathering in my eyes. I felt like that was all I had done the last few days—cry and apologize.

Before the tears could fall down my cheeks, I was engulfed in my mother's arms. I buried a sob into her shoulder, unable to control the emotional outburst. A few wet sniffles from both of us and my dad joined the hug. There was water collecting at the corners of his eyes. Strong arms wrapped around us, holding us together. He had the kind of arms you could lean on and would always be there to catch you when you fell. Dependable. Solid. Tough.

I lost track of time. The one thing I didn't have much of. I couldn't bring myself to leave their presence—physically or emotionally. They brought a steady calm to the violent storm brewing inside me, and I wanted to hold on to that feeling for as long as possible. Telling my parents had been difficult, if not downright tear-jerking. I had known they were going to be upset, but nothing prepared me for their sorrow. Losing their first-born was an emotional pill to swallow.

Actually, I think they gagged on it.

I was so angry at this curse for hurting people I loved. My parents tried to be strong for me, but they fooled no one.

Later, when I lay tucked as cozily as possible in my bed, I thought of Seth. Alone, my tired mind went straight to him, and I pictured him a hundred different times. When we were just kids on the playground. Finding the clearing the first time and the thrill that quivered in our blood. Forming the circle under Seth's guidance. Our first kiss just a few months ago. The severe feelings that filled me when he said the vow. So many memories...

The needed to hear his voice spread through me like wildfire, joining the poison coiling inside me. What a concoction. I knew, though, that if he heard my voice, he would be unable to stop from rushing to my side. And anyone who stood in his way be damned. The last thing I wanted was Seth to see me sick—to watch me die.

I wanted his last recollections of me to be happy ones, not of me frail and lifeless. I wanted him to remember me as I had looked when we had been together that night, with love shining in my eyes. I couldn't bear to see pity, sadness, or regret in that face I cherished so much.

A quick glance at my wrist revealed that I had lost another star. Three to go. Tick. Tock. Tick. Tock.

Seth

When Kat didn't show for class today, I knew something was wrong—horribly wrong. Honestly, I knew this morning when I had opened my tired, bloodshot eyes and saw another star was missing. She was fading from me. It sat at the pit of my gut, weighing me down.

I couldn't swallow, filled with fear, but it did not stop my eyes from constantly seeking her out. Of course it did not help my paranoia that she wasn't answering her damn phone. I cursed at her under my breath for scaring the ever-loving crap out of me. More than anything, I wanted to believe that she was okay, just taking a mental health day. I did not want to admit that the curse might already be working its venom on her.

I made it through three periods before I lost it. Mrs. Carson was going on and on about some kind of macroeconomics mumbo jumbo. Who really needs this crap? Certainly not me. My mind was crammed with thoughts of Kat, and I had to see her. Grabbing my books, I stood up in the middle of Mrs. Carson's lecture and walked out. Yeah, even Zeke's questionable scrutiny couldn't stop me. I was a man on a mission.

"Mr. Nightingale," she called. "Where are you going?"

I ignored her, barreling through the door. It wasn't the first time I'd walked out on a class. The halls were empty as I all but ran from the school, my shoes echoing off the walls. I squealed out of the parking lot in a mad dash to Kat's house, leaving behind a scorch of black marks.

She could hide under the covers if she wanted, but Kat wasn't going to escape me forever. We were technically tied beyond the boundaries of this world. As soon as I pulled up to her house, I knew that my gut feeling had been right. Kat wasn't okay.

The ground went topsy-turvy. My hand shot out, stabilizing myself on the hood of my car. A third star had dissolved. Knowing that the end of Kat's life was evitable didn't make it any less earthshattering. I had loved this one girl since I took my first breath. I was born loving her, and now she was slipping through my fingertips.

Pushing off the truck, I made it to her front door. If her parents even thought about standing in my way… Yeah, not going to happen. They were lucky I didn't just bust in. There was nothing rational about how I was feeling right now. Patience? I didn't have any. Sanity? Not today. Rational? Yeah bloody right.

Her mom answered the door, and it only took one glimpse to see that Kat had told her parents. Her mom's reddish hair was disheveled, and she looked like she hadn't slept in days. I knew the feeling all too well and imagined I looked similar. "Seth." She sighed, dropping a shoulder against the doorframe. There was almost a relieved quality to the raw texture of her tone.

Dark shadows lined under her eyes, and seeing them made me feel small. It wasn't that she condemned me on the spot, just the opposite, but in my head, she should have. I ran a hand through my messy hair. "I need to see her." Pressure clamped down on my chest. If she refused…

She nodded, forcing a small smile. "Of course you do. She is in her room."

I half expected her dad to pop out around the corner and break my nose. If it had been my daughter, I would have done a hell of a lot more to the boy who stole my little girl's life. With a hand gripping the banister, I turned around. "I-I'm sorry that I failed. More than I could ever say."

Kat's mom laid a soft hand on my shoulder. "Seth, you have protected my daughter at all costs, even at the expense of your happiness. You have nothing to apologize for. I know how much you love her. Kat has always been stubborn and reckless. She told me to not let you in."

No surprise.

"And I assume by your lack of surprise that you figured as much. I think she is afraid to let you see her. Modesty has never been one of her strong suits," Kat's mom finished.

"When she didn't show up for school today, I thought..." I couldn't bring myself to say it.

Her mom inhaled. "She is really tired. Her body is shutting down. I won't sugarcoat it, Seth. It's not going to be pretty, but whether she is willing to admit it or not, she needs you."

Let's just hope Kat came to realize that revelation. It would be easier on both of us if she did.

I stood in her doorway soaking up the sight of her. A mountain of blankets dwarfed her. Rainbows were splattered over her floor, climbing up her bed. Kat always had a thing for pretty colors and her room was a testament with its glass wind chimes and bottles. Her usual sun-kissed skin was pale and her light blue eyes were sunken. Icy fear drenched my veins.

The frame creaked under my weight, and her eyes fluttered in my direction. "Hey." Yeah, that was all I got. Lame. There were a gazillion words flying through my head, but I couldn't figure out how to form them without losing my shit.

She rubbed her eyes. "Seth? What are you doing here?" Her voice sounded faint and sleepy. It was sort of cute.

My lips twitched. "You didn't show for school today, and you've been not so subtly ignoring my calls."

"It was that obvious, huh?"

I crossed the room and sat on the edge of the bed. "Really, Kats? Did you honestly think that I would stay away from you?"

She combed her fingers through her hair, looking shy and self-conscious, so unlike the confident Kat I was accustomed to. "I didn't want you to see me like this. Is that so wrong? To want you to remember me the way I was before?"

I couldn't stop myself from touching her. My hand caressed her cheek. "You can't believe that I am that shallow. It doesn't matter to me. You of all people should know that what I feel for you is so much deeper than physically appearance. Don't push me away, not now. I need you, Kats." My voice was gruff with feelings

I couldn't control.

Her eyes glistened. "Being with you, Seth, was the greatest, happiest time of my life. I don't regret any of it. Not for a split second. You made me feel...loved. Whole. Like I mattered. I haven't felt like that in a very long time. And I know why now. I was missing you."

A giant ball of emotion clogged my throat.

Each hour, every minute and second that ticked by drove me frickin' insane. Not knowing which might be her last breath was killing me. I didn't want her to suffer, but on the other hand, I couldn't let her go. I couldn't lose Kat.

Taking her small hand in mine, I stared at our joined fingers.

"Only two left," she said with a sad smile.

Ugh. I couldn't think about *that* without growing claws and wanting to lash out. There was a good chance I would never come to terms with this. I knew that when I left Kat today, I was going to hit something or someone. It had been a long time since I had gone looking for a fight—too long. Tonight my knuckles would get a workout. My hands flexed as if they were anticipating the need to bloody some poor sap's lip.

At the tension escalating in my hands, Kat's eyes narrowed. "Seth." My name came out more like a warning.

"What?" I replied, trying to keep the gruffness from my voice. I got the don't-play-dumb-with-me look. Man, I was going to miss her looks.

"Whatever you are thinking about doing—don't." Her voice was soft, even as she tried to sound stern.

I smirked. It was nice to hear that she still had spunk. "How do you know what I am thinking?"

She rolled her eyes. "I might be bedridden, but I can still sense your turmoil. Your anger is like a heat wave inside me."

I played with her fingers. "Sorry. I'm still not used to this." And nor would I have. She would be gone before I had the chance to really explore our link. My chest ached at the desolation.

"It makes me angry too. Sometimes when I'm by myself, I just want to throw something or hit someone."

Knots formed in my stomach. "Hit me."

She snorted. "Tempting."

"Come on, Kats. I can handle it." Yes, I was baiting her, but at least it brought a little color to her cheeks.

Her little nose twitched. "Next time I get the urge, you'll be the first person I call."

I rubbed her palm along my jaw. "I love you."

She hissed, and her eyes darkened. "Ditto."

***

Katia

I didn't have to open my eyes to know that she had arrived. Wherever she went, she carried a warm glow, the scent of apples, and unconditional love.

It appears that when you are on your deathbed, everyone comes to say their goodbyes, but this one person I welcomed.

A genuine smile touched my lips. "Grandma," I whispered. The sound of my scratchy voice shocked me. It had been hours since I'd spoken.

Handing me a glass of water, she gave me a tender smile with deep dimples on either side. Long gray hair was pulled back into a twisted bun at the nape of her slender neck. Crinkles appeared at the corners of her soft blue eyes.

After I took a sip of water, cooling my scorched throat, she took the glass and set it aside. "Now, tell Granny how the hell you ended up activating the curse." Her willowy hand captured my cold one.

I laughed, then gripped my side, wincing. Laughing was out of the question for my sore muscles. Leave it to my quirky grandma to get right to the juicy points. No pleasantries about the weather or how school was going. It was what I loved most about her. She gave it to you straight, no BS. "Where to start?" I mumbled.

She angled her head, a twinkle glinting in her eyes. "Where it always starts…with a boy."

Wasn't that the truth?

"He's not just any boy, Grams. He is *the* boy."

"Seth Nightingale, I presume?"

"Mom told you."

With a secret curl to her lips, she patted my hand. "She didn't have to, honey. I've always known. It was clear from the day you two were born that you were infatuated with each other. Of course your mom and dad panicked."

I rolled my eyes. I might be bone-tired, but I could still give some good eye action. "Why am I always the last one to know?"

"Love is blind dear."

I snorted. "They also say love can kill."

Nothing fazed my grandma. "And you think you are going to die?"

I lifted my brows. *Duh.* "It's doesn't really matter now what I think. The curse already has its claws in me." I flipped my wrist over. The second star was barely visible. By the end of the day it would be gone.

She ran her fingers over the stars. "Ah, the family curse. She might have pierced the flesh and injected the poison breaking down your body, but your fate is still in your hands."

I blinked. "You're losing me. My fate was sealed the second Seth and I said the words that bound us."

A secret glint shone in her eyes. "That is what everyone else believes, but not me."

She had piqued my interest. My grandma might be on the peculiar side, but she was the most intuitive nixie I knew. Her instincts were always on point. If she thought there was a way to change my predestined outcome or, dare I hope, stop the curse, I owed it to her, to me, and to Seth to listen. "What do mean?" I asked. A rush of possibility warmed my core. Where the heck had the woman been a month ago? It would have save me a lot of heartache.

"Just like your parents, I had prayed this curse would never see the light of day. I made a promise to your mother about your gift, because she was afraid. The uncertainty and the unknown are scary. However much I disagreed with her decision, I kept my promise. Until today. You have a right to know, Katia. Our family has been waiting for a power like yours."

My eyes narrowed. What she was saying was crazy. My powers were a dud. They didn't kickass like Seth's. They weren't lifesaving like Elena's. I sure as heck couldn't manipulate people's minds. "I don't understand."

She brushed the hair from my face. "You are special. The gift you were given isn't something to snub your nose at. You have it inside you to rid our family of this curse for good."

I held the blanket close, confused. "How is that possible?"

"You are an unweaver."

I wracked my brain, trying to recall if I had ever read of such a thing in all those mystical books Seth had made me pore over. "Um, what does that mean?" *Please don't let that be some kind of magickal disease.* That was the last thing I needed.

"It means that I believe you have the power to undo this curse. What the others didn't know, or failed to realize, is that Arachne was a great weaver. It is in your bloodline, Katia. You have the cure inside you. A twist that eluded Isa when she unleashed the curse. You can undo this spell."

Granny was off her rocker.

Yep, that was my initial reaction, and she saw it in my scrunched face. It was her raspy laugh that had me reconsidering. "Don't dismiss the idea so quickly, love."

My grandma wasn't known for being a liar. Honestly, she was probably the only person who was truthful with me. So why was I having such a hard time believing this?

I contemplated what she was implying. Could I undo spells? A string of different memories came back to me. Little things I had never really second-guessed. A love spell gone awry. Faulty test taking charms. Both times I had been able to break through Zeke's memory erasing. Every spell that had gone *oops* made me wonder if I had a hand in its failure.

Suddenly, a seed of belief took root in my belly, sprouting and growing branches. "How?" I asked.

Grandma gave me a wide grin. "That's my girl. It is just about figuring out how to solve the counteractive magick. The cure lies inside you, Katia."

That really wasn't a whole lot of help. So I could cure myself. Great. It still didn't explain how I went about doing so. Where was the instruction manual for unweavers? Because I needed one pronto. My timetable was ticking. Sure, I might have unwoven spells before, but never consciously. I just sort of picked apart this nagging inside me until it disintegrated.

Not exactly rocket science, but maybe that was the key.

Was it possible the all I had to do was concentrate on the curse instead of just lying here letting it eat me alive? I am sure it was much more technical than that, but if I could find a lock on it then just like any problem, any puzzle, I just had to put the pieces together.

One.

Fragment.

At a time.

Chapter 26

Katia

My room was immersed in darkness as night descended. The conversation I had with my grandmother rolled around in my head. Seriously, the last thing I wanted to do right now was muster up the energy to use magick. I was just so tired. My eyes were half-lidded, but I was deathly afraid—pun intended—that if I closed my eyes, I wouldn't open them again.

But if there was the slimmest chance I could do this, save myself, then it had to be tonight. A sense of urgency pushed inside me, but my brain mulled over a thousand questions. How did I begin to dissemble a dark curse? What if I couldn't do it in time? Or do it at all? Why me? What made me so special from the others who had lost their lives to this killing curse?

I huffed, staring at the ceiling. My mind was reeling, and I was amazed I could actually see straight. Under this amount of stress and fear I wouldn't be able to tie my shoe, let alone break a curse. It was utterly insane to think that I could do this.

I wanted to hurl.

Instead of dwelling on my death, which had been on my mind nonstop, I focused on relaxing my breathing. I thought about things that calmed me. A bubble bath. Shopping. Buy-one-get-one-free sales. White chocolate cheesecake. Okay, so that last one just made me hungry. My stomach growled, reminding me that I hadn't really eaten anything all day. My appetite had vanished with the curse.

Well, this was going swell.

So far all I had managed to do was piss off my stomach.

Frustrated with myself, I wanted to yell at the top of my lungs. This might be a good time to take up Seth on his offer. I could really use someone as a punching bag. If I couldn't figure out how to control my own gift, I would not just be letting down myself, but all the people who loved me. No pressure.

I was just about to give up for the night and maybe by an act of God, I could try again tomorrow, but then…

Really on pure accident, the rage that was scalding inside me, allowed me to latch onto the heart of the curse. Just like Zeke's spell to wipe my memories, there was a passageway blocking and clogging my organs instead of my mind. Once I located the source of the foul magick, I did what I did best. I picked, prodded, and chipped through the obstruction.

Tingles of energy pumped through my blood, stronger than I'd ever felt. Zeke's mind spells were powerful, not as potent as the curse, but I had broken them. All my life I had been using my gift without intentionally knowing what I was doing.

That was pretty kickass.

And slightly disturbing.

I pushed and pushed myself. Each time I didn't think I could go on, I dug deeper, pulling just enough strength. Hours could have befallen, but I knew I was making headway. The harder I plowed at the curse, the harder she shoved back. I even started to hear the chattering of what I thought was spiders.

Ugh. What was with this bitch and spiders? Did she think it was poetic because Arachne had ultimately gotten what Isa thought she deserved—justice when Athena turned her into part spider?

I'll never understand goddesses.

My whole body erupted in what felt like tiny little legs crawling over every inch. I wanted to jump out of bed and run from the room. The creep-scuttling feeling in my hair was the worst. But I had to push further. If I gave just a centimeter, she would take a mile.

Receding inside myself, I waged a war with the curse. We went head to head in a battle of magick. She slashed out, squeezing my lungs with her curse to the point where I was gasping for air. Still I clung to the energy inside me, refocusing on the pressure in my chest until I could breathe with ease.

And so the game went. She attacked. I defended. But finally, in the struggle for power, I felt the first inkling of victory when I was the one attacking, putting her on the defensive. A surge of hope gave my magick a boost.

Bone tired and on the verge of passing out, I finally closed my eyes, incapable of doing anything else. I wasn't a hundred percent positive that I had broken the curse, but I knew I had given her an epic fight. I had done all that I could, and I prayed it would be enough to at least let me see the light of another day to try again. Within minutes, blackness submerged me.

Bleary eyed, my eyes fluttered open, and the first thing I noticed was the sun—golden and bringing glints of color into my room. Clearing the gunk from my eyes, I slowly pushed myself up, leaning against the headboard. My limbs were wobbly and weak. I had a throbbing headache, but other than that, I felt like I'd just had the worst flu of my life. In spite of all the aches and the general dizziness, there wasn't any magicky fog dogging me down.

Inhaling, I took a moment to take inventory. First on the list: my wrist.

I was down to one lonely, little star. But on the upside, it was as bold as ever—no fading—yet. It still lifted my spirits. Actually, the solitary mark made my spirits soar.

Also the buzzing had stopped ringing my ears, and I couldn't have been happier. How much creepier could it get than hearing the rapping of eight legs times a thousand spiders. It would be a hair-raising experience for anyone.

Ick. Gawd, I hate spiders.

Swinging my legs to the edge of the bed, I tested my stability. When I didn't fall flat on my face, two thoughts entered my mind—shower and food. In that order.

The water hit my face and I sighed, sinking against the tiled wall. Before long, the bathroom was nice and steamy, just what my chilled body needed. As I let the water beat down on my face, I thought about the last few days. My mind spun, unloading a bunch of crap on me. A few hours ago I hadn't been sure I would even open my eyes again. My demise still might happen, but, inside, something told me I was going to be okay.

Only time would tell.

I had been in the shower for more than twenty minutes, wallowing in something as simple as hot water. I looked worse than a prune. And I loved it. Turning off the faucets, I shut off the water, and my hands trembled a little. Not a hundred percent. Nowhere near, but the fact that I wasn't a sack of potatoes anymore, well, I'd take it. Even the familiar scent of my shampoo gave me comfort.

As I was drying my hair, something caught my eye in the mirror, a flash of black. Anyone else might have thought that it was a beauty mark or a mole, but at closer inspection they would see the detailed shape. There was a second star on the inside of my wrist, which could only mean one thing. I had broken the curse.

Holy shit.

After an excited/panicky moment, my lips split into a stupid grin. "I did it. I freaking did it." Yeah, I totally wanted to jump up and down like a girl and chant some lame cheer. My stomach had other ideas, rumbling so loudly I could hear it over my hairdryer.

Turning off the switch, I couldn't take my eyes off the twin stars. I knew that I needed to give it a few more days, gain my strength and make sure the curse wasn't screwing with me. My initial reaction was to run to Seth, but I didn't have it in me to lift his spirit only to crush his heart again if something went awry. Seth had suffered enough because of me.

The house was quiet as I tackled the stairs. And yeah, it took me forever without tumbling down, and I had to balance myself on the railings. By the time I reached the kitchen, I was out of breath.

Holy honey bunches of oh's.

Mom and Grandma Rose were at the table staring into their still full coffee mugs. Their expressions were desolate

"Someone die?" I asked, jokingly.

Heads flew in my direction at the archway. "What are you going out of bed?" Mom asked, jumping to her feet to help me.

Grandma's eyes twinkled.

I dropped into the closest chair. "I've seen nothing but the four walls of my room for days. I can't take it anymore," I complained.

"Katia—" Mom began to scold.

"Mom," I interrupted. "It's ok. I-I think I may have broken or at the very least weakened the curse."

Her eyes clouded with confusion, and my grandma just leaned back in her chair grinning. I told Mom everything that happened last night. How I attempted to use my magick to exile the evil inside me.

And for the first time in days, I saw a glimmer of hope in her eyes.

***

A week went by…

Only two stars remained; the others hadn't returned—yet, but neither did the sickness. One thing that had returned was my appetite. It came back with a vengeance. I literally ate everything in sight. Claudia would have had a stroke.

Speaking of friends, mine had been knocking on my door and blowing up my phone for days. It kind of felt good, knowing they cared, but I had given Mom strict instructions to let no one in. I wasn't ready.

But now, a week later, with a clean bill of health, I figured I needed to rejoin the living, because it looked like I had a future. I chewed over the lie I was going tell everyone but the circle, who knew the truth. I needed a darn good cover story for missing school unexpectedly. A family death seemed too morbid considering how close I had come to dying.

I was finding it excruciatingly difficult to concentrate on anything but Seth. It was hopeless to even try. My brain, my body, my heart were all Seth-starved. I was having withdrawals. There was only one thing to do. I needed to see him. Now.

I took more time than necessary on my makeup, covering any lingering shadows, and I took twice as long on my outfit. This reunion was going to go down in my history book. I wanted to remember every detail.

Nerves started to come into play as I left the house. Would Seth be happy to see me? Would he believe that I had broken the curse? Would he still want me? Butterflies and grease swarmed in my belly. Maybe that cheeseburger hadn't been the best idea, but it made Mom so happy to see me shovel food into my face. How could I possibly disappoint her? She was given a second chance with her daughter. My waistline was the least of my concerns.

Before long I was leaning on the side of Seth's truck with my ankles crossed and a grin so big my lips hurt. Eddy's Auto Repair never changed. It had never been remodeled. No updates. It was like time had stood still at Eddy's. A giant round sign with Eddy's name splashed in the middle stood on an old-fashioned gas pump. Classy. It was one of the very things I loved about Vermillion. Small-town charm and people you could count on.

Tiny sparks lit the star-strewn sky. The night was a smoky dark blue and the moon a globe of pale yellow. By my calculations, the shop closed in about thirty seconds, and then Seth would be all mine. He just didn't know it yet. My patience was unrepressed, and I was about one second away from tossing this silly romantic plan I had concocted in my head. The whole wind in my hair, running at each other in slow motion, and then him sweeping me off my feet.

Storybook.

It was actually a miracle that I had lasted a week before seeking him out. Mom had told me that Seth called every day to check on me, and I could tell she hated hiding the truth. I wasn't dying. But I had made her promise, at least until I was really sure. After a week I was chomping to get out of the house.

Seth had kept a secret for seventeen years. I didn't know how he did it. Seven days and I was ready to yell it from the top of the Eiffel Tower. Then, when I didn't think I could wait another nanosecond, my heart thundered in my chest and my palms began to sweat.

Seth

What a night.

Not even having my elbows deep in brake fluid and tire muck could take my mind off Kat and what she must be going through. I glanced at my wrist so much during the day that I pulled a muscle in my neck, but home was no better. If anything, it was worse. Nothing but time, and time lately was my enemy.

Walking outside, I rubbed the cramp at the base of my neck. I had taken no more than a few steps when something suddenly caught my eye. A vision. My brows knitted together. "Kats?" There was no hiding my shock, and for a split second I thought my mind was playing cruel games with me. Making me think I was seeing Kat.

Just freaking dandy.

I stood in the parking lot staring at her. She gave me a come-get-me grin. I blinked, and she was still there, except now she was running straight at me. Then she leaped into my arms. "Kats," I murmured her name, burying my face into her neck. I lifted her off her feet, and she clung to me like ivy.

"Don't let go," she whispered, her voice thick with tears.

Every cell in my body warmed. "What are you doing here?" I asked. I never thought I would see her again, let alone looking so vibrant with pink cheeks and bright eyes. I had barely come to terms with a life without her, and here she was, doing funny things to my heart. It jumped in unrestrained excitement and, at the same time, squeezed in panic.

Her feet touched the ground, but I kept my arms around her. "I had to see you."

"But the—"

She put a finger to my lips, silencing me. "I never want to hear that word again."

Whatever she wanted. I'd stay just like this forever. "How is this possible?" She didn't look like the same girl I had seen just over a week ago. Kat looked vibrant and very much alive. I hated that my heart was hammering in hope.

I didn't think her grin could get any wider. I was wrong. Dimples deepened on her cheeks, highlighting her mouth. Her fingers framed my face. "I kicked the curse's butt."

Did I hear her correctly? My ears must have deceived me, because I think she said that she had broken the curse. But it didn't make sense. How had Kat been able to do what many others never could? "How?"

"Apparently I am an unweaver."

I raised a brow.

"My grandma informed me that I have the power to undo spells. And "

That actually made sense now that I had a moment to think about it, and I didn't know why I hadn't put it together sooner. "I can't believe this is real."

She looked up at me. "Oh, it's real. Should I pinch you?"

I smirked.

Then she pressed her mouth to mine in a soul-burning kiss. Her lips were like satin under mine, demanding and potent. No sooner had our lips sealed did I feel the tingles of magick. Our bond was spurring us on. A small squeak of surprise escaped Kat and was drowned by my lips. The tingles that I know we both felt were followed by the reappearance of a third star. We were cementing our connection.

I couldn't believe that the pandemonium was really over. Pulling back just a tad, I stared down into her flushed face. "I still can't believe that this is real. That you are real."

"Here. Let me help you with that." She pinched me.

My lips curved. "Point taken." I dropped another kiss on her lips.

She looked up at me with huge owl eyes that glinted in the moonlight. "I take it that means you still want me?"

Please. Who was she kidding? "I want a lifetime with you. A multitude of kisses."

"Then we will have just that," she said.

And I believed her. Ours was an undying love.

Epilogue

Katia

So you want to know what happened after Seth and I broke the curse, defeating the odds? Wondering what happened to the circle of five? Did Seth and I ride off into the sunset, make a gazillion little nixie babies and live happily ever after?

Well those are adventures for another day.

And the best part… We are all alive to tell them.

THE END

Look for:

MOONDUST

The conclusion to the Luminescence Trilogy

AVAILABLE MAY 2, 2014

~*~*~*~

Connect with me online:

(I'm serious – I would love to hear from you.)

My Blog: http://jlweil.blogspot.com/

Twitter: https://twitter.com/#!/JLWeil

Facebook: http://www.facebook.com/#!/jenniferlweil

Goodreads: http://www.goodreads.com/author/show/5831854.J_L_Weil

CPSIA information can be obtained at www.ICGtesting.com
Printed in the USA
LVOW05s2318021014

407081LV00013B/329/P